**The love** of Mezzaluna, holdi...  ...g ...to each other's eyes re-opened Dario's barely healed wounds and forced him to seek solace in his office. The full-length mirror he passed in the foyer reflected a well-dressed, successful restaurateur, but he knew better than to believe the illusion. The clanging of dishes and murmurs of the restaurant staff muffled through the wall.

He dropped into the leather chair. The unopened bottle of the Frangelico on his desk taunted him. Combing his hand through his hair a few times, he tried to remember the sweet, nutty taste of the liquor on his tongue. His mouth salivated at the thought. If he popped the corked and took a sip, he wouldn't be able to stop until he consumed the last drop. He shifted his focus on the gypsy stone on the table. Fourteen years later and he still couldn't part with the damn thing. Now it was nothing but a paperweight for the restaurant's stack of bills, and a constant reminder of his pain. The only keepsake him and Irena had shared...or half of it. Did she still have the other half? So much for the gypsy's prediction.

If there was a rewind button on the life he would've pressed it long ago. He straightened, leaning against the backrest, the coldness of the leather seeping through his thin cotton shirt. Better get his thoughts back on the job. Damn bills won't pay themselves.

# Dangerous Benevolence

## by

## Zrinka Jelic

**Dangerous Benevolence**

Cover Art by *Kim Mendoza*

The Wild Rose Press, Inc.
PO Box 708
Adams Basin, NY 14410-0708
Visit us at www.thewildrosepress.com

Publishing History
First Mainstream Thriller Edition, 2018
Print ISBN 978-1-5092-1983-4
Digital ISBN 978-1-5092-1984-1

Published in the United States of America

## Dedications

To my husband and children
who were neglected while I wrote this book.
~*~
And to critique group at Kiss of Death
and especially my critique partner T. L. Walsh,
thank you for kicking my butt to finish the story.

Chapter 1

The lovers at the secluded table of Mezzaluna, holding hands, gazing into each other's eyes re-opened Dario's barely healed wounds and forced him to seek solace in his office. The full-length mirror he passed in the foyer reflected a well-dressed, successful restaurateur, but he knew better than to believe the illusion. The clanging of dishes and murmurs of the restaurant staff muffled through the wall.

He dropped into the leather chair. The unopened bottle of the Frangelico on his desk taunted him. Combing his hand through his hair a few times, he tried to remember the sweet, nutty taste of the liquor on his tongue. His mouth salivated at the thought. If he popped the corked and took a sip, he wouldn't be able to stop until he consumed the last drop. He shifted his focus on the gypsy stone on the table. Fourteen years later and he still couldn't part with the damn thing. Now it was nothing but a paperweight for the restaurant's stack of bills, and a constant reminder of his pain. The only keepsake him and Irena had shared...or half of it. Did she still have the other half? So much for the gypsy's prediction.

If there was a rewind button on the life he would've pressed it long ago. He straightened, leaning against the backrest, the coldness of the leather seeping through his thin cotton shirt. Better get his thoughts back on the job. Damn bills won't pay themselves.

He grabbed the yellow purchase order from the top of the stack and scanned over the page. Why did he bother? His accountant had warned him of the declining sales over the years due to the bad economy. Many businesses around his restaurant folded, he struggled to keep the prices low to attract patrons, but people's disposable income shrunk and they rarely dined out.

The door to his office flew open and Ante stepped in, two uncapped beer bottles in his hand. He kicked the door shut behind him. "I knew you'd be hiding in your cave."

Annoyance replaced Dario's brooding "Your only saving grace is that we're family or I'd fire you for bursting into my office without knocking. You think I put that sticker on the door saying keep nuts out because I'm allergic?"

"Ha-ha." Ante approached the desk. He plopped one beer in front of him and lowered to the chair facing Dario. "Never drink alone." After taking a long swig from his bottle, Ante pointed at the tall bottle on the table. "Going back to hard liquor? You know what that shit does to you."

Dario tilted the brown glass. Last time he had fooled his younger brother was in grade school, not likely he'd buy the lie now, but it was worth a try. "Wasn't gonna drink it."

Ante arched an eyebrow, looking at him with that who-are-you-kidding-bro look. "You enjoy torturing yourself by staring at it?" He gulped a few more long pulls from his bottle and swiped the back of his hand over his mouth. "We did great tonight. Wait staff is happy with tips they got and we're ready to close. Mom must be proud."

Ante raised his bottle and Dario clicked his beer with his brother's in a toast to their parents, their nightly ritual at closing.

Ante nodded fast a few times, drained his beer, licked his lips, and then deposited the empty bottle on the table. "So, coming to the party?"

Dario thumped his beer on the desk and pressed his finger at the stack of bills. "I suppose you'll take care of these?"

"Oh come on. Leave the work for one night. It'll still be here in the morning." His brother tapped his foot against the desk, annoyance filled his tone.

"Exactly." Dario leaned over, his finger still on the top bill. "And doubled if this stack doesn't get taken care of tonight. We receive deliveries every day." He flashed one bill in his outstretched hand. "This one's for bread." Picked up another and waved it in the air. "Beer." Then another. "I don't know what this one's for, but it's for something. Some days it feels like everyone wants our money and all I do is write checks."

"Okay, you proved your point." Ante pointed at the stacks of papers on Dario's desk. "This is just an excuse. You think I don't know you. Ana's been asking about you."

Dario turned to the computer screen, guilt brewing in the pit of his gut. Whenever he thought of Ana that night came to mind...the night he preferred to forget. "I can't imagine why."

"The two of you made a good couple, everyone thought—"

"Well, try paying your bills with everyone's opinions." Dario dismissed him with a wave of his hand. People and their ideas. Who asked them for the advice? The assumption that they knew what was best for him irked him no matter how hard he tried to ignore the rumors.

Ante loosened up his tie. "You dated Ana because she kind of resembles Irena, but what happened? One minute you two were kissing and the next, zilch. The break up was so sudden."

Dario scrubbed his hand over his face. So the bitch had not told, yet. Surprising. He pushed the beer bottle across the desk. "Too much booze and with her fake blonde hair close to Irena's, I cried the wrong girl's name in bed."

Dumb mistake. Anna's bleached hair could not compare to Irena's tresses—rays of sunshine reflecting off the surface of the water. Neither could be captured in a bottle of hair dye. God, learning to live without her had been harder than saying goodbye. He'd tried to stop comparing every girl to Irena to no avail, for fourteen years he was left to grapple with their split-up.

"Aw man, that stings." Ante got on his feet and took the empty bottle. "Still, you should get out instead of living in this office, like some hermit. I hear Irena's parents aren't doing well. Maybe she'll come home to see them one last time."

Dario shook his head. "Knowing her parents, the world wouldn't blame her if she didn't."

Despite his words, a hint of hope kindled inside him, but he extinguished it fast. No, if she returned, she'd find a way to contact him. Unless... She'd fallen out of love with him. After all, it'd been fourteen years. Unimaginable, they had promised their love would live forever, but they were young and green. He could still recall the sweet scent of her hair, the feel of the soft skin pressed against his body.

"People said teenagers are not mature for marriage." Ante's voice pulled him out of his reverie. Again, goddamn people and their thinking.

"No, I was too poor, not book smart and no promise of a great future. Her parents never liked me, thought their daughter could do a heck of a lot better. Back then, her parents were right and made damn sure to put as much distance between us as possible by sending her off to Canada. The night we split up, my toes pushed through the holes in my socks. Yet I wanted to give her the world, hell, I couldn't afford a new pair of socks." Dario powered down his computer, hiding his face from Ante. Their parents had provided food on the table, a one bedroom shack that he and his brother slept on the floor, and plenty love, but there was not much else. "Ironic, now I have everything money can buy, but I don't have her." He raked his shaky hand through his hair. "Don't know why I still hold on."

"No need to explain it to me, bro, I understand you, and those who don't..." Ante clicked his tongue. "Well, no explanation is possible. Back then everyone took us for two good-for-nothing SOB's, but we proved them wrong, didn't we?" He pointed at the picture of their parents' house hanging on the wall behind Dario, which he'd painted from an old photo and his memory on the long and slow tanker voyages. "Now others beg us for a job. Speaking of which, you won't believe who came asking for work earlier today."

Dario leaned back in his leather chair and pressed his chin on his laced fingers. "Humor me."

"Who was the one guy the most likely to succeed

since grade school?"

"No, oh-ho, no," Dario chuckled. "What's that saying about the wheel of fortune? You're right, I don't believe you. He had a name for us, Lepers brothers? Yes, that's it. Didn't the snob get a scholarship of some kind?"

"Yeah, that blew up his already overblown ego. In the end, what good did that do him?" Ante shrugged. "He's unemployed and from scanning over his resume also unemployable."

*So expensive education and no common sense or job.* "What did you tell him?" Laughter still rumbled Dario's chest. Since they'd opened the restaurant, people gossiped the two brothers wouldn't make it. Now five years later, those who pointed fingers and ridiculed them knocked on their door looking for work.

"That we're fully staffed." The corners of Ante's mouth curved in a mocking grin. "Anyway, why would we give him a job when he wouldn't let anyone use his pencil eraser? Plus, I'm not joking, we are fully staffed." Ante unbuttoned the collar of his shirt. "I'm gonna change into something more casual. I do like these new suits you've got for the staff, by the way. The vests are accentuating the waitresses' bosoms."

"Good grief, I can't believe you're still holding that high school grudge over a pencil eraser." Dario snorted. Yes, his brother could hold a grudge for life. "Anyhow, that is why you're in charge of hiring. I would've given the poor sucker a job." Dario leaned on his elbow, staring at the white chef's jacket draped over the hanger on the dark door of his office.

"Didn't you want me as a manager because I can come up with the biggest BS?" Ante scratched his head and grabbed the back of the chair with the other hand.

"That too."

His brother gave a quiet chuckle. "If only you'd snap out of your mood and come to the party. Man, think about it, the girls are waiting for us. The whole town is out tonight."

"Don't have time." Dario released a huff of air. "Plus, I'd give anything to have what you have. Reconcile with Martina and get your daughter back. Stop throwing it away by hitting a skirt every night."

Ante's shoulders slumped. "She wanted freedom, so I gave it to her. If she wants me, I'm here and all hers. So until she does, I'll take my pleasure where I can find it." He puffed his chest and tilted his head. "Come to the party. The masquerade is perfect. For one night you can be whoever you want to be."

Dario hid his face behind the stack of bills.

Ante marched out of the office, leaving Dario to his thoughts. Younger, that was what he wanted to be. No mask could take him back in time.

Could Irena have returned? He'd never find out if he stayed hidden in his office. She wouldn't know he owned the most successful restaurant in Zadar, but she could find out. Anger burned through him. He would show her parents they'd been wrong to break him up with their daughter, he would get her back. No other girl imprinted herself into his heart like her. Since her, he'd dated casually, but that gig ran old some two years ago.

Dario cast another glance at the talisman he'd split with Irena at the fair. The clinking of the gypsy woman's large hoops hanging from her ears and her raspy voice with a funny accent surfaced. Oh yes, her scary face with deep lines was etched in his memory. It replaced Irena's face in every dream. The woman tried to tell him something, but no words came from her moving mouth.

The smell of burning incense had barely masked the stench of horses' shit inside her colorful tent. The amulets in her collection rattled as she pushed the box and made them pick one, then broke it in two. Her large and strange rings only made her fingers appear more gnarled. She had him convinced the lines in the talisman predicted their love was written in the stars and nothing would keep them apart. But the good luck piece proved to be more of a misfortune... he was foolish to have believed the fortune teller. It had been fourteen years. He was making his own path in life and kept busy. Hell, he'd said this for so long he even convinced himself.

He pushed away from his desk, allowing the chair to roll on its coasters across the tiled floor, put his foot down before he hit the wall, then got up and turned off the lights. A faint yellow glow emanated from the talisman. He approached his desk and picked up the trinket. The surface radiated a soft heat. The mass could've absorbed the warmth and the light from the lamp on his desk.

*Irena's parents aren't doing well, maybe she returned to see them one last time*, Ante's words stirred a hunch in him. His walls softened. Could she have come back home? What would it be like to see her again? He squeezed the amulet, then placed it back at the top of the bills.

If he was to find out answers to his questions, he should not spend this night alone in his penthouse.

Perhaps the Fates would finally smile upon him.

****

Dario stared at the crack in the letter P of the neon purple light above the wide entrance. Several years since a drunken brawl that had spilled onto the street and caused the damage and the new management still hadn't fixed the sign. They seemed to think the fissure gave the place character, but he disagreed. The ancient building of the Old Town drowned out most of the noise—an attractive feature for bar and night-club owners.

The old stomping ground of Dario's gang had seen change of ownership and a few facelifts over the years, but kept its name. The pack gathered here on their nights out and if the saying that old habits die hard was true, and Irena was back, she'd visit this place. All over the town posters advertised tonight's venue at the Papillion, she would expect to find him here.

The blending light gave the illusion the large butterfly above the archway of the blues lounge, Papillion Bleu, flapped its oversized wings. Boisterous laughter drifted from the long line of patrons braving the cold night. Damn, he'd freeze his balls off out here. Stupid to leave his jacket in his car so he wouldn't have to cart it along. Why hadn't he listened to his brother and came with him? Ante's connections got him into many places no matter how long was the line.

In a few strides, he stepped up to the main door and nodded to the bouncer, his high school buddy. The bald man nodded back and opened the thick, red rope strung over the doorframe.

"Not fair! Come on, man, I'm waiting for almost an hour." The first guy in the lineup took a step too

9

close.

"Take it up with the boss." The bouncer thrust his thick arm at the pushy patron. Dario lowered his head and slipped inside, embraced by instant warmth.

Neon strobe lights throbbed in rhythm with the base. As always, the live band packed the house. Dario followed the lit path, meandering among the filled plush booths toward the circular bar in the middle. A couple left for the dance floor, leaving two stools empty. The bartender flashed a beer bottle at him just as he settled on the seat. He nodded and the bottle slid along the smooth surface at his open palm.

He took a sip and scowled at the overly bitter taste. After years of sailing on foreign ships, he got used to finer brews. Domestic beer no longer suited his taste buds, but he didn't feel like bothering the bartender for something else. The guys behind the bar barely kept up with the orders barked at them.

The music beat caught him, and he tapped his foot while nodding in cadence with the weeping guitars. Nothing expressed his mood like blues and this tune was his favorite from his secret 'brooding playlist.' He pivoted the stool away from the bar and scanned the crowd for familiar faces. His brother's thick hair stood out among the manicured ladies. Which one would wake up in his bed come morning? Fools should know better. Ante loved his ladies, but his heart belonged to only one. Hopefully, he'd change his ways before Martina found someone.

The song ended, but the long applause prompted the band to keep going and they picked up the rhythm with BB King's classic.

"Dario, I didn't expect to see you here." Ana's

slurring voice rose above the noise. She plopped her silver clutch purse on the bar and braced her hip against his stool. Her smeared lipstick and runny mascara revealed her sorry state. She shook her empty glass in front of his face. "I could use another one."

"Sure, what are you having?" Telling her she had enough would infuriate her. He flagged the bartender.

Her frown deepened lines around her lips. "The stronger, the better."

He nodded at her, leaned over the bar and gave the order to the bartender. When the man raised one eyebrow, Dario nodded. "And make it a double."

The bartender set to work and slid the cocktail glass toward Ana. She grabbed the drink and slurped, then coughed. "This is stale, cold coffee."

"And it's pretty strong, I bet." He pushed a bottle of water in her free hand. "Drink this too. Tomorrow will be hell to pay."

She puffed her cheeks and blew out a hot breath. He frowned at the smell of stale booze carried to his face.

"Oh, I get it." She set the drink down, shaking the plastic bottle at him. "You're still pissed at me about the money."

"Was it the money you asked to pay for your child's doctor bill, but you spent it on a new pair of shoes? Or was it the time you asked to buy things for your son's school supplies and somehow ended up on a shopping spree for your darling self?"

She shrugged and shook her head. "What was I to do? Tom paid for those things."

Six months later and her callousness still bugged the hell out of Dario. However, he had only himself to blame. After the first time she'd spent his money on other things rather than her child as she'd claimed, he should've denied her and taken the boy to buy what he needed. But it was easier to give her a few bills to stop her from whining. Well, at least, her child had one responsible parent. "The right thing would've been to return the money."

"Meh." She shrugged one shoulder, licked her parched lips, then pulled out a pack of cigarettes from her purse and slid one out.

"If you needed money, ask. Don't lie about your child." He plucked the smoke from her crooked lips and crushed it. "It's a non-smoking bar. If you don't stop with this drinking and partying crap, you're going to risk losing custody of your child."

She frowned. "I could live with that. The little brat is costing me some serious cash. He wants this and that and what's left for me? Nothing."

"That's the price of parenthood." Dario patted her arm, understanding it was booze that spoke. "You tricked me two times, never again. Being a single, unemployed mom is hard. Focus on your kid."

Damn it, she made him furious with her pity party for one. He needed to get away from her. He plopped his beer on the bar. "I have to go look for Ante."

Sniffling, she wiped her hand under her nose. "I don't want to be a waitress anymore. I'm done with that crap."

He leaned closer to her ear. No point advertising her misfortune to those standing by. Her unsteady legs and loud voice already drew attention. Perhaps she was better off not working in the restaurants where she'd have a free access to booze. "Get your act together, prove it to me, and I'll pay for your college. Get that nursing diploma you always wanted."

"I don't want any job or go to school. Why can't I get a man to look after me?" She hiccupped and took a step forward, lost the balance and stumbled.

Dario grabbed her elbow, steadying her on her feet. "You need to go home."

Yanking her arm away from his grasp, she pushed on his shoulder. "Stop pretending you care about me, you didn't want me. Let me be and go with your precious Irena. Oh, I forgot, she's gone. She left you."

Damn it, Ana. He came out tonight with hopes to find Irena, however impossible that seemed, not to get guilt-tripped. If Ana planned to hurt him with her careless remark, she pierced his heart, though her accusatory tone stung the most.

"Ana." A woman's voice boomed. Dario snapped his head toward Ana's sister. "It's okay, Dario. I'll take her home."

He nodded and got to his feet. Judging by Leila's scowl, she was getting fed up chasing after her sister and dragging her drunken ass home. "Go home, Ana."

"One more drink." Ana jerked away from Leila's hold and took a step toward the bar.

"You had enough." Leila wrapped her arm around Ana and nudged her toward the exit. "Let's go home now."

Dario returned to his seat, the band's music drifted past him, but he couldn't place the song with Ana's words replaying in his mind. He breathed deeply and took a slug of his beer, scowling again at its bitterness. A person clad in a red cloak approached, the deep hood hid the face, but the swaying of hips under the cloth reminded him of Irena. She still wore her mask even though it was after midnight when true identities were revealed. She squeezed between his stool and the one next to him. The citrus perfume was Irena's branding.

Holding her glass, she faced him. Her hood covered most of her features, but something about her deepened his suspicion that Irena stood before him. She downed the orange drink, then licked her full lips. With the glass pressed to her chest, she uttered a deep moan for the appreciation of for the cocktail.

"Easy there, there's plenty of night left." He tilted his head, trying to catch a different light to see her, but it was too dark to make out her features around her mask.

"No worries, I only drink half a shot of vodka." She placed the tumbler on the bar and flashed him a smile. Her accent seemed foreign and so did her treble, unlike Irena's alto. Who was this woman?

But her drink, or the way she liked it, had him sitting on nails. Half a shot of vodka in her screwdriver...he'd only known of one female who drank it that way.

The girl took two steps away from him, halted and turned her head to look over her shoulder. Was she waiting for him to follow her? *What are you waiting for?* He set his drink on the bar and got on his feet. She continued on her way, keeping a slow pace, squeezing between the crowds. He stayed a few steps behind.

Ante intercepted him at the main door, shoving a brown bottle at him. "Leaving already? You forgot your beer."

"Hold it for me." He waved him off, never taking his eyes off the red hood, slowly disappearing into the crowd outside.

"Hold it for you? Oh, you're expecting to find beer left when you get back?" Ante's shout grew louder with every word.

Dario glanced at him. "Fine, drink it up."

When he raised his glance at the crowd on the street, the red hood had vanished. Damn it. Had he seen a ghost? It couldn't have been too much beer. He'd barely taken a couple of sips. No, she was real and she couldn't have gone too far. He stepped out on the cobblestone paved road of the old city. At the corner, he spotted her cloak and followed her. In an instant, she ran into the narrow alley.

"Wait," he called, catching up with her. Grabbing onto her shoulder, he turned her around. The girl uttered half a scream and pierced him with do-I-know-you stare. He spotted the differences between this girl and the one at the bar. The blue mask encircling her eyes and half a nose had shiny studs, not red feathers. She stood a good two inches shorter than the other girl and wore no lipstick.

"So sorry, I mistook you for someone." He released his grip on her shoulder and took a step back. What were the odds they'd be two girls in red cloak tonight?

Wondering where to look next, he rubbed his neck, walking slowly back toward the Papillion Bleu.

"Psssst…"

He pivoted at the piercing sound and there she leaned against the whitewashed wall of a Gothic church, several steps from him. Some unexplained power rooted him to the spot. Would she run away if he approached her? She gathered her cloak around her and continued down the alley.

"Wait, don't go." He called after her, but she spun in his direction and placed her gloved finger to her lips. The deep hood still hiding most of her face, the large plumes of her mask covering her eyes fluttered in the air.

Then she took a sharp left turn, skipped the two steps and entered a dark vault of the 'City Gates,' a tunnel leading beneath the ancient, stone-built medieval walls once erected for protection, and one of many perfect hideouts for the couples of old and modern times. The secret make-out hole he'd taken Irena to spend time alone, away from prying eyes.

He approached with hesitation. His heart pounded, ready to jump out of his chest. Could it be her? "Who are you?"

She panted in the corner, her breathing audible in the quiet of the night. Her shoulders rose and fell with each breath she took. Slowly she turned and faced him, and pulled the hood and the mask from her head, revealing the rest of her. "Have I changed that much?"

His heart stopped for a moment. Even in the dark, her blonde hair would stand out, not now. Her head blended with the darkness. The length of her hair seemed odd, cropped too short. Still, the tresses framed her petite face. A face that haunted him for the past fourteen years finally stood in front of him.

Chapter 2

The girl retreated into the darkness of the vault, away from the patch of light coming in from the street lamp. Dario took in the vision before him, his breathing subdued. He couldn't speak, his mouth had dried up and his mind drew a blank. His legs froze. *Is it truly Irena?* Everything about the woman convinced him it was her, except her hair color. Instead of her silky, golden locks, short brunette tresses barely reached her eyebrows. Her once slim frame seemed fuller in all the right places.

If he approached her, would she vanish? He took a tentative step. A piece of broken glass scraped the ancient cobblestone under his shoe, he halted.

A slow smile curved her ruby lips. Her hand, clad in the white, knitted glove reached from under her red cloak. "It is me."

He took her offered hand, her fingers curled around his. "Tell me this is a dream. I don't want to wake up."

"Then keep on dreaming." She cupped his face with her free hand, her perfume the subtle hint of citrus strongest on the inside of her wrist, intoxicating. "Thank God I found you."

He threaded his fingers through her thick hair. Could he get used to this dark tone? "Your hair, it's different."

"I'm trying to get used to it. It's temporary, needed

17

a change." In the next instance, her lush lips lifted to his. At first, her lips merely brushed his, then he wrapped his arms around her waist and pulled her to him. The fear he'd wake any second and discover she'd turned into a wisp of smoke gripped him, but he pushed down on the tightness in his gut. This was real, not his imagination, and hell if he wasn't going to make the most of it.

The cold stone wall stung his back through the thin denim fabric of his shirt. He couldn't remember when she'd backed him against the building. Once she deepened her kiss and her tongue slipped into his mouth, he uttered a deep moan and wrapped her in his arms. His body had not forgotten her, the tingle of nerves returned and assured him his girl was back in his arms. It wasn't until her frantic fingers moved to the buttons of his shirt that he regained a smidgeon of composure. He wanted to peel her clothes off, taste every inch of her, leave her limp and begging for more.

"M-m-m…Irena, babe." He breathed next to her lips. "As much as I'd love to relive our teenage days, I'd like to get away from this cold air."

She pulled back, her beautiful pale blue eyes fixed on his. "A few things are worthy of discomfort, but if you can, sneak me into your room—"

Laughter burst from his chest. The days of sneaking her into his parent's house through the window were long gone, but Irena wouldn't know his life had soared from the threshold of poverty. "I can do much better." He placed a kiss on her cheek. "I'm parked two blocks from here."

Her gaze lowered, but not before sadness filled her eyes. A mysterious smile played on her lips. She traced her finger down his torso, her voice almost a whisper. "Incredible, your dad's old Skoda is still drivable. We made some grand memories on the back seat."

He swallowed audibly, restraining the urge to take her here. It wouldn't do, in his fantasies, he took her to his bachelor pad and made love to her all night in every conceivable position. "No, babe, rusty Skoda was towed to the salvage yard years ago. It was hard to part with that car. When she left it felt like my memories went with her." He took her hand and laced his fingers with hers. "I drive a black BMW now. Let's move on, the night won't wait."

She tugged on his hand and made him stop. "We can't be seen together. I'll meet you by the bridge in twenty minutes."

"What?" Confusion mixed with sudden panic. He shook his head. "No. I'm not letting you go."

Her sigh told him she didn't want to part either, but the resolve in her unyielding gaze convinced him that now was not the time to argue. "What if you aren't there? Where can I find you?"

"I'll be there." She pulled the hood over her head. "Go now. And make sure you're not being followed."

Tension filled his chest and stiffened his neck. "Who'd follow me?"

"You're wasting time with questions." Nimble like a shadow, she bolted out of the vault and kept to the high medieval wall lining the road along the harbor, street lights reflecting on its still waters. Her feet made no sound on the stone paved street of the Old Town.

A heavy sigh failed to relax tension in his shoulders on his way to his car. The way she'd acted suggested she was afraid. He halted. What kind of man was he, fetching his car instead of following her in case she got into a trouble? He turned in the direction she'd left, but he couldn't spot the red cloak. His only option was to wait for her at the meeting place.

His heart pounded and his hands shook. He barely fit the key in the ignition. The engine purred, and he drove like a maniac through the abandoned streets, the lights and shadows changed in equal intervals.

He arrived at the bridge in less than ten minutes, but there was no red cloak. His happiness plummeted to his stomach. Stupid, why on Earth had he let her go?

A group of young and rowdy partygoers made their way toward him. Irena, in her red hood, tugged a couple of steps behind them, pretended to be a part of the group. Smart, if she was hiding from someone, she was less likely to be spotted in a crowd. Reaching his car, she slipped inside. No one in the bunch turned their heads at her action.

"Drive," she ordered, strapping the seatbelt.

"Who were those guys?" He turned the car around and drove away.

She shrugged, not meeting his eyes. "No idea, I used them for my cover."

He gave her a side-glance. "Would you care to explain what's going on?"

"Someday. Right now, I want to enjoy your company." She glided her hand over his thigh. "My, there's some leg muscle under these pants."

The roses in her cheeks and her pale blue eyes sparkled like two jewels made him suppress taking her into the backseat and ravishing her. He still had trouble believing this was not one of his make-beliefs. Many nights he'd walk the empty city streets alone and pretended she was right beside him. Not tonight. He should press her for an explanation, but knowing her, she'd come clean on her own terms.

Now alone with her, both his hands on the steering wheel, not touching her, sitting next to her, keeping control of himself and the speeding vehicle, proved harder than anything he'd ever tried before. She wasn't making it easy with her closeness and her busy hands fondling his thigh. Thank God for the transmission and parking brake between them, or he'd let the car go off-road. No matter how much he desired her, the hairs on the nape of his neck were on full alert. Something was wrong…very wrong.

She giggled a throaty, naughty chuckle. He groaned in frustration. She glided her hand to his groin and gave him a light squeeze on his swelled cock. "Where's the fire?"

"In my trousers, you know it full well, you little vixen." Oh good, the light ahead was changing. He pressed his foot on the brake and brought the car to a screeching halt. Then he leaned toward her, cupped her chin and pulled her to him.

"Come here," he whispered, capturing her lips with his. Her tongue met his and he caught it between his teeth. She rewarded him with another dose of her husky laughs.

His trousers would burst before he got her to his pad. The shrill horn of the car behind them jolted him. Irena moaned and leaned back against the seat. "Didn't we pass the road to your house three blocks back?"

After shifting gears, he took her hand and kissed the soft mohair of her glove. "Babe, there have been many changes. My parents passed away six years ago.

Ante and I sold the shack we grew up in and opened the restaurant. Who knew my mom's traditional recipes would turn into an overnight success? We're no longer the two dirt-poor brothers." He gauged her reaction from the corner of his eye.

"I'm sorry to hear about your parents. They were such nice people." She turned to the window and after a long silence faced him. "Better than mine, but I don't want to resurrect the past, not tonight." A soft smile formed tiny dimples in her cheeks while she glided her hand over the smooth leather interior. "This is a nice ride."

He raked his top teeth over his bottom lip. "Wealth comes with a price. Suddenly everyone's a bosom friend with me and Ante."

She snickered. "Knowing you, you'd give them everything you've got."

"You know me, babe." He pulled into the parking spot designated for visitors in front of his building. "Let me show you where I live now."

Easing out of his car, all tension left him. She skirted the hood and wrapped her arms around his waist. The way she molded her lithe body to his made him forget all the unasked questions swarming his head. He glanced at the top of the twenty stories high building. The moon reflected off the dark windows of his penthouse. A few more steps to the entrance and he'd start peeling her clothes off in the elevator so he could lay her on his bed as soon as he got her through the door.

She glanced over her shoulder, and again after a couple of steps.

He narrowed his gaze, peered into the darkness

beyond the parking lot of the condo building. Other than the sanitation had not picked up the garbage for the second week, nothing seemed out of the ordinary. And even the piling trash bags were becoming the norm. Turning to her, he pulled her closer. She'd been acting strange, avoiding talking about her past fourteen years. But he wouldn't let her get away that easy. "Let's get up to my place and then you're going to tell me what's going on."

Inside the condo lobby, the stainless steel door of the elevator stood wide open. Dario quickened his steps, ushering Irena toward the car. He pressed the button for the penthouse. She wrapped her arms around him and cast him a seductive smile. Her eyes sparkled with desire. God, she was beautiful.

Their embraced image reflected in the shiny door as it slid closed. He leaned toward her and placed a gentle kiss on her forehead. He'd never burned with such intense desire. Every nerve in his body vibrated with aching need.

She sighed and pulled back, her tongue moistening her luscious lips. "Fourteen years without a kiss is a long time."

He gave a slight tilt of his head as her words sank in. "You mean, you never..." Unable to finish the sentence, he glanced down to her heaving chest. This news filled him with joy. Still, sorrow swirled through his heart. Although she'd said she could never love Fred, as years passed by, Dario assumed she had accepted her commitment. Had she suffered and cried many nights? Her hopeless past would stay in the past. From now on, her future would change for better.

"Yes, from the get-go I knew I'd spend my life in a

loveless marriage. Only, I've expected to be free of Fred sooner." She whispered in his ear, wrapping Dario again in her enchantment.

"Surely, on your wedding night, you must've—"

"My wedding night." She dragged the words out, corners of her mouth slid down and her nose wrinkled. "What a joke. I spent it in the bridal suite, alone, flipping channels on the TV."

Relief chipped away some of Dario's worry. Often he cringed at the thought of her enduring Fred in bed with her. Though the rumors about Fred put Dario's fears at ease, he was never too sure. "And the groom?"

"The groom?" She snorted. "He was on another floor's executive suite in the arms of the priest who performed the wedding ceremony."

Dario's mouth dropped, and he stared at her, wide eyed. "I'm sorry you have to suffer like that. Your parents thought they secured you a fairy-tale future."

"They only cared about the payment from Fred, which they never got. Serves them right." Her seductive whisper sent another shiver through his body before she caught his lobe between her teeth. A promise she'd soon answer all his questions lingered in her kiss.

He barely held onto the little control he had. Damn it, why was the elevator going down? The door slid open on the underground parking level, and a plump guy staggered in, cinching a sleeping boy higher on his shoulder.

Irena pushed away from Dario, pulling her deep hood over her head. She retreated into the corner and stared at the elevator's floor tiles.

The man nodded and pressed the button, lighting number four on the panel, then cast aren't-you-gonna-introduce-me look to Dario.

Dario feigned indifference, but a stone dropped through his gut. Irena acted strange as if she didn't want to be seen with him. The man's expression changed to fuck-it-I'll-introduce-myself. He adjusted his hold on his son and extended his hand. "You must be the newest fling of our city's most eligible, yet sworn bachelor. I'm Stan by the way."

Rage flamed inside Dario, and he fisted his hands. If not for Irena's presence and the sleeping child, Stan's teeth would meet his knuckles.

"Nice to meet you, Stan," Irena murmured, glancing at the intruder, but not accepting Stan's hand. "Your boy looks cute asleep on your shoulder."

"Ah, yes, party animal, just like his dad once was. I thought he'd never go to sleep." Stan's deep laughter boomed in the elevator.

"Too much excitement?" Dario kept his gaze at the round number on the elevator's control pad. Stan's floor dinged as the elevator stopped and the door slid open.

"Too much sugar," Stan answered Dario's question and put one foot out. "But you know the saying, what goes up, must come down. Have yourself a great night." He was about to step out, but he halted and faced Irena again. "Sorry, I didn't catch your name."

"Claire." She nodded, casting another glance at Stan.

Stan murmured something under his breath and finally left, leaving behind the stench of body odor.

"Claire?" Dario raised a questioning eyebrow.

She lowered her hood and pressed her body to him. "He didn't need to know. I'll explain. Later."

Dario traced his finger along her smooth forehead. God, she was that one person who fed his soul and gave him the reason to get up in the morning, face the new day, and even smile. After all these years, she was back in his arms, all grown up and beautiful as ever. Fear shadowing her big eyes couldn't escape him.

"What are you afraid of, Irena?" The elevator chimed in time with his question, the door silently slid open.

She grabbed his hand while he still brushed her hair from her face, placed a kiss on his knuckles and tugged him along. "Let's leave the questions."

Holding onto her hand, he approached the single, cherry color door on the top floor, and fumbled for his keys inside his jeans pocket. "My unit is the only one on this floor. Just wait until you see the view."

His hand shook while he inserted the key. The lock clicked and he pushed the door open, extending his arm, his palm facing up. "Welcome home."

Her slow steps carried her deeper into the penthouse. He followed the trail of her perfume and stared at her from the door. She descended the three semi-circular steps spanning the width of the ten-foot wide landing. Her slippers sank where the hardwood floor met the plush cream carpet. Judging by her mouth hanging open and eyes wide, she was amazed by his new place.

"Gorgeous," she breathed, approaching the window spanning from the floor to the ceiling. The twinkling lights of the city spread before her.

In a few strides, he was at her side and pointed at the distance. "And you can see all the way to the islands. See that moving light? That's a fishing boat in the channel. The lights beyond that are in the village of Kali on Ugljan."

"Amazing." She turned to him, a smile lingering on her lips. "You've done quite well."

He cupped her petite face in his hands, placed a soft kiss on the top of her little nose. "All with you in mind."

She froze, if not for her slow blinks, he feared she stopped breathing. "I thought of you every day. Can't tell you how glad I am to find you single. I was afraid you'd be married with a couple of kids by now."

"No babe. It was hard at times, but I held on to the prediction that we'd be together again." Her eyes glazed over and he forced himself to step back, give her space. "Where are my manners? Let me take your cloak. Can I get you something to drink?"

A nervous smile appeared on her lips, her white teeth flashed in the dim overhead pot light. She pulled on the string of the red cloak and shrugged out of the cape, then peeled off her white, mohair gloves. Stones on her ring twinkled as she draped her garments over his offered arm. He caught her hand, staring at the jewel on her finger. The question pressed on his mind, but the words wouldn't form.

"It's fake." Her words pulled his gaze to her face. She shrugged. "Just like my marriage. But I can see it on your face. You wonder why I still wear it. Because…" She took her hand out of his and yanked the ring off her finger. "It hides the real one. "

She raised her hand in front of his face and flashed the yellow pipe cleaner he'd wrapped around her finger the night they'd parted.

"I hardly take it off. Only when I need to wet my

hands, still it held up pretty well over the years." She paused, exhaling a shaky breath. "All I ever wanted was home and family with you and…I…"

Molten lava erupted deep inside him and boiled to the surface, making him drop her cloak and gloves on the heap next to his feet. For the first time in his life, the shame of growing up poor spiraled through him. Today he lived a very different life, but he'd never forgotten where he came from. His breath hitched as pain sliced his chest and constricted his throat.

Her heaving chest and face tense on the verge of tears. "No, baby, don't." Her voice strained, she swiped her thumbs under his eyes.

"Oh, Irena." He croaked, pulling her into his embrace. The emotions he couldn't keep bottled up any longer erupted. He forced the words out. "I promised you a real ring. I lost all faith you'll be mine and…"

She combed her fingers through his hair while he rocked her trembling body. Her tears soaked the fabric on his shoulder. "The ring doesn't make a marriage. Now, where's that drink you offered?"

He pulled back, but still held one arm wrapped around her while the tight bend loosened up his chest, and flashed a grin. "This occasion calls for a champagne, unfortunately, I don't have any. How does a glass of wine sound?"

"White if you have it." She bent to pick up her things where he'd dropped them. Her teary eyes deepened his pain. Knowing her, she'd need a moment alone to regain her composure.

"Glass of white coming up." He stepped into the kitchen. Lights appeared misty, reflecting on the black granite countertops. The wine cooler built under the kitchen island was a perfect refuge to gather the last of his composure. After some careful consideration, he settled for a bottle of Malvasia Istriana. She'd love its floral and fruity aroma and crisp taste. He grabbed a corkscrew and two long stem wine glasses and joined her on the balcony.

"I see you found the way out. The view from here is even better." He handed her one glass and placed the other on the wide railing, then proceeded to uncork the bottle.

Her perfume drifted stronger, and he became aware of her closeness. "Yes, the view is marvelous, but I much rather memorize your body in the light of candles."

His hand turning the corkscrew halted, and he met her lips with his. In an instant, their bodies molded together, squeezing the bottle between them.

"M-m-m...babe," he whispered next to her lips, placing kisses on her cheek. "Let's not allow this wine to go warm. It's best consumed chilled."

Licking her lips, she pulled back and raised her empty glass. "Then, by all means, pour."

The pale yellow straw colored wine tinged with green filled her glass. He filled his, then held it up for a toast. "To our beautiful future together."

A dark shadow crossed her eyes, but she clicked her glass with his and downed the drink in a few gulps. She extended her empty glass to him. "I know this wine is for sipping, but I couldn't help it. Tastes fabulous, clean and zesty, yet it's light bodied."

He tilted the bottle over the rim of her glass but didn't pour. "More?"

"Only a dribble, so you don't have to drink yours

alone."

"Say when." The liquid barely filled the bottom; she waved her hand for him to stop.

He placed the bottle on the small table in the corner and wrapped one arm around her shoulders. She tilted her head toward the sky.

"I forgot what the night sky looks like here. In Toronto, the light pollution is too great to see a single star." She rubbed his hand, then laced her fingers with his.

"Ah, this is nothing," he said, tilting his head at the starry vault. "I know of the place where you can see stars better. The sky appears so low. You'd think you can just reach up and grab them. I want to take you there. To the stars, that is." He took another sip of his wine. Her closeness and warmth worked its effect on his already primed body.

"Dario," she said, turning to him then placed a kiss on his neck. "Make love to me. Now."

He swallowed, repressing the urge to strip her of her tight jeans and the fitted sweater right there on the balcony. To satisfy fourteen years of drought in love making would put a great pressure on any man, but he was up to the challenge. He took her hand and pulled her into his embrace. She smelled of heaven and home, and everything he always wanted. As if recognizing the scent of her arousal, his cock sprang full mast and threatened to burst out of his pants. *Easy boy.*

He traced his thumb along her cheekbone and she narrowed her eyes to almost almond shape, he could still get under her skin. Cradling her head in his palm, he swayed with her to the gentle blues rhythm drifting from the speaker in his living room. His lower abdomen contracted as he brushed his thumb along her bottom lip. The stir of her breath on his face when she leaned closer set his heart on a wild race. Her lips touched his, pressing, caressing, tasting.

Drawing her closer, she wrapped one arm around his neck, deepening the kiss, and reached her other hand to his crotch. The sweet hint of wine still lingered in her mouth and incited him on.

He slipped his hands under her sweater, finding the clasps of her bra, and whispered, "This night may not end here, but I want to start fulfilling your wish on the balcony."

"No, Dario. We spent too much time here already." A hint of fear in her voice caused the tiny hairs on the back of his neck to stand on end. "Let's take this to your bedroom where no one can see us."

## Chapter 3

Dario led the way to the loft, his hand tight around Irena's. With every step he climbed, he gazed over his shoulder. She claimed she hadn't made love in fourteen years. Why had she waited all this time to leave her husband? Or had she left him? Dario couldn't wait to show her how good it could be, with the right person. He remembered her sparkling eyes and the mysterious smile lingering on her lips from the last time they had sex. Hell, that felt like a millennium ago. She was hungry for his attention.

"Welcome to my bedroom." He cringed at the messy sight. "My alarm didn't go off this morning, I had to rush." The only time the king size mattress appeared tidy, was when he placed a fresh set of sheets on it. He dimmed the light on the nightstand and straightened the yellow cover, then put away his dumbbells he'd left carelessly in the middle of the floor, and was about to return the balance ball to its spot in the corner, but she tugged on his arm.

"Looks okay to me." She drew closer to him, a shy smile stretching her lips. She glanced at the bed. "We're going to mess it up again." Her sultry whisper sent pleasant vibes through him and he kicked the ball away. She swayed her hips against his pelvis, teasing him. Her eyes smoldered with lust. "So, was that guy right about you breaking young girls' hearts?"

"Ah, don't believe my neighbor." Damn Stan. Dario clenched his jaw. "I've dated on and off over the years, mostly off."

"It's all right, I didn't expect you to stay celibate." She closed what little distance remained between them. Her arms encircled his waist. He felt her hands explore the muscles of his back. "Anyone I know?"

Though her question carried a teasing tone, he gave a slow nod, afraid how she'd take what he was about to reveal. "No one serious for years. Then briefly Ana."

Her sudden silence worried him so he continued, "She pursued me after I made my small fortune. Before that she couldn't spare me a glance..." He tightened his hold on Irena's hips. Her eyes seemed to lose the fire, and curiosity flashed in them, searching his face for an explanation. "I fit her bill for a wealthy man, but enough about her."

Irena pulled back, pursing her lips as she huffed out a breath. "Ana always wanted everything I had. Her fascination to look like me was creepy. She kept telling me how you'll hurt me and urged me to dump you." Irena lowered her head. "I almost caved once. Though when the parting time came, it would be easier on both of us, but couldn't let you go. Not really." She tapped her fingers on her chest. "Not in here."

He muffled Irena's further words by planting his lips on hers, coaxing them apart. Their tongues met in a slow dance. Fuzziness spread through him, settling in his groin.

Irena's hands caressed his body through the thin cotton of his shirt. His desire hardened against her thigh. The thought of entering her core made his heart pump faster. No other woman made him feel this way.

"I missed you," she whispered, her lips moving against his.

He slipped his hand under her sweater and brushed her soft, warm belly. She shivered and grabbed his wrist when he was about to pull his hand out. When his fingers wrapped around the button of her jeans, she helped him with the zipper then lowered the pants below her hips.

His fingers slipped inside the band of her panties, finding her moist enticed him to glide farther down, searching for the top of her folds. His thumb massaged her nub, while a finger moved inside her, first one, then two, filling her, stretching her.

With a whimper, she arched her pelvis, giving him greater access. "Faster, harder, baby."

Her demanding whisper caused him to stop. So love-starved, she'd shatter before he got her naked. She had the same effect on him, his body shook with desire, every nerve alive and vibrating.

With a head shake, she raised a questioning brow. "Why did you stop?"

Wrapping his hand around her slender neck, he tilted her head and licked the exposed skin. He reached for the hem of her sweater and pulled the wool garment over her head. "Let me see you."

She stepped out of her crumpled jeans and tucked her thumbs inside her panties, ready to slide the lace down her slender thighs. He cupped her buttocks and she shimmied, working her underwear to her ankles. When she kicked her leg, he grabbed the purple garment and pressed her soaked thong to his nose. Her citrusy perfume mingled with the smell of her natural essence and sent another rush of ecstasy to his groin.

He let out a long grunt.

Instinct drove him to explore all of her, to increase her pleasure. To give her what her husband never had.

His hands dropped to his sides as she unbuttoned his shirt and peeled the cotton off his shoulders. She glided her hands over his skin. "My, you have grown."

He reached for her boobs still shielded behind the silky brazier, but it was her muscular frame that caught his attention. "So have you."

"Here, have a better view." She flipped her hair and puffed her chest, reaching her arms behind her back to undo the clasps of her bra. She pulled the straps down, her full tits just inches from him. He cupped them in his hands, flicked his thumbs over her nipples, making the pink buds stand to attention. She winced and flashed him a glance, her fingers busy with the fly of his pants.

Her tight muscles flexed with each move. "Let's make it fair and free you of your jeans."

"By all means." He helped her with the removal of his pants.

He glided his hand over hardened muscles of her abdomen. Whatever kind of sport she was in required commitment, money, and many sacrifices until it became a second nature. Not for someone leading a *normal* life. She trained for her self-defense. But, why? Her husband? Was he as abusive as her father had been? From the little he knew about Fred, the man preferred the company of men and couldn't care less about her. However, Dario didn't want to waste time badgering her with questions. Later, he'd find the answers, after they made love. His voice hitched as she worked her fingers around his shaft. "Oh, yes, babe, it knows your hand."

He lowered to the mattress, taking her with him. Her slow, exquisite stroking of his chest, sinful in its effect, transported him into a forgotten, intoxicating realm. Seeking his hand, she wrapped her fingers around his wrist encouraging him back between her legs. He increased the depth and pace of his strokes. His fingers moved, faster, short strokes, coaxing moans out of her. She swayed, straddling him, thrusting her hips to meet his fingers. If her arching back and throaty noises were any indication, she couldn't hold on much longer. He moved his mouth to her nipple sucking her breast until it pebbled, and nipped the hardened nub, making her flinch.

"God," she panted. "I'm crazy with need for you...primal."

"Yes, we are." He sat up, wrapped one arm around her waist, and flipped her onto her back, then covered her naked body with his. In one strong plunge, he entered her warm channel.

"Ah, yes..." she cried, wrapping her legs below his butt. Her hands stroked and touched everywhere, sending waves of desire through him. His shaft, sheathed inside her narrow core, swelled and lengthened. With each thrust, the embers of passion ignited within him. The need for release had him in a sweat as he fought to hold himself in check. A warm flutter low in the pit of his stomach spread like a bush fire. A wave of heat washed over him. Shattering bursts of pleasure infused his body. He let out a primal growl as he bucked on top of her. Lights exploded behind his closed lids, taking him to the height of pleasure. Euphoria took him out of this world and for a moment he experienced weightlessness, while ripples of orgasm slammed his pelvis against her hips.

Irena writhed beneath him, panted and raised her hips meeting his thrusts. Her chest glistened in the dim light. Their melded bodies were a perfect fit, always had been. He laced his fingers with hers, kissing her neck and face while her tense body relaxed in his arms.

Slowly, she opened her eyes, her gaze fixed to the ceiling. A wide smile stretched her lips and she uttered a low, gruff moan. "I almost forgot what an amazing lover you are."

He kissed her. "Will you stay with me? Let me love you every night until the dawn?" He brushed her sweaty hair off her neck and placed a kiss on her hot skin.

She traced her finger along his temple. "I will."

Sadness filled her eyes, causing his guts to coil in a tight knot. Why wouldn't she open up to him? If there was something or someone after her, she should know he was on her side.

She tangled her legs with his, her breasts begging for his attention. God help him, at this rate he wouldn't get any sleep, but he didn't care. In fourteen years, he hadn't taken a single day off. By all that was holy, he deserved a day to himself as he worshipped Irena in every way she wanted. Lazily, he traced the swells of her boobs, while her chest rose and fell with each breath beneath his hand.

She played with his hair. "Where's that wine? I'm so thirsty."

"I left it on the balcony." He swung one leg over the edge of the mattress. "I'll go get it and some water. You won't kill the thirst with wine."

"Sounds good." Her bite on his arm ignited a fire in his loins all over again. "Hurry back."

He scrambled down the carpeted stairs, opened the balcony's sliding door and snatched the bottle from the glass top table. A thin line of light appeared on the horizon behind the islands in the distance. Dawn would reach them in about an hour. He'd better make the best of what was left of the night. In a few strides, he crossed the floor to the open concept kitchen and let his feet slide on the cream tile, stopping by the brushed chrome fridge door. The light came on inside the appliance and made him squint while he found the green bottle of mineral water. He filled the two tall glasses with ice and carried everything upstairs.

His insides melted at the sight of sleeping Irena. How could he have forgotten, she loved to snooze after lovemaking? He placed the glass of water on the nightstand by her side of the bed. She'd be thirsty when she awoke.

After turning the lamp off, he lay next to her, pulled the covers up and planted a kiss on her soft, warm shoulder. Tomorrow, he would make love to her again and later feed her a big breakfast, they would get her things and she would move in with him. Under no circumstance would he let her stay with her parents, no matter how old and feeble they became. He'd get them hired help if he must, but Irena was his. His bachelor days were finally over. At the press of the button on the remote control, the blinds lowered, darkness engulfed the room. Tonight he'd sleep like he had not slept in years.

**** 

Something smacked him on the shoulder, shaking

him awake. "Wake up sleepyhead. It's nearly three in the afternoon. Are you okay, bro?"

His hopes to find Irena's naked body stretching under the covers shattered when he jerked to sitting and came face to face with Ante. "What the hell are you doing here?

His brother straightened and took a step back from the bed. "Staff called me after you failed to open the restaurant this morning." He put his hand up. "No need to thank me. I managed through the lunch rush just fine. You didn't answer my phone calls so I started to worry. You left the penthouse door unlocked." Ante tsked and shook his head. "Do you want to get robbed?" But in the next instance a stupid smirk appeared on his lips, he winked. "People saw you following Little Red Riding Hood last night. You missing work for the first time ever, guess she showed you a great time."

Dario fisted his hands. For a moment Ante's chocolate colored eyes and mahogany hair reminded him too much of himself and it restrained him from knocking that ridiculous smile off his brother's face for such a rude awakening. After all, he'd let him sleep through the day. Last night's events replayed in his head. The indent on the empty pillow was still there. She couldn't have gone far.

"Irena," he called, kicking the covers off and jumping out of bed.

Chapter 4

Dario snatched his rumpled jeans off the bedroom floor. His boxers still tucked inside, the way they had crumpled off his hips under Irena's gliding hands. He hopped into the pants, shoved his arms through the sleeves of his sweatshirt and yanked the fleece over his head. *Damnation*, how could he miss her leaving? Sleep had found him at dawn, and while it wasn't the first time he'd stayed up all night, the slightest sound should've woken him from his slumber.

Maybe having Irena in his bed had relaxed him. He couldn't remember the last time he'd slept that heavy.

Judging by Ante's hanging mouth, his brother was stunned at his admission that he'd spent the night with Irena.

"No time to lose. We have to find her." Dario pulled on the same socks from last night. Irena's naked body spread on the top of his black bed cover surfaced in his mind. The way she licked her lips while he kicked off his socks and climbed on top of him sent a shiver of pleasure through him, but urgency pressed him on. If he was to have her in his bed again, he better get his ass in gear.

"Are you sure it was her?" Ante cleared his throat. "I mean, it could've been Ana. You know how she has some weird fascination to look like Irena."

"It wasn't Ana." He barely spared half a glance at

Ante while doing up his pants zipper and button, then flew down the stairs. "I think I know what Irena and Ana look like to tell the difference. And Irena's brunette now."

"Whoa." Ante trailed behind him. "No way would Irena do that. Her hair made her stand out in the crowd."

Dario paused on the bottom step and gaped at his brother. "That's it. You just unraveled a part of this mystery. Irena's golden-blonde hair was always easy to spot. Now as a brunette, her hair is ordinary." *But why?*

Ante shook his head. "She loved standing out. I can't see it."

"She didn't say much, but from what I gathered, she's on the run. From her husband, I assume..." At Ante's questioning stare, he continued. "I must find her."

Ante spread his arms wide as if to encompass the city. "Where would we start to look? And why'd she run out on you?"

Dario took a step back and bit back a truck-load of swear words. "I bet she's at her parents' place."

"No," Ante gasped, his jaw dropped. "You wouldn't go there. Her mother despised you. She won't be of any help. The woman always thought of us vermin." He scrunched his nose. "As if she was better than the rest of the world just because she was a teacher."

Dario half listened to his brother's rants while searching every place he kept his car keys and coming up empty. Mrs. Novak had a superiority complex, but she lived in a time when teachers were to be feared and respected. "Help me find my keys, I misplaced them."

41

Ante tossed the car keys at the Dario from the kitchen table where they laid. "Irena sneaking out explains the unlocked door. About going to see her parents, you may want to reconsider."

"I'm not afraid of her mother. Not anymore. Go press the elevator button." He stepped out of his apartment and locked the door, stopping his hand mid-turn of the key. What if Irena returned after he was gone? Not likely, he checked that the door was fully locked. If she should come back by some miracle, he'd have the porter let her in with his spare key.

Ante might've bought his bluff, but cold snakes stirred in his stomach at the thought of facing the stern woman. Irena's mother had pulled on her teacher's connections to get his report cards and shoved them under Irena's nose as a proof that he'd never amount to anything with his barely passing grades and absenteeism. Little did the educator know he'd spent most mornings tending to his ill father and worked wherever he could find work to pay the bills. His mother had provided food from the little patch she called a garden, but the meat was a rare treat on their table. Thankfully, fish from the abundant sea made up for the absence of Sundays' roasts.

He followed Ante into the elevator. Just last night he was here with Irena, kissing her senseless while she drove him wild with desire. Now he was sharing the ride down with his brother. Not how he imagined his date would progress.

The bell chimed at the ground floor and the door silently slid open. Dario shot out of the elevator, racing for the main entrance.

"You didn't park in the underground parking

42

garage?" His brother's voice laced with astonishment drifted from behind.

"I took a visitor's spot." Outside, the overcast sky hung low with gray clouds promised imminent rain. Ante's hurried footsteps thumped on the stone walkway leading to the parking.

"My, you left your baby out here." Sarcasm dripped from Ante's voice as he placed a hand on Dario's shoulder. "I understand you, bro. Driving all the way down to the underground garage takes too long and Irena is worth having your car vandalized or stolen."

Dario approached the driver's side of his two-seater BMW and glared at Ante. "Okay, I get your mockery. Yes, I'm overprotective of my car, or as you call it my baby." He pointed at him. "You of all people should understand. Growing up we had nothing and appreciate every little thing we got."

"I hear you, bro." Ante slid into the passenger's seat.

Dario slid the key into the ignition. At the first click, the panel light came to life. "Got your cell with you?"

"Of course." Ante buckled his seatbelt.

A knock on the driver's side window made Dario jump. Stan's fat, round face filled the frame. "Hey, neighbor."

Chatting with his nosey neighbor was the last thing on Dario's list right now, but he lowered the glass between them. "Hi, Stan. I'm in a hurry."

Stan stepped away, hands in front, fingers spread. "No worries just wanted to tell you your visitor stormed out of here some two or three hours ago. Almost didn't recognize her, she wore a black coat, but it was her, all right."

Dario's heart lurched and he could almost kiss Stan, his nosiness could save him time. "Did you see which way she went?"

"She had her phone pressed to her ear and didn't hear me when I wished her good day. I'm sure she was getting a cab, but she dropped this." Stan pulled a business card of the Lulu Taxi Company.

Dario let out a long sigh and took the card in his hand. "Thank you, Stan."

"Hey, don't mention it. That's what neighbors are for. Got to go, my little one is on the swing by himself." He touched his meaty finger to the brim of his baseball cap and took off for the playground.

Dario passed the card to Ante. "Your buddy is a dispatcher for Lulu Cab, can you get him to check drivers' logs and find out if they picked up a passenger at this address today and where they dropped her off?"

"Piece of cake." Ante slid his cell out of the shirt pocket. The light of the screen lit up his face while he scrolled through his contacts, then pressed the phone to his ear. "I hope my buddy's not asleep." He lowered his chin when the person on the other side of the line answered. "Hey, bud…sorry for waking you up. Yes, I know you pulled the double shift, but I need a favor from you, big time. What's that? Um-hum…okay…listen, man…stop talking for a moment."

Dario eased out of his parking spot, praying Ante got a lead on Irena. He pulled onto the street. The digital numbers on the panel clock displayed 3:25. Afternoon rush hour traffic would start in less than an hour. He stepped on the gas pedal.

Three blocks from Irena's parents' apartment building, Ante was still on the phone, tapping his fingers on his knee while his buddy was on the landline phone with the day dispatch to check the records. A parked police vehicle flashed its blue lights and blocked the road.

Dario brought the car to a stop, blowing hot air of frustration through his nose. "Now what?"

"The cop is re-directing traffic to the side street. Something big must've happened." Ante rolled the window down and stuck his head out. "I don't see any wrecked cars on the road. Maybe they took them away. Hey, isn't that Rob? Rob, my man, come here."

Dario extended his neck, peering over the steering wheel at the guy in uniform. Their high school friend waved to them and moseyed toward their car.

"Maybe he'll tell us what's going on." Ante returned his attention to the phone as the voice replaced the tune coming from the device.

"I doubt he is at liberty to do that." Dario rolled his side window when Rob approached.

Rob nodded to him and leaned his arm on the roof of the car. "Sorry, Dario, hate to send you down that narrow street, but that's the only detour."

He flashed Rob a tight smile. "Thanks for the heads up. You wouldn't be able to tell us what's up, would you?"

Rob leaned closer, poking his head through the open window, and lowered his voice. "You didn't hear this from me, but it's gonna hit the news fast anyways. A woman blew her brains out in the parking lot, left a note. Hitting a pedestrian a year ago apparently put her in financial ruins. Oh, remember that girl you dated in high school… well her mother was the one hit."

"Such unfortunate tragedy. I'm sorry the woman ended her life like that." Dario clicked his tongue, shaking his head. The connection to Mrs. Novak's accident stirred bad premonition inside him. "Thank you for the information."

A sudden urgency pressed on Dario's shoulders. He gunned the engine and took the detour. Ante hung to the handle above the window, pocketed the phone and shouted over the noise of the speeding car. "The cabby dropped her downtown. No specific address. However, you are in luck, the man was clocking out for the day and the dispatcher asked him. He saw her going into the Hotel Bastion. No need to go to her parents'."

A block away from Irena's old apartment building, Dario parallel parked his BMW between a delivery truck and a motorcycle. Parking on the street wasn't the safest, but there were no other options in this older part of the city. He drummed his fingers on the dashboard, gathering the courage to face Irena's mother.

He turned to the newsstand. Clear plastic covering over the stacked magazines to protect them from imminent rain, swayed and crinkled in the wind. After fourteen years, the small metallic structure still stood here, a new sign displayed at the top and a person clad in jean jacket hovered behind the closed sliding window minded the business. Fond memories flooded him. An image of his young self in a worn out T-shirt and jeans floated in front of his eyes.

Ante stirred in the passenger seat. "I don't get you, bro. Irena's not here. Why do you have to go through this?"

He snatched the keys out of the ignition.

"Something tells me the woman in the parking lot did not commit a suicide, nor was Irena's mother hit by accident a year ago. The driver who had run her over failed at her job."

"Look," Ante said, grabbing his shoulder. "Just because you think some foul play is going on, perhaps you should leave the investigation to the police."

Dario brushed his brother's hand away. Irena's husband wouldn't have any trouble lacing a few pockets for things to work his way. "Think about it, man. Irena's parents forced her to marry for money. She said the fact her parents will be taken care of for the rest of their lives gave her strength to go through the ordeal. What do you think she meant?"

Ante shrugged. The corners of his mouth dipped. "Sounds like her parents sold her into this marriage."

"I'm sure money was promised. Her parents would want to secure their future and marrying Irena to a rich guy did that. I'd bet anything in this world Fred's on the hook for payment in some way or another." Dario grimaced, rubbing the stubble on his chin. His theory developed in front of him. Her parents had gone to great extent to keep them apart, despite their daughter's reluctance to marry the guy they had chosen for her. "I don't know the whole story yet, but pieces are falling into place. I'm speculating they outlived someone's patience. Her mother's *accident* was supposed to make the problem go away if you know what I mean. Instead, Mrs. Novak now has bigger medical expenses and it's more of a drain on Fred's pocket. He waited this long to get rid of the driver so it wouldn't come too soon, too suspicious."

Ante's thick eyebrows drew closer, resembling a

caterpillar. "Are you batshit crazy? How long have you been thinking about this?" He waved his hand and opened the car door. "Let's get this over with."

Dario eased out of the car. He skirted the hood, meeting Ante on the sidewalk. Old, familiar buildings had barely seen a fresh coat of paint. A couple of new stores and a café opened since he last ventured up this road. "The army barracks are now turned into the city's library."

"It's nice to see the trimmed bushes replaced the ungodly iron fence and armed guards." Ante's lips thinned into a white line.

"We were still kids when army occupied these buildings." Dario's footsteps halted as he neared the weather-beaten doors of the building where he'd spent many nights kissing Irena. Often well after her curfew, thankful that her parents valued their sleep more than enforcing their rules. The memory of their parting for good squeezed his throat. If he never boarded that tanker, today his life wouldn't change much. At least the ship captain had recognized his cooking skills and recommended him for culinary college. It had taken twice as long to obtain his degree due to the ports his vessel docked in, but he persisted and in the following years rose to the position of Chief Steward.

No matter how busy his life had kept him, he'd missed Irena so much he wanted to pick her from his dreams and hug her, instead of his pillow. And he should be running to her, not going to face her mother, but an unexplainable urge moved him forward.

He swallowed hard and tilted his head toward the second story balcony. Empty planters piled up in the corner against the rusting railing.

Inside the foyer, the walls had seen a fresh coat of paint, but the staircase was the same, cold, hard cement, thin iron spikes held the black top of the railing. The soles of his sneakers squeaked on the wet steps.

His feet carried him to the second floor to the green apartment door. Mr. L. Novak was displayed on the small, gray plaque. He pressed the button, holding it down. The shrill chime filled the long hallway.

He waited. No answer.

"Oh, well," Ante breathed, turning for the stairs. "Looks like no one's home. At least you tried."

"She's in there. She may not be fast on her feet anymore." He rang the bell again. Two short rings this time.

"Who is it?" A weak woman's voice came muffled from the other side of the door.

"Mrs. Novak, it's Dario. Can we please talk, but I don't want to talk through the wood."

"What are you doing here?" Her voice took on a sudden deep tone as if she tapped into the fountain of strength. "If you're looking for Irena, she's not here. Unless you know where she is, be gone, you vermin. You caused enough trouble."

It had been so long since he heard those words spoken in the harsh tone. Years ago she would send him scrambling, but not anymore. Like a sword, he too had been forged in life battles and Mrs. Novak no longer epitomized someone to fear. So, Irena had not visited her mother. How did the woman know her daughter was missing? "I'm not here for Irena. Please, just open the door."

"Go away and don't come back here." Silence followed only broken by the slow shuffling of her feet.

"I told you there was no point in coming here." Ante tapped him on his shoulder and hurried down the stairs to the first landing.

Dario's chest tightened as he turned to follow his brother. Before he reached him, the rattling of chains and clicking of locks filled the hallway. He paused and waited. The door to Novak apartment opened and Irena's mother shuffled out, leaning heavily on her walker. Liver spots covered her hands and face, deep wrinkles sagged her skin. Her faded yellow flannel gown floated around her thin frame as if it hung on the hanger.

"If you find her," Mrs. Novak said, a pleading in her voice. "Tell her she must return to her husband. What kind of woman leaves her man? Her head is filled up with nonsense. Every wife has to endure her husband's wrath." She lowered her gaze at her feet in worn out slippers, their color was not distinguishable. "Tell her, her father had to go to a home." Her voice trembled as she began to weep. Moments later, her frail body shook with her sobs. Strange, Irena had said her mother had not shed a tear over her leaving home, yet here she bawled for sending her abusive husband to a nursing home.

*Horseshit.* Dario clamped down his lips and cast her a tight smile. Had Mrs. Novak truly loved her husband to the point of blind devotion? Or was her speech just to put up appearances? He'd bet all his money on the latter. "If I find Irena, I'll pass on the message."

"If she doesn't go back, her poor father will not receive the care he needs. We can't pay for the home and my medical expenses." She turned toward the open door. "Such an ungrateful daughter, God cursed me with, after we gave her everything."

Dario fisted his hands, but couldn't restrain his tongue, not when Mrs. Novak's words reopened the barely healed wound. "Everything, Mrs. Novak? It's obvious you want to find her for your own gain."

She halted and pivoted on her good leg. "Her husband is worried about her. She's sick and needs medication. He came here, believing she'd returned home to aid me. When he saw the misery I live in, he graciously offered to pay for my knee replacement surgery *if* I find her."

A surge of anger flooded over Dario. Irena's husband had come here, looking for her. He didn't love her, so why follow her across the world? When Mrs. Novak was about to disappear inside her apartment, Dario shouted before she shut the door. "The woman who hit you committed suicide today."

Mrs. Novak threw her head back and huffed. "As she should," she said, her voice peeved and shrill with irritation. "I wouldn't be in this predicament if she didn't wave for me to cross the street at a pedestrian crossover. Once I put my foot on the pavement, she hit me. Later the stupid woman changed her story. She lied and said I jumped in front of her car."

The door closed, cutting off the stench of urine and decay wafting from Mrs. Novak's apartment. He faced his brother's wide eyes and half-frown. "Well then, who's batshit crazy now?"

"Your theory could be right." Ante shuddered. "I can't shake the feeling we're in over our heads. What are we to do now?"

"Get the rest of the story from Irena. What else

does her husband pay to her parents? I have a hunch there's a life insurance policy on them with a big payout in his favor. He wants them dead and lacing doctor's pockets would be a piece of cake. How difficult would it be for a doctor to claim the old woman's heart stopped while under general sedation? It happens all the time. No one would even suspect a foul play." Dario ran down the stairs and stepped into a puddle in front of the door. His cloth sneakers soaked. Rain pelted him, and he pulled the hood of his jacket over his head. It must've rained for a while. It was hard to ignore the squishing sounds his shoes made and the drenched socks sticking to his freezing toes.

Ante pulled his coat over his head and fell into step with him. "Everyone's bribable today. Heck, when our mom was dying in the hospital the nurses and doctors couldn't be less pleasant if they tried, but they quickly changed their tune when we slipped them a few bills."

"Don't remind me." Dario fished out the keys from his jeans pocket. The last thing he needed was to think of their mother's death and pompous hospital staff who couldn't bother to change the patient's bed sheets until he laced their pockets. Everyone expected to get his or her hands greased these days. Small wonders, many workers had not seen paychecks in months and when they did, extra for overtime they put in working on weekends or evenings often got omitted from the pay.

Ante shivered in the passenger's seat. "Turn on the heat, I'm soaked."

Dario pulled out of the parking spot in a hurry, good thing the delivery truck left open space in front of his car or he'd cause some damage to bumpers of both vehicles. "Irena must've found our restaurant's web page with links to the attractions in the vicinity. The Bastion hotel was only open in the last few years."

"Why didn't she contact us? We would have been glad to help her." Ante sounded hurt.

"I'm sure if she could, she would've. There's more to this than what we know." Dario ignored the pang in his gut. Ante was right, damn it. Why hadn't Irena chosen to ask for help from him? Maybe she didn't want to burden him with her problems. Then, she wouldn't know he was no longer that poor teenager who couldn't buy her a drink. Or perhaps she didn't want him involved. Her constant glancing over her shoulder and edginess meant the things could get dangerous.

"The cab driver saw her going in, for all we know she might've eluded him to think that's where she was staying." Ante placed his finger on the radio button.

Dario shoved Ante's hand away from the dashboard. "How can you think of the music right now?" Listening to the drone of his engine and rain pelting against the car suited his racing mind.

The rest of the drive around the harbor to the Old Town was spent in silence, except for the white noise of the car and swish-swash of the wipers on the windshield.

He parked at the back of their restaurant and eased from behind the steering wheel. If only this rain would light up, he could search for Irena faster and easier.

He approached the red-brown building built on the remains of the medieval fortress from the thirteenth century converted into a hotel. Thick white trims framed the four floors of windows. Though the main entrance was narrow, it led into a spacious foyer. White curving marble stairs with black cast iron balustrade stood to the right from the reception desk.

A tall, thin man in dark brown suit leaned over the mahogany desk. Two burly guys in black suits a few steps behind the man, facing the entrance of the hotel. Dario paid them no heed on his way to the reception. However, the tall man seemed familiar. Older, receding hairline revealed pink scalp under the fake sun-bleached blond hair with graying roots, but that face still belonged to Fred. Dario's initial instinct was to punch the man's teeth, but his bodyguards would be on him faster than he could swing his arm. Yep, he'd be the one spilling bile on the parking lot if he approached the scum. Better to play cool and see what the man was up to.

Fred tapped his manicured fingernails on the wood while the receptionist finished his phone call.

The young man in navy blue vest bearing the hotel's logo returned the receiver to the cradle and faced Fred. "I'm sorry sir, but as I said, we don't have a guest with that name. Are you positive the lady was staying at this hotel?"

Fred reached into his suit inner pocket and produced the leather wallet, pulled out two hundred dollar bills and flashed it in front of the man's face. "Check your computer again."

The receptionist stared at the crisp bills clasped between two bony fingers. At the currency exchange rate, two hundred dollars could be more than this man earned in a month. Dario prayed the youngster wouldn't risk his job by taking cash and giving out confidential information, and that his salary exceeded the offered bribe, and that he received the paycheck regularly.

The receptionist gulped, drew in a long breath and turned to the monitor. "Can you spell the name of the guest?"

## Chapter 5

Every click on the keyboard by the hotel receptionist tightened Dario's chest. The raindrops pelted the glass dome window in the lobby and lightning flashed, followed by another ground shaking thunder. He crossed his fingers that the storm would knock out the power any moment and then the employee couldn't give Fred any information on Irena.

The receptionist snapped his gaze from the computer screen and nodded at Dario. Dario nodded back. "I can wait. Help this gentleman first."

The employee raised his hand and turned to the rack behind him. He plopped a hotel card key in front of Dario. "Your key, sir."

*My key?* Dario clamped his lips tight so not to blurt out anything and dropped his glance at the thin plastic rectangle in front of him. The side displayed the hotel logo. He coughed up a thank you and scooped the card in his hand. Turning to Ante, he nudged his head toward the curving staircase and took notice of the two burly guys in black suits and dark sunglasses.

Once out of the sight, Dario halted and flattened his back against the stucco wall, motioning Ante to do the same.

"What in the name is going on?" Ante whispered, but Dario pressed his index finger to his lips.

The voices in the lobby drifted from a few steps

below.

"Sorry, sir, there's no guest with that name staying here." The receptionist raised his voice.

"Very well. Someone else wouldn't mind earning this." Fred's tone turned sharp. "Is there another hotel near?"

"Many small hotels are closed for the season. Your best bet would be Hotel Kolovare, it's large enough to stay open all year." Judging by the receptionist's steady voice, he had no intention of taking up the offered bribe.

Footsteps on the marble floor grew fainter as the trio left the lobby. Smart, the receptionist was sending Irena's husband and his cronies to a hotel outside the city. Dario flipped the card key in his hand. Was Irena waiting for him in room 253?

He pushed away from the wall and skipped over the stairs to the second floor.

"This is getting stranger by the minute." Ante whispered, out of breath trying to keep up.

"You can say that again." Dario followed the direction of the black arrow on the wall's sign indicating the room she may stay in was to the left of the stairs. Fear mixed with anticipation of seeing her again. What if this was all some sick prank and Fred's dogs waited to beat the crap out him? There was only one way to find out. He pushed his legs faster.

He lowered his gaze at the card in his hand again. She must've arranged this knowing he wouldn't give up looking for her after last night. A fuzzy feeling in his gut brought a smile to his face. The game of cat and mouse was Irena's favorite. He was about to cage that little escaping mouse in his arms and never let her go.

Zrinka Jelic

He halted in front of the door and pressed his ear to the cold wood. Ante's eyebrows seemed permanently stuck in an arch since the receptionist plopped the key in front of Dario. His heart squeezed. Not a sound. Perhaps she wasn't there after all, or she rested. Last night they had kept each other plenty busy. Not knowing what he'd find on the other side, he signaled Ante to stay put.

Dario was about to knock on the door, then poised the card over the slit of the reader above the round knob. Whoever waited in there expected he would let himself in. Ante grabbed his forearm before he could slide the card through. "What if this is a trap of some kind? How will I know you're in trouble?"

Dario pushed his breath out. "I'll call you." If it was a trap and someone was waiting by the door with a club to knock him out, Ante wouldn't know. Better make a plan B. "Take the key after I open the door. Wait a minute or two and come inside. Be careful."

Ante swallowed audibly. "You too."

Dario slid the card all the way into the reader. Three red lights changed to green and a loud click indicated the door unlocked. His heart pounded in his ears. He pushed on the handle, opening the door wide enough to poke his head through. The first place he checked was behind the door, only an empty urn decorated the spot. A hunch told him not to let Ante in before he made sure the area was clear. Dario passed the card to Ante, stepped in and scanned the room with one hand still on the doorknob.

A hard kick at the back of his knees came so sudden he didn't have time to register which direction it flew from. His legs folded beneath him and with a

58

groan, he crumpled to the carpet.

Through his teary eyes, he made out the shapes. A teenage version of Irena dealt him another blow to his chest. He recognized the karate move, but his neglected training kicked in too late to block the punch.

"Oy," she shrieked, slicing the air with her rigid hands and gripping his neck in a vice.

"I'm a friend." He managed to say before his windpipes constricted and he wheezed.

Irena ran out of the door adjacent to the bedroom, thin spaghetti straps of her yoga top crossed her shoulders. "No, Ella. It's Dario."

The girl's hard face mellowed and she released her iron clutch. He gulped air, but his chest still ached from the blow.

Ella turned to Irena. "Mom, why didn't you tell me Da…Dario was coming here?" She pivoted to him, wrapped her hands around his arm and helped him get on his feet. "I'm so sorry. This is not how I imagined we'd meet. How embarrassing. It's my mom's fault. She should've told me. I'll get you an ice pack."

Mom? He would ask had his voice recovered from the blow. Irena was a mom. The same color almond shaped eyes, pointy chin and petite nose, there was no mistaking the girl was Irena's daughter. But, hadn't she said she stayed celibate all these years?

"I'm all right." He groaned, cringing at the pain in his knees.

The room door flung open and Ante barged inside, his fists in front of him, rage on his face.

"Mother fucker, let go of my brother," he roared but lowered his arms at the sight of Irena.

"Ante!" She threw her arms around his neck.

"Irena, my girl, am I ever glad to see you. Sorry for bursting in like that." He wrapped her in his arms and spun her around, then lowered her to the floor. "I almost didn't believe that miserable bastard of a brother that you were back. Only you can pull him from his brooding." Ante glanced over at Dario and frowned. "Bro, you're looking a bit pale. What happened?"

Ella helped Dario to the recliner next to the couch occupying the middle of the floor. She settled on the armrest, taking his hand in his and making him squirm in discomfort. "Are you sure you're fine?"

"Quite sure." Scooting away, he increased the distance as much as the sofa allowed. The girl seemed a tad too affectionate. Okay, she kicked his butt and was regretful now. The strange attention she gave him, along with glee in her pale blue eyes, made him question if he didn't, in fact, suffer a hard blow to his head.

Ante approached. "And who's this beauty? Don't tell me. It's like I'm back in high school. You look just like your mom. Except for the cropped hair. For a second there I mistook you for a boy."

"That's the idea. Mom says you're so funny, un—"

"Ella," Irena snapped before her daughter could finish. Her tone mellowed as she continued. "This is Dario's brother, Ante."

"I'm so glad to finally meet you both." Ella stood up and shook her hand with Ante. "Mom told me so many stories about you." Irena's citrusy scent engulfed Dario. Ella sat back on the armrest of his chair and wrapped her arm around his shoulders. The girl wore the same perfume or maybe stole her mom's, since he assumed Irena wouldn't let her teenage daughter use makeup or attractive scents.

"Wish we could say the same about you." Ante settled on the settee facing them. "But I hope we'll get to know each other."

"Well, I see your neighbor found the taxi company card I dropped. It took you longer than I expected to find me. You're losing your touch." A warning flashed in Irena's eyes as she turned to her daughter and the girl eased away from Dario. His mind still struggling to wrap around the fact Irena had a teenage daughter.

"So you're a mom now, Irena? Wow, and to such a beautiful girl. You'll have to fight the boys with a stick before they knock your door down." Ante winked at Ella, making her blush.

"Boys don't interest me, Un…Ante." Ella flashed a sheepish smile. "Is it okay if I call you Ante? Or would Mr. Vitez be too formal? Mom says your last name means a knight."

Dario chuckled at Ante's frown. The teasing they'd endured in the schoolyard because of their last name still stung. The two brothers from the gutter with a noble family name, in people's mind just didn't compute. Seeing Ella's eyes lit up as she said it out loud as if she wanted that name for herself, almost made all the hurt of lashing tongues go away.

Ante waved his hand. "It does mean a knight, but no one calls us by our last name." He leaned closer. "We're not knightly."

"Ella Vitez." A dreamy grin lit up her face. "It sounds so romantic. I'd love to have such a last name instead of Novak." She turned to Irena. "Mom, what do you think?"

"Ella, honey, please curb your enthusiasm." Irena

gave out a sigh of exasperation. "I'm sorry, Dario. She's been dying to meet you two. She's impossible."

"Looks like we got a fan. Our late mother's name was Elia, but people called her Ella too. You have your mom's last name, not your dad's?" At Ante's bold question Irena and Ella only exchanged smiles. Irena nodded to some unasked query from her daughter.

Ella turned to Ante. "My dad? Oh, you must mean Fred." She dragged the words out. "He's not my dad. Mom also told me all about your parents. Ella is my middle name. No one but Fred calls me Dawn, by his late mother."

Dario flashed a confused glance at Irena. She huffed. "Fred's mother insisted her first granddaughter be named after her if only she knew."

A knot in Dario's chest loosened. Still, if Fred wasn't Ella's dad, who then? Wait, how old could the girl be? Careful not to draw her attention, he gave her a quick once over. Early teens. Could he be her dad? He dismissed the panic bell somewhere in the recess of his mind. There was not a trace of resemblance to him in the girl. Then again, some people have said they did not see themselves in their children yet their sons and daughters were spitting image of their parents. No, if he fathered Ella, Irena would have told him, she wouldn't keep that from him. Except...no, he must stop this insanity.

Ella laced her fingers with his and he couldn't help but stare at their joined hands.

"Have you seen much of the city yet?" Ante asked.

"No." Ella pressed her lips to a thin line. "We arrived two days ago. Mom won't let me out on my own and all we ever do is train in this room."

"Train for what?" Dario used the moment to disengage his fingers from Ella's.

She slid her hand to his knee. "I must be prepared for any unexpected visitors. How are your legs? Hope I didn't break anything." Thankfully, she sprang on her feet moving her hand from his leg. "Jeez, I totally forgot about the ice pack I was gonna get for you. Where's my head?"

"I'll be fine." Okay, the girl had some teenage crush on him. Whatever had her mother put in the girl's head? Ella saw him as a real knight in shining armor on a white horse. He must ensure she understood he liked, no, loved her mom. And he'd love her like a daughter he never had, but this fondling and strange attention had to stop.

"Ella," he said getting on his feet. His knees protested, mostly due to long sitting, so he shook his legs lose. "I'd like a word with your mom. Irena, is there a place we can talk?"

"There's a small balcony off the side." Irena turned to Ella and tilted her head in warning typical for moms. "Remember what I told you. No prodding."

"No worries." Ante winked at Ella, making her blush a new. "So, your mom told you stories about us, eh? Bet she conveniently forgot a few where she embarrassed herself."

Ella's adorable giggle lit up the room, and Dario couldn't help but laugh along. She parked her bottom next to Ante. "Do tell and don't leave out anything."

Dario cringed and turned to Irena. He almost smiled at the future retribution in the glare she sent his brother. Okay, this was a bad idea leaving Ante alone with her daughter. Who knew what stories he'd spout?

However, Irena followed Dario out to the balcony and closed the glass door. He skirted around a hot pink yoga mat rolled out on the narrow patch of cement.

"Now you know why I had to run from your place. I left her alone for too long." She crossed her arm over her ample chest. "Don't worry about Ella's attention. She adores you, that's all."

"Why didn't you tell me you had a child?" He didn't intend for his tone to come out as scalding, so he tucked loose strands of her hair behind her ear and softened his expression. "Yes, I find her attention rather intimidating. Kids scream their lungs out over some teenage pop star."

"Ella's not your typical teenager. When she was little, she wouldn't go to sleep before I told her at least one story of our youth. Today's kids don't have what we had. Freedom from all this technology, that kind of life it's foreign to them." She drew in a long breath and blew it out. "So much has happened I'm afraid I don't know where to start."

He took hold of her trembling shoulders. Perhaps he'd over analyzed Ella's reaction. Poor girl must be craving a fatherly figure in her life and assumed he'd fill in the position. And he gladly would if Irena would let him. "From the beginning, or in our case a new beginning."

She only chewed her lips and turned her head away from him.

Her silence unnerved him. "Come on, Irena. You know you can always count on me. Babe, you're shaking. Are you cold? Stupid of me, you're wearing a tank top and yoga pants and I didn't think before we stepped out into the cold air."

She wrapped her bare arms around his chest and he pulled her to him. A part of his body reacted to her closeness. Dammit, now was neither time nor the place, but she always had such effect on him. He took off his jacket and draped the bomber over her shoulders.

"It was a mistake to return to my home town. It doesn't take an idiot to figure out I'd run back to you. I never should've sought you out, but I just couldn't help it. And I didn't know where else to go. We've been on the run for so long."

"No love." He kissed her forehead. "That's crazy talk. Whatever kind of trouble you're in, I'll help you."

She tilted her head up, worry lines marring her beautiful face. "I was afraid you'd get involved, but it's dangerous. You risk losing everything you worked hard for and perhaps your life and the lives of your loved ones."

"That is why you need to tell me everything. I need to know what I'm up against. I figured you're on the run from Fred and…" He didn't know whether to tell her, but judging by the receptionist's reaction, she already knew. "We bumped into him in the lobby. You're lucky that young guy was working the front desk. What would happen if there was someone who would've accepted two hundred bucks Fred offered in exchange for the info? Fred already paid a visit to your mother. You're not safe here or any hotel. Please, consider moving in with me."

"You went to my mom's? Oh, my God, after all she put you through?" Irena pulled away from him and gripped his jacket tighter. She turned and faced the cast iron railing, her shoulders rigid. "God, this is so hard. I knew I shouldn't have involved you in my mess."

"Your mess is my mess now." He placed his hand on her shoulder. "Please, there's plenty of room for you and Ella and you can train in the rec room in my building."

She tilted her head, placing her cheek on his hand. "Fred is very cunning, all he has to do is ask around this town. Someone will tell him where you live."

Thankfully, no one could enter his condo building without punching the code into the security system or if someone buzzed them in. And that was the flaw, for gullible tenants often pressed that buzzer and let door-to-door salesmen inside.

Dario cupped her chin in his fingers. "What does he want from you?"

She closed her eyes and pulled her lips, stifling a sob. "It's a long story. Come. Let me ask Ella if she'd want us to stay with you, although, I already know the answer." Halting by the balcony door, she turned to him. "Did my mother have a word for me?"

"Of course she did. Fred has agreed to pay for her knee replacement surgery. If you return to him. If you don't, he will stop the payments to your father's nursing home." Dario propped his hands on his hips. Should he tell her the rest? Better not, it would only upset her more. Over the years Irena had plenty of reasons to go insane, but her mind seemed rock solid as always. No, Fred spread lies about her being mentally unstable. Irena was a pure diamond that couldn't be cracked under pressure.

"So my mom confused me for an obedient, gullible daughter? They don't need Fred's money." Irena pushed the door open and stepped inside the hotel room.

Ella's back slid down the chair. She held her stomach and shook with laughter. She sat upright and wiped her eyes, ending her merriment with a long sigh. "Is it true, Mom? Did you slip at the classroom door and skid to your desk on your butt? Oh, if that was me I'd change schools."

Irena glared at Ante. "I knew we shouldn't leave you in charge."

"And you treated us with some epic falls nine more times that day as I recall." Ante pointed at her. "No one's beat your record. Yet."

Ella threw her back against the chair as she erupted in a new set of giggles. Irena's shoulders shook and she joined in with her daughter. "It's all funny now and it's great to laugh with you again."

Irena's merriment loosened a knot in Dario's chest. This short moment took him back to their careless teen days of endless summers and innocence. She reached for her purse and pulled out her wallet. "I'll call the front desk and ask them to have my invoice ready." She handed a stack of bills to Dario. "Will you pay while I talk with Ella?"

He pushed her hand away. "Keep your money. I'll take care of your stay here. Just pack up and come down."

Ella sprang to her feet, glee on her face. "Where are we going, Mom?"

Irena darted her gaze at him and he shook his head. If she told her daughter they'd be staying with him, the girl would never stop hugging him. The day was wasting away and they had many things to accomplish.

"I'll tell you in a minute. Go pack." Irena walked him to the door. "We'll be down in a few."

"All right." Dario kissed her lips and nudged Ante to follow him to the hotel's lobby.

Once outside Irena's room, Dario turned to his brother. "Ella's behavior strikes me as odd. I don't know what is going on here. Have you seen how she looks at me?"

"I see that kind of look every time my little girl looks at me." Ante's lips stretched into a mocking smile.

Dario dismissed his brother's comment with a wave of his hand. "No wonder, genius, your child is looking at her daddy."

"And Ella is looking at hers."

Chapter 6

The sand colored walls of the hallways in hotel Bastion Hotel closed in on Dario. His legs felt like pudding beneath him, and he gripped the wall for stability. Still, the thought he could be Ella's dad made him smile. He'd guessed as much, but until he heard it from Irena, he would not make assumptions. His brother's offhand remark infuriated him, he restrained from punching the smirk off his face. After several blinks, Dario's vision cleared. He glanced at Irena's room door, ensuring the ladies weren't about to step out. It wouldn't look good if they walked out in the middle of his and Ante's brawl. The white wood panel remained closed.

Dario placed a firm hand on his brother's shoulder, gave him a hard squeeze. "The thought crossed my mind, but I know Irena. She would get the word to me that I'm a dad. Besides, there's not the slightest resemblance in Ella to me."

Ante shoved Dario's hand off his shoulder. "Irena's situation was hard, that's why she didn't or couldn't tell you."

Ante's reasoning calmed Dario's initial panic. He took a long step back and an even longer breath. "I can't imagine why Fred would want to raise my child?" Dario shook his head, calling Ella his child didn't sit right just yet. He wished it to be the truth, but he would hate to find out that his joy was premature. "From what Irena said, Fred likes...how should I put this? Well, let's say...girls don't excite him."

Ante raised his finger. "Didn't I say as much? We never saw him dance with a girl, in fact, we never saw him do anything with a girl. But when the guys got tanked and stupid, Fred would join in their drunken dance."

Dario pondered Ante's theory. "I wasn't paying close attention to Fred's follies back then." In fact, he'd barely noticed the guy. A costly mistake. Irena's parents spend too much time hanging out with Fred's family. They were often seen strolling together along the lower promenade. They must've debated the details of their children's marriage. "A few guys from our gang said he grabbed their butts. We laughed it off. It's not like it's a crime if guys turn him on, but why then did he need a wife?"

Ante raised his hand as if asking a permission to speak. "Here's a thought for you. Fred has the hot's for men. Chances are his parents knew of their son's sexual orientation and that he'd never get a wife on his own accord so they found him one. They denied any rumors about him." Ante screwed his face. "You know the kind of gossip—could he be queer? So they married him off and a few months later his wife is pregnant. Whoa, whose son's a gay now, eh? Rumors stop and he goes on, has a boyfriend on the side. Irena raises the baby on her own."

"Jeez, you may be onto something," Dario whispered. His throat tightened. Irena's parents had married her off to keep him away, because all he could give her was poverty, yet doomed her to the miserable life with a rich husband. Doubtful Fred would provide for her and someone else's child. The fact she raised the child on her own told him she worked for her money.

He nudged Ante toward the stairs. They'd spent too much time pondering, he risked Irena and Ella coming out of their room and finding them there, instead of at the reception desk settling her hotel bill. "I can't imagine the hardship she's endured. I wish she got a word to me somehow. It would be easier to take the news in earlier. So, I could be a dad."

The thought sank in and started to take hold, but another memory sluiced the fuzzy feeling around his heart. "No, this is crazy. Irena was afraid—terrified actually—of getting pregnant. Her dad would kill her, she said she rather commit a suicide. She wouldn't sleep with me until her eighteenth birthday. Once she turned of legal age, she wouldn't require her parent's consent to ask her doctor for the pill, but her parents would need to sign the form."

A smirk appeared on Ante's face. He laced his fingers over his stomach, corners of his mouth dipped and he drew in a long breath, just like their late mom when she was about to give them a lecture on life. "And did you make love on your last date?"

Despite the sorrowful parting at dawn, warmth flooded Dario with the memory of their last night together. "Yes, several times, in fact."

"And did you use the protection?" Ante mimicked their beloved mother's voice and stance whenever she posed such question. Bless her. Mom had always made sure her boys stayed true gentlemen, even if chivalry was going out the window. She had voiced her displeasure about them having unwed sex, but Mom wasn't a prude either. What he wouldn't give if she could see her granddaughters, she'd wished to be a grandma.

Dario snorted at Ante's imitation, he nailed it every time. "Of course I did…well, except for the…oh, God." He'd lost control and couldn't…shit. Irena wasn't freaking out, so he thought she may be close to her time of the month. A strange thought occurred. Maybe she wanted to get pregnant, but why not tell him? She knew she'd be welcomed in his home. Mom loved her like a daughter. Knowing Irena, she wouldn't put an additional burden on his parents. Their meager checks from social assistance barely fed them. What kind of job could he lend with high school diploma in the post war-torn economy?

"You'll find all the answers soon. Took me a while to believe I was a father and I knew of my Jasmin since that stick turned positive." Ante pointed his chin at the reception. "Go settle Irena's bill. I'll bring the car around."

"Sure." Dario dug the keys from his jacket's pocket. "Careful around the corners."

"Quit with the driving lecture. I've been driving longer than you." Ante shook his head, turned for the exit and waved over his shoulder. Dario glared at his back. Ante had to rub it in he'd gotten his driver license before him, his older brother.

Dario stepped to the reception desk, pulling out his wallet. The same receptionist raised his head and glanced at him, flashing a smile.

"Miss. Claire called, she said you'll be settling her bill." He placed his thin hand over the tray of the printer. "How will you be paying?"

Miss. Claire, the name she'd given to his neighbor. Dario should've known, she wouldn't check in under her real name. Ella wouldn't be checked in under her name either. Smart. Irena knew her husband would try bribery and she protected herself and the hotel staff with an alias.

Dario opened his wallet. Would he have enough to cover their stay? Paying via credit cards would leave a record of the transaction under his name, and if Fred was as resourceful as Irena had said, he wouldn't have problems tracking him down.

The receptionist plopped the sheet of paper under his nose and pointed at the bottom line. Dario pulled out all his cash. He gave the clerk a pitiful smile. "I'm twenty Euros short. Ante would have some if you don't mind waiting a few minutes."

The young guy scooped the money from the counter. "Don't worry. I know you'll come back with the rest."

"How do you know?" Dario shoved his now empty wallet into the back pocket of his jeans.

"One has to be living under the rock not to know you. Or not live in this town. You're Dario."

Dario shook his head. Okay, he couldn't remember everyone's face, but he never imagined the younger generations would know him. "And you are?"

"Andy Paleca." The youngster said his name as if Dario should know him.

Dario rubbed the stubble on his chin, trying to recall meeting the youngster, but couldn't, though the last name seemed familiar. "Sorry, have we met?"

"No, but you were in the same classroom with my mom, I'm Tamara's son. She asked if you could get me a job here."

A light went on in Dario's head. Still, he couldn't quite place the youngster. He'd helped many get the job. "Sorry, can't remember you, but I know your mom. No need to thank me. Tell your mom I said hi."

Andy nodded, but his glance darted at the foot of the stairs as Ella appeared, a heavy bag bouncing on the shoulder strap. "Hi Miss Danielle, can I take that for you?"

Danielle? Of course, a fake name. Dario rushed to her, grabbing the strap as it slid from her shoulder. "Why didn't you call the bellboy?"

Ella snorted. "You're kidding, right? Mom wouldn't leave the bags to someone else's care. That is why we had to cross the Atlantic on a ship instead of a plane. It was cheaper, plus she didn't have to check in our valises."

Andy cleared his throat. "I'm sorry you're leaving. If you want to go out sometimes, call the hotel and ask for me. I'd love to show you the city."

Ella's cheeks blushed, and she averted her gaze to her shiny, red sneakers. "I'd like to, but my mom won't let me."

Dario put his hand around her shoulders. Suddenly hugging his girl didn't seem odd. He'd tease her about turning Andy down later, now she'd need some encouragement. "If we ask your mom nicely, maybe she'll consider."

A smile lit her face, and she beamed at him. "Really, Da...um, Dario?"

"I'll talk to her." Dario patted her shoulder. Ella's slips were getting worse, soon she'd blurt dad instead of Dario.

At the phone's shrill ring, the receptionist nodded to Ella before he scurried behind his desk. "See you later then."

"Talk to me about what?" Irena took the last step to the hotel lobby and plopped a brown suitcase in front of him. "Hope this will fit in your car. Good thing it's not too heavy."

"Not a chance." Dario eyed the monstrosity. "What have you packed in there?"

"Sparing gear takes lots of space. Our clothes barely fit in corners. We only brought a few essentials."

A few? Dario scratched his head. How to transport that huge case to his place without damaging his vehicle?

"I parked out back...holy." Ante's feet halted and the soles of his shoes squeaked on the polished floor. "I should've brought my truck."

"I have an idea. Why don't we go to the restaurant? I'll cook you up a nice early dinner. I'm starving, hope you guys are too." Dario tapped Ante's shoulder and pointed his chin at the suitcase. "You can carry this, right? Oh, and I was short twenty Euros. Can I bum some cash from you?"

"Ah." Ante gave a sigh of exasperation, pulling his wallet out. "You guys go ahead. I'll catch up with you. Your bags are safe with me."

Irena flipped her hand at Ella and they both covered their heads with the hoods of their raincoats. Though the downpour ended, heavy drops dribbled from the rooftops and branches. Still the way their faces hid behind the fabric, one would think they expected to walk out into a storm of Biblical proportions.

At the service entrance, Irena halted. "We'll follow

you a few steps back. Don't turn to look at us. Pretend we're not together. We may be watched by Fred's men."

He stared at the two women who unexpectedly entered his life. Ella's face turned serious. It was hard to watch her so rigid. Just a moment ago she'd blushed when a boy asked her out, now she appeared ready to kill. Judging by the strength of her punches, it wouldn't surprise him if she delivered a deadly hit.

Dario pointed at the metal container on the hotel's narrow parking lot. "If we're being watched, I should go out through the main door as I came in. When you see me walking past the dumpster, start on your way, but keep your distance."

"I know how to find your restaurant. It's only a block from here. Go now. We'll get there." Irena stepped to him, rose on her toes and kissed his lips.

He reached out to pull her to him, but she slipped away faster than his hand could react. Damn it, he wanted to kiss her senseless. Ella's giggle put a lid on his desire. A bit of affection Irena allowed him in front of her daughter, told him she didn't want the teen girl to see her mom in love. It showed in the way those two sparkles lit in her eyes and in her genuine smile.

His long strides carried him toward the Mezzaluna. As hard as it was not to turn and check on Irena and Ella, he followed their reflections in the wide shop windows lining the narrow streets. The cobblestones pavement glistened in the recent downpour, while the gray sky promised more deluge to come.

\*\*\*\*

Ante pulled up behind the restaurant. The soft roof of Dario's car lowered and Irena's suitcase stuck out from the backseat. His brother had said the truth, her bags were safe with him, but Dario's car wasn't.

Ante opened the car door and leaned out, a grin on his face. "I managed to squeeze that trunk into your car."

"Idiot, I thought you'd carry it over not force it into such a small car." Dario fumed, unlocking the restaurant door. "Anything damaged?"

"Relax man." Ante jerked his head in Irena's direction. "Are they coming in?"

"Yes, they are playing it cool. Just give them a minute."

"Why?"

"We may be watched. So act normal." Dario pushed Ante away from the front door and flipped the sign on the window to open.

His brother's wide eyes and arched eyebrows gave him a comical look. "Watched? Who's watching us?"

"Fred's men." Dario hung his jacket on the rack by the door. "Lead the girls to a table behind the wall. It's pretty secluded."

Through his restaurant's bay window, lights flickered on in the establishment across the street and drew Dario's attention. Odd, the place stood closed for over a year. "Hey, have you heard of LaGrotta re-opening?"

"No, the owner couldn't come up with the money to pay the stiff fine from the health inspector." Bottles clunked behind the bar as Ante stocked the beer fridge. "Serves the dumb ass right, he tried to save a few Euros re-selling the booze as a house brand. Apparently, some glasses had lipstick stains on them when he poured the leftover wine into a carafe instead down the drain."

"He might've found money. Looks like they're about to open." Dario scurried from the window, tapped Ante's shoulder. "The girls are coming in. You're the manager, go greet them. And it's purely business."

Ante straightened and picked up the menus.

It was strange to listen to the talk between Irena and Ante as if the two total strangers exchanging pleasantries. But whoever watched them, sure by now must be bored and decided nothing out of the ordinary was happening. Nonetheless, Irena and Ante put on a worthy performance. While Ella's wandering gaze surveyed the restaurant's moon décor.

Ante seated them at the secluded table, took their drink orders and left them perusing the menu. Dario tuned the music system on and soft guitar tones filled the dining room. He left for the kitchen, grabbed the white apron from the shelf and slipped the top loop over his head, then tied the strings around his waist. The oven had not preheated yet when two long honks from the car drew him to the small window. A shiny red two-seater pulled up next to his black BMW. Ana got out, tightened the collar of her short fur coat. Her high heels matched her designer's bag in her other hand.

What the hell? Had everyone suddenly come into money? Tying the apron strings behind his back, Dario stepped out on the stone patio before she reached the rear door.

"I didn't think you'd be open yet, but I saw your car parked here." She halted by Irena's suitcase sticking out from the backseat. "Are you traveling?"

Damn you, Ante, for leaving the luggage. Something suspicious was going on, Ana didn't appear in a new expensive car and wardrobe on a whim. He gazed over the patio's railing mulling over the most plausible answer. "Ante has Jasmin over the weekend and wants to take her camping."

Ana exposed her straight and white teeth with her smile. What the hell, just yesterday her mouth was full of yellowed and uneven teeth. "So nice of him to spend time with his daughter."

"What's going on, Ana?" Dario motioned to the car. "Where did you find the cash for all of this?"

"I finally found the right man." She shrugged. "You wouldn't believe it. He used to hang out with us. I said some awful things about Irena when I found out she's to marry him. I was jealous then. The stupid cunt left him and now he is free and loaded." In the next instant, her grin vanished, replaced by some fake concern. "However, her husband is worried about her, though I don't know why." Ana's lips thinned into a pink line on her skinny face. "Fred is so generous. He even helped your next door neighbor pay the fine so he can re-open the restaurant. I can't imagine how anyone could leave him."

Dario gripped the cold railing of the patio. How could he forget her lashing tongue? She lived for the gossip. "Ana, don't get involved with that guy. He's not a right man for you at all. He can be dangerous. You're looking for love in the wrong place."

By Ana's arched eyebrows and round eyes, he said too much. "Love? Pfft, what would I do with love? I only love money. You don't know Fred like I do?"

"I think I know him better. He was always weird. Why is he back? What does he want from you?" As if that was hard to guess, but Dario had to play dumb.

"I already told you, he's worried about Irena.

Thinks she may need medical help and something, I wasn't really listening after he handed me the keys to that beauty over there." Ana pointed at her new car, then turned to Dario. "I'm sure she must've made a contact with you by now."

*You traitor, sold your soul to the Devil for a few expensive gifts.* Dario wanted to slap her but shoved his fists under his armpits. "I haven't heard from Irena. So she either is not in town, or she doesn't want anything to do with me. Whatever, I don't care. She wounded me when she accepted Fred's hand in marriage and I moved on. If I see her, I'll let you know, but don't hold your breath."

Ana's lips upturned and her eyebrows drew closer. "Right, you're not fooling me. You're so hung up on Irena that you once called me by her name in bed."

Dario chose his words carefully. After all, Fred could've slipped a bug in Ana's bag and listen on to her conversations. Why else would he spend the money on a twit? "I was drunk and that was a long time ago. Yes, it took me years to forget her, but I'm over her."

Worry lines appeared on Ana's forehead and her face dropped. Perhaps she bought his act. She grabbed his forearm. "Please, Dario. Fred will take all of these nice things away if I don't have a satisfying answer."

"You should've thought about it before you accepted his gifts." Dario removed her hand from his arm and returned to the kitchen.

Ana stood on the patio for a few minutes, appearing uncertain and scared. Had she not sold herself to the highest bidder, she wouldn't be in this predicament. She slowly turned on her unsteady legs and trudged to her shiny car. What would happen to her? Dario's chest squeezed. He couldn't bear to be responsible if harm came to her. Perhaps she would listen to reason and return the gifts. If she was lucky, Fred would let her go unscratched.

Ante came through the swivel kitchen doors and raised the writing pad to his face. "Okay, here we go. For Irena no dairy, nothing fried, no chocolate, no heavy sauces, no salty food, no…" He dropped his hand to his side. "She just wants a small salad."

Dario's eyebrows crept up his forehead with each item Ante recited. "Who eats like that?"

Ante shrugged. "Someone whose health consciences, I suppose."

"Hmm…all those food restrictions limit her to a poor diet." Dario rubbed the stubble on his chin. Maybe Fred told the truth. Irena could be sick, but not mentally as her husband had claimed.

Ante nudged his head for Dario to come closer. His brother pressed his finger to his mouth and held the flip door open. "Listen."

"Ella, no." Irena's snappy voice echoed in the restaurant's dining room. "It's not the right time."

"But, Mom," Ella whined. "They suspect already. What if Dad asks and you deny it? Then later, how will you tell him, oh, by the way, you were right? It wouldn't look good on either of us."

"Oh baby, you're too smart." Irena's voice mellowed. "But patience, please. We may not live to see later."

## Chapter 7

Keys clinked while Dario unlocked the door to his penthouse. The elevator doors slid open, and Ante trudged out, grunting under the weight of the bags. "Okay, who mistook me for a mule?"

Ella snorted and slapped her hand over her lips, but her giggles continued. "Unc—"

"Ella, watch your tongue," Irena hissed and grabbed Ella's wrist, an angry scowl marring her face.

"Um, sorry, I meant to say Ante…he's so funny." Ella lowered her gaze, her tone subdued.

Dario gave her a sympathetic smile. Poor child, Ella's giddiness vanished.

"It's fine, sweetheart, you can call me Uncle if you want." Ante rubbed Ella's arm and shrugged at Irena's sharp stare. "What? I always wanted to be a cool, overindulging uncle."

Irena's shoulders relaxed. "I can live with that. I guess." Her stern expression returned as she glanced at her daughter. She waved her warning finger at Ella. "Don't get carried away."

Dario pushed the door open and ushered them in, hoping to defuse the tension between mother and daughter. He figured Irena agreed for Ella to call his brother an uncle out of respect. Youngsters referred to grown up men as uncles had nothing to do with being related. "We're home. Make yourselves comfortable."

Irena embraced Ella. "Sorry, baby. I shouldn't have overreacted. Come, you'll love Dario's place."

"It's okay, Mom." Ella held her mom's hand and followed her inside the condo.

Despite Irena's predicament, Dario's lips were stuck in a permanent smile ever since she accepted his offer. Ella's burst of enthusiasm when her mother told her the news made him chuckle. She had grabbed the first chance to wrap him in a tight hug. Instead of stiffening, he embraced her like a dad. Just to think, a few short hours ago her attention had seemed odd and made him uncomfortable. Could it be his dad's instincts were awakening?

Ella's eyes widened as she slowly descended the stairs from the foyer to the open concept living room. "This is great. I love your place Da...Dario."

"Thank you, Ella." He gave her hand a soft squeeze and winked at her. His heart clenched. The girl was dying to call him her dad. He'd have a serious talk with her mother. Persuade her he was okay with finding out about Ella, despite the fact she hid Ella from him still hurt. Her predicament hadn't been an easy one, he must keep that in mind.

Ante puffed and allowed the bags to slide off his arms and shoulders, leaving them piled at the front door. He let out a sigh of relief as he sprawled out on the couch. "Get me a cold one, will you?"

"What am I? Your personal servant?" Dario threw the words over his shoulder, heading for the fridge. Irena and Ella would be thirsty after the lunch he'd served them. Irena's long list of restricted items troubled him. He never knew her to fuss over her food. The subject would require some delicate broaching.

"Ladies, what can I get you?"

"Just water for me." Irena patted her stomach. "I stuffed myself. You should've let me do the dishes so I wouldn't be this sluggish."

"It was my pleasure to cook. It's not often I get to step into the kitchen unless something needs fixing." Running a restaurant required him to wear many hats, but he never imagined he'd have to deal with faulty plumbing and wiring. The damn espresso machine had more parts than a motorcycle. He had to become the master of all trades or his profits would diminish under the repair bills.

"Ella, you can sleep in my home office," Dario said, filling the two tall glasses with fizzy mineral water. "There's a nice pull-out couch and you are welcome to use my computer."

"Thanks." Ella wrapped her hand over the knob of a balcony door, ready to pull the glass panel open. "Wow, the view from here's amazing."

Irena offered him her warm smile when he passed the glass to her. Her swallows echoed through the room. She licked her lips and closed the blinds. "The view is much better at night when the lights of the city twinkle. You can step out on the balcony then. Right now the sky is gray. I hate rain."

Ante's phone beeped and he pulled the cell out of his pocket. "Good, the kitchen manager clocked in. We're covered for tonight's dinner. Never thought the cold rain would drive people out for dinner, but it is Valentine's Day." He cleared his throat and got to his feet, then turned to Irena and Ella. "Can Ella come along and meet my little girl?"

Irena flashed him a look of surprise. "Wow, Ante,

a daddy? Can't imagine. I still picture you as a goofy teenager. When did you get married?"

*This should be interesting.* Dario crossed his arms over his chest and arched an eyebrow. Would his brother fess up? Neither he nor Martina are without blame for splitting up shortly after Jasmin was born, but Ante should snap out of his life-is-a-party attitude and accept that raising a child would test his limits.

"We broke off the engagement." Ante's face soured. "I hope we can work out issues someday soon."

Irena clicked her tongue and the corners of her lips dipped. "Sorry to hear that. How old is your little one?"

Ante flashed a lopsided grin. "Jasmin will be four this summer." He tweaked his head, a Cheshire cat smile beaming on his face. "She's my pride."

*Well, well, what do you know?* Years of harping seemed to have worked. As the saying went, constant dripping hollows out the stone. There was hope for his brother's future with his woman and the child they've created.

Irena patted Ante's chest. "That's the winning attitude."

Ella took her mom's hand, pleading in her round eyes. "Please, Mom, can I go with Uncle? I'll be extra careful, I promise."

Deep lines appeared on Irena's forehead. "Oh, I don't know, baby. It's not safe."

"Come on, Irena. Why wouldn't it be safe? We won't be gone for long." Ante extended his hand to Ella and waved her to him. "Let's go, your mom is overly protective."

"Wait! I…you can go, but first…" Irena hurried to the front door where Ante had piled up their bags. A sound of zipper sliced the air and she rummaged through the contents. "Here," she said, pulling out the nun-chucks. The two-foot-long smooth wood pieces swayed on the chain draped over her fingers.

Dario exchanged a worried glance with Ante then pointed at the oriental weapon in Irena's hand. "Does she know how to use that?"

"She's an expert." A proud smile lit Irena's face and she wrapped her arm around her daughter's shoulders. In the next instant, her smile vanished. "Still, be careful. Check and re-check your rear-view mirror and surroundings. Pay attention to anything unusual." She kissed Ella's forehead and embraced her as if this could be the last time she'd see her daughter alive. "Take care of your...uncle."

"Mom, you're exaggerating and not to mention scaring Dario and Ante." Ella took the nun-chucks from Irena's hand and tucked the weapon inside her jacket.

Ante stood frozen at the bottom of the steps. At Irena's throat clearing, he jerked and scurried up the stairs. "We're all set then. I have nothing to fear."

"You're well protected." Dario placed the unopened beer bottle back in the fridge. Obviously, Ante planned to spend the night with them, as he often did when he cared for Jasmin and Martina partied on town. Dario didn't mind them, but tonight would be a special for him too. Still, he hadn't in his heart to turn his brother and his niece away.

The click of the penthouse front door jerked him back from his reverie. Irena stood at the bottom of the four stairs, staring at the door. He closed the fridge and approached her. "Ella will be fine, you worry overmuch. Besides, I need to talk to you. I'm not sure I can do this with her present."

Irena brushed her fingertips down his cheek, sending pleasant vibrations to his chest. "I need to talk to you too."

He took her hand and kissed her palm. She moved closer, pressed her lips to his neck and trailed kisses over his collarbone. His mind clouded with the ache in his loins as the urgency to make love to her stiffened him. Now, what was he gonna do? He lost his train of thought as she molded her body to his. *Talk, that's it.* Their lips met, a quick peck at first, then longer contact as she parted hers welcoming his tongue. He slid his hands into the back pockets of her jeans and gave her tight buttocks a firm squeeze.

He had to stop before Ante burst inside with the impressionable young girl in tow. As usual, by the time his brother reached his car, the dolt would realize he'd forgotten something, like his keys. Irena's soft moans hardened Dario, but he pulled back. She leaned forward to capture his lips again with hers. He placed his fingers on her chin, stopping her.

"What about that talk we need to have?"

"Later," she whispered, attempting another kiss.

He indulged her with a peck to the corner of her mouth. It was typical of her to avoid hard questions by distracting him with her body. "No, now."

How he kept his voice and composure unyielding he would never know. Smoldering desire vanished from her eyes and deflated his ardor. With a long sigh she trudged to the couch then dropped on the cream cushions. She closed her eyes and drew in another long breath. What could be hidden behind her knitted brow?

"There's so much to tell." Her gaze stayed on her

laced fingers.

"What happened fourteen years ago, after I walked you home at the crack of dawn?" He huffed and ran a hand through her hair.

"I got cold feet once I saw my packed suitcases in the hallway. I ran away and walked the city streets. I wanted to go to your house, but couldn't. Kept reminding myself how I'd be nothing but a burden to you and your parents." Her voice shook and grew fainter.

He lowered to the thick glass top of the coffee table, facing her, and took hold of her fidgeting hands. "Babe, you were always welcome in my home. You know that."

"Hanging out at your place on occasion wasn't the same. If I moved in, things would change fast. I'd be yet another mouth to feed. With only a high school diploma and no connections, could I hope for a job?" She wrapped her fingers around his, her gaze still not meeting his. "My dad would not let us be. He would cause all kinds of trouble for us and your family. He knew people in power who owed him favors, and he threatened to cancel your dad's social security checks if I disobeyed him." She shook her head, fluttering her hair. "I couldn't allow that. Me noncomplying with their plan would destroy your family."

"They made sure you obeyed." He swallowed against the dry throat. Poor girl had not been left a choice. "Then what did you do?"

"Somehow, I found myself in front of your house. My feet just took me there." Her breath hitched, sadness filled her beautiful blue eyes when she finally granted him the look. "Your dad sat in his wheelchair in front of the house. He said you left three hours ago, maybe longer."

"Oh, babe. I had a bus ticket for the noon departure, but I couldn't sit and wait. My buddy drove me to the port the ship I boarded was anchored at. We must've been miles away by the time you arrived. Had you found me at home, I never would've left."

She nodded, gazing over the condo. "Perhaps it had to happen. If we weren't torn apart, would you have anything you have today?"

"That day I vowed to get my ass out of the gutter and make my fortune. I guess I needed the good kick to get me going." He swallowed and placed a kiss on her trembling fingers. Had he never have boarded the ship, his life would've stayed on the same path of poverty. In a strange way, her parents gave him the chance he wouldn't dare to take had they let him have their daughter. The long voyages on slow tankers would mean months of separation. The impatience would cause him to jump overboard and swim back to her.

"Can you get me another drink? All this talking is making my throat dry."

"Sure," he said, getting to his feet. He'd let her go on with her story. The burning question about Ella put at the back of his mind. "Would you like a glass of wine?"

"No, the mineral water is good." She joined him at the kitchen island. Her hand glided over the onyx marble top. "I didn't know what else to do, so I went home. My dad raised his hand to slap me for coming home so late, but Fred stopped him. He would have some hard questions to answer at the passport control if my face was bruised." She snatched the glass from

Dario's hand and gulped the clear liquid. Her lips glistened in the low-hanging light, inviting him to kiss her. He cupped her chin and brushed his thumb over her lower lip. She closed her eyes as he placed a soft kiss to the corner of her lips.

Irena traced her finger over the shapeless forms on the counters. "But he promised to give me a good beating once we're in Canada. My dad seemed satisfied with that."

Rage burned in Dario. Though the events she divulged took place fourteen years ago, he wished he could wrap his hands around her father's neck and squeeze the living daylights out of the weasel. By all that was holy, he would get his hands on both men.

"Did Fred keep his promise to your dad?"

She shook her head. "He never touched me; he had his hounds to do the dirty work for him."

Okay, his relief was premature. Fred's name got bumped to the top of the list of men he'd love to beat to a pulp. "Coward in any case, and those who work for him."

Her silence rattled him. By her tight expression, she had more to tell. Her gaze wandered to the ten-foot window, as darkness slowly replaced what little daylight they had today.

Dario straightened. "Ante has this theory. Fred needed a wife to ward off rumors about him being a gay."

Her slow nod was barely noticeable. "And to play his dutiful wife whenever his parents visited. Visit? Pfft…what am I talking about?" She dismissed the notion with a wave of her hand. "They came in for an inspection. His mother opened the cupboards and drawers and ran her finger over the furniture to see if I dusted since her last scrutiny." Irena braced her hip on the kitchen island and crossed her arms over her ample chest. "Each time she'd ask at the door if I was with a child already. Once I announced my 'delicate' condition, she stopped asking. You can't imagine how much I disappointed her by giving her a granddaughter."

Damn it. That should've been his mother showing off her grandchild, not Fred's. "Such an old and skewed belief. The way some people of that generation behave, one would think our parents still live some hundred years behind our times."

A tiny smile stretched Irena's lips. "Your mom and dad were ahead of the time though many dissed them as lazy for living off social assistance. Everyone was quick to forget your dad fought the war and lost his leg for this country."

"It took years before we saw money trickling down to us. By then, Mom's health deteriorated and it only got worse." Dario spun the glass in his hand, making the liquid swirl. It had taken Dad longer to fight the red tape than the war lasted, often leaving him wondering was it worth to take up arms and defend the country. Their poor mother had hidden her illness for who knows how long to not to put more strain on the already thinly spread income. The extended family rarely helped and with Mom's illness, they turned completely away. Nowadays, cousins come knocking on the door, reminding him of the importance of the family ties. Good thing Ante was there to remind them of times where they seemed to have forgotten their beliefs.

"I'll never be free of Fred." At Irena's loud exhale,

he glanced up at her beautiful face. She tapped her fingers on the counter.

Dario straightened and took her hand. "I wouldn't bet on that. Ana already dug her talons into his wallet. She showed up at the restaurant, she seems to come into money, Fred's money that is. And the guy across from the Mezzaluna reopened today. After a health inspector closed them for almost a year. Ana tells me Fred's generously paid for the guy's fine."

Irena harrumphed. "That owner doesn't know it yet, but Fred bought his restaurant he didn't just pay a fine. Omibo Corp, his company, 'helps' the struggling businesses. The truth is, they take them over and incorporate." She froze, and her eyes took on a sharp look as if a realization struck her. "Wait. You said Ana has a boy. How old would he be?"

Dario shrugged, frowning. "I'm not sure, grade school. Twelve maybe. Why?"

"Oh, dear God." She placed one hand on her heaving chest, her color drained from her face. "That boy is in danger. Is there someone who could take him? Hide him from Fred?"

Dario's back stiffened, trying to comprehend what Irena was implying. "What? Fred would…no…that's sick…the boy's just a child."

"If not Fred, there are plenty on his secret list who would. He or rather his company sponsors a private boarding school. For all intents and purposes, it is a school during the day. But at night, a different curriculum is taught there." Her voice lowered and she glanced over her shoulder as if expecting someone to be listening on their conversation. "Powerful men, and some women too, those with deep pockets, satisfy their twisted perversions with minors. After quick cash exchange, they are shown to the kids' bedrooms. Their visits are recorded on camera. That is how Fred has them in his fist and can manipulate and blackmail them. Things are done his way or...well, you can imagine the damage he could cause them. The media would have frenzy."

Dario couldn't blink. The news she relayed still had not wrapped around his mind. "No one suspected?"

"There are speculations, but so far no one's been able to prove a thing." Her hand shook as she poured the remaining water from the bottle into her glass. "It's a well-guarded secret."

"Where do they get the kids from?"

"For the most part, they are employees' children. Parents jump at the opportunity of free secondary education. The students returned home in an awful mental state, but parents are scared to speak out. In the past, those who opened their mouths not only got fired but soon after they suffered terrible fates, fatal car accidents, debilitating illness, sudden heart attacks, severe allergic reactions. Fred's company keeps health files on their employees, they know everything." She stared at the air bubbles in her glass racing to the surface. "All received hush payments that came with a confidentiality agreement."

"How...how did you come into this information?"

"As I said, it's a long story, so let me start from the beginning." She drew in a long breath and took another sip of her water, licked her lips and continued, "I was given a room in the basement of Fred's house, a maid's quarters really, with a small bathroom, but didn't need anything more. The neighbors knew me as his maid.

Thought he'd humiliate me by giving me a janitorial job at his office. He couldn't stop my paychecks, wasn't enough to support myself and Ella, but enough for necessities. One day I was wiping down toilets when I overheard the two women speak Croatian. I gathered some courage and approached them." Staring at the glass, she gave a small laugh. "Tanja, the manager, was looking for a new assistant, so she gave me a chance. She encouraged me to take evening classes. I progressed slowly. Fred was rarely at the office and didn't seem to care. He was not much at home either." Leaning her elbow on the counter, she rested her chin on her curled fingers. "When he was there, he threw parties that often turned into full-blown orgies. I'd go out during his party nights, found a coffee shop that stayed open all night. Across the street was a martial arts school. They had the help wanted sign for weeks. I was reminded of you in your karate gi so I went in…and asked what kind of help they required. I washed windows and cleaned then later filled in at the reception when needed, but I earned free lessons. The sensei took me under his wing. The rest is history."

Dario rubbed her shoulders. It must be hard for her to spill all this out. Under his gentle fingers, her muscles slowly relaxed. She leaned into him, pressing her back to his chest. He inhaled her citrus scent and wrapped his arms around her slender waist. "I feared Fred would not be a loving husband, but I made a peace with the fact you were in a better place than I could provide. Have you cried many nights?"

"I did at first. Not because Fred didn't love me, but because you and I were an ocean apart. Soon I realized tears were of no help, and that was what Fred wanted:

to see me broken in spirit." She shook her head, her lips pressed into a tight line. "I wasn't going to indulge him." Then she licked her lips and continued with her story, "A year ago, I found the truth about Fred's prestigious school. I'd been promoted to a team leader and was given access to some files. I was searching for a specific spreadsheet when I stumbled upon something." Her body stiffened again, she took a few steps back and leaned against the wall. Her chin shook and her lips quirked. "Pictures of young girls and boys, old men hands held them in compromising positions. You can see the fear in kids' eyes, some clearly cried. Things, like sex props…used on them." She gasped, her breath shook on exhale, while tears spilled out of her eyes. "Dario, those teenagers were still kids. I can't imagine fear and pain they endured."

Not wanting her to continue, he stepped to her and pulled her to him. Obviously what she had found was still haunting her. Someone had either planted these files for her to find or whoever put them there wasn't the brightest light on a string. "Shh, it's okay babe. You're here, they can't hurt you."

"Oh, but they can, and they will. Fred inherited everything after his parents' death. He no longer cares who knows of his sexual orientation. The deal was I stay as his wife until he gets it all." She dabbed her hand under each eye, but tears kept coming.

Dario handed her a box of tissues from the counter. Anxiety knotted his stomach. He anticipated some ugliness in Irena's story, but he never imagined she'd had to flee for her life. "You played your part. Why is he after you?"

She took a long step back, her eyes big and round,

fear on her face. "He doesn't care about me or anyone else dumb enough to defend me. We're only obstacles to what he really wants."

"And what is that?"

"Ella. Virgins like her are a prized possession. A congressman is offering a hefty sum to have her first." Irena's glance darted at the clock on the wall. "Speaking of which, where is Ante? He'd been gone for over an hour. Didn't he say he'd be back in a few minutes?"

## Chapter 8

Heavy rain pelted the window panes. Dario matched the steady drone by tapping his fingers on the marble countertop of the kitchen island. Phone stuck to his ear, he listened to the endless rings. *Damn you, Ante, where the hell are you*? Irena ceased her pacing. Her pallid face and furrowed brow indicated her concern.

"Why isn't Ante answering?" Her voice was barely above a whisper.

"He won't pick up if he's driving." Dario tapped the end call button on his cell and speed-dialed Ante's number again.

Irena exhaled a shaky breath and resumed her pacing, chewing her fingernail. "I never should've let her go. What was I thinking? If something happens to Ella... Oh, why did I let her go?"

Dario rushed to Irena and wrapped his free arm around her shoulders. "Nothing's gonna happen to our...um...your daughter. They'll be here any moment. You'll see."

He squeezed Irena's shoulder. Her rigid posture indicated she knew he suspected Ella was their child. She would tell him everything on her own time. But time was a thief, it had already stolen over a decade he should've spent loving her.

Muffled buzzing had him turning in the direction

of the sound. Was it coming from the couch? He approached and lifted the cream cushions. Ante's cell chimed with Dario's name displayed on the screen. How had he missed hearing it numerous times he'd dialed his brother's number? He ended the call and the low tone stopped. "The idiot most likely doesn't know where he left his phone."

"That makes matters worse." A deeper crease formed between Irena's knitted eyebrows. "If they are snatched off the streets—"

"Let's not get crazy. This is a small town where everyone made it their business to know everyone else's. No one gets kidnapped here." Dario swallowed a knot in his throat. What he described used to be this city. It had grown over the last decade and a half. These new people who moved in were a different sort than those he'd grown up with. There was a time he could swear on people's dependency. Not anymore.

He wrapped Irena in his arms and rocked them for a few long minutes. Her body shook and his gut clenched. *Where are you, Ante?* "I bet Martina didn't have Jasmin ready and made them sit while she packed. She does that. It's her chance to talk with Ante. She's trying to restore their relationship, but he can be a real prick."

Irena nodded but didn't say anything. Her silence tightened the knots in his stomach. He should keep talking to pass the time. He might have Martina's phone number in his missed calls list. Long ago he'd learned not to meddle in Ante and Martina's business and never answered her calls. Fool of his brother mistook her caring for controlling and checking up on him by calling Dario's number. When his brother returned, he'd punch his nose for taking his sweet time.

"How much does Ella know about this school? I don't want to blurt something in front of her. You know…I don't want to frighten her."

"She knows everything. I've seen a few of the teens returned to their parents." Irena stepped away from him and shook her head. "It's not living, Dario. They are husks of what once were vibrant children, now frightened, broken, all using drugs to forget the demons."

His chest squeezed. What kind of men could do such things? They were someone's daughters and sons, sent to school to get a better education, not to be used in the vilest way. This was the outcome when no one speaks out. The crime goes on and more innocent lives got destroyed. "It won't happen to Ella. You have my promise."

"Dario, you can lose everything. Even your life. And not just you, Ante too and everyone he loves."

"Babe, we came from nothing. If we lose it all we know how to rise again. As for getting killed, you know I'd give my life for you and…" He cleared his throat. "And Ella too. Ante is resourceful. Don't fear. He'll protect his own and fight for us."

"I can't shake the fear off." She paced again, one hand on her hip, the other by her mouth as she chewed her thumbnail. "I knew you'd risk it all for me. That is why I stayed away from you this long. I could live with us being separated, but can't live if I lose you for real."

He put his hand up, palm outward to stop her talking nonsense. "Babe, you're not going to lose—"

They both spun toward the front door as girls' giggles and Ante's deep voice bounced off the walls in the hallway. Dario reached for the door handle. Ella opened the door before he could turn the knob, a white grocery bag in her hand. Her face lit up with a cheeky grin. Keeping her eyes on Jasmin, she slipped the nun chucks out of her jacket and into the duffle bag still by the front door. Ante balanced the two large pizza boxes in his hands, Jasmin's sparkly princess bag dangled from his elbow.

He kicked the door closed with his foot. "Woo-hoo! What a deluge."

Dario fumed. The dimwit had not realized he gave them both such worry. Then how could he? His brother didn't know the danger lurking around Irena and Ella.

"We waited in the car, but this rain isn't easing off." Ante passed the pizzas to Irena, shook the water off his jacket and clicked his tongue before hanging the suede coat in the closet.

Dario strode toward him, his fist ready to punch the grin off his brother's face. The idiot worried about his jacket. "You mor—" He swallowed the curse as Ella flashed him a smile.

"Uncle Dario." Jasmin ran up to him, reached her arms above her hand, her signal for him to pick her up for a hug.

In an instant, his initial anger defused, he picked his niece up and her thin legs and arms wrapped around him. "Hi, sweetheart. I missed you."

His gaze tracked Ella as she placed the bag on the counter. Irena's face relaxed, her color returned, and a soft smile lingered on her pretty lips while she stared at him and Jasmin. Perhaps she envisioned him and Ella. Damn it, why couldn't he hug his daughter as freely as he hugged Jasmin?

"You gave me such scare." Irena grabbed Ella into a tight hug then pulled back and examined her face. She rubbed her thumb over Ella's lips. "What is this? Lipstick? You're wearing makeup?"

Ante lifted the lids on the pizzas, the aroma of freshly baked dough and melted cheese wafted from the two boxes. "Martina's friends had some fun with her. Doesn't she look great?"

It must've been Irena's sharp scrutiny that made his brother swallow and turn to Dario.

"You said you'd be back in a few, it took you over an hour." Dario took a step forward.

Ante gave a sheepish smile and a shrug. "Look, I thought Dario would know. I had to sit there and wait for Martina to get Jasmin packed, never mind that I told her million times to have her ready." He picked up a slice of pizza and took a big bite, then sucked the strings of melted cheese hung from his fingers.

Ante pulled another slice from the box. "At least I had time to place the order for our pizzas. Before I've picked up my order, we stopped by the Mezzaluna to see that everything was running smoothly. The place is packed. I was gonna call you, but, hey!" He patted his shirt and pants pockets. "Have you seen my cell?"

Dario shook his head but decided not to answer. Let his brother sweat a little, see if he could find his phone on his own. "You should've told me you were going to take a scenic route. We were worried."

"We're alive and kicking. No one followed us. And I'm a bit disappointed that I didn't get to see Ella in action." Ante flashed a mocking frown that irked Dario. Hopefully, his brother noticed a promise of future retribution in his narrowing gaze.

"Can I keep my makeup for a little longer? Please, Mom." Ella's pleading tone worked because Irena's shoulders lowered and she smiled.

"Make sure you wipe it off before bedtime." Irena let go of her daughter and stepped to the counter. "What's in the bag?"

"Some junk food and pop. Isn't Jasmin the cutest thing ever, Mom?" Ella placed her thumbs at temples and wiggled her fingers at Jasmin, making the younger girl giggle. Dario kissed his niece's soft cheek and placed her down.

"She is," Irena said, crouching in front of the little girl. "She reminds me of you at this age with her pig tails."

Ante produced two DVD cases out of the deep pocket of his jacket. "We'll make it a movie-fest tonight." He held out a cartoon. "For the kids, and this one's for later." He pointed at the action movie in his other hand.

"Right, for later." Dario snorted, staring at pizza boxes from the famous restaurant. Extra thin crust with goat cheese and porcini mushrooms in one, and in the second one plain cheese and pepperoni pizza. Oh, the smells. They made his mouth water. Now he didn't mind his brother returning so late. The Providenca had the best pizza. "You'll be asleep halfway through the kid's movie."

Ante plopped his butt on the stool at the kitchen island. "Your prediction may be a correct one, in fact, I'd bet my money on it." He gave a nonchalant shrug. "Come on, kids, let's eat. Pizzas are getting cold."

Irena helped Jasmin out of her little faux fur coat and sat her at the table. "Are you hungry, love?"

Dario smiled, passing out the plates. Irena's aunty instincts kicked in instantly. Her hard circumstances toughened her demeanor, but motherhood also made her soft inside. The combination of both turned her more feminine than ever.

Jasmin nodded. "Can Ella sit next to me? Daddy says she's my cousin." She turned to Dario. "Uncle Dario, can I show Ella your collection?"

Dario gauged Irena's reaction. She appeared unmoved by Jasmin's remark of Ella as her cousin. "Sure, honey, but remember," he waved his finger, "what do we never do?"

"We don't mess things up, only look." She bit off a piece her pizza, a corner of the crust sticking out between her lips as she tried to fit the whole thing into her mouth.

Ante took a seat at the dinner table. It must've been Ella's questioning gaze that prompted him to continue. "Jasmin loves to peruse Dario's old photo albums. He's old-fashioned and keeps what little pictures we have from our younger days instead of getting them scanned."

"What you call old fashioned, I call nostalgic." Dario bumped his shoulder against Irena's. "Grab some food before Ante gobbles up all of it."

Irena reached for a slice but pulled her arm back. "I couldn't possibly. I'm still digesting my late lunch."

"Here, Mom." Ella scraped toppings off the slice and handed it to Irena.

"Thank you, honey." Irena took a bite and chewed slowly.

Ante's jaw dropped. "What? You just gonna eat the crust?"

Irena took another bite and shrugged. Ella licked her lips and put the slice in her hand on the plate in front of her. "That's all Mom can eat."

Dario raised one eyebrow, staring at the blushing Ella. Was the girl lying for her mother? Not liking pizza toppings and not being able to eat them were two different things. Irena had food issues, just how bad, he'd find out soon.

Irena patted her stomach and blew out her breath. "That was great. Anyway, I'd love to look at those pictures."

"Me too." Ella piped. "Maybe some of the moments from mom's stories are captured in those pictures." She turned to Ante. "Sorry about ruining your movie night, Uncle."

"Ah, nothing's ruined." Ante dismissed her with a wave of his hand. "You'll be done with the pictures in twenty minutes."

Ella wiped Jasmin's hands and face with a napkin. "Your daddy's always so funny."

"Where is your daddy, Ella?" Jasmin asked with an innocence of a three-year-old girl, but her question brought uneasy silence.

"I...my dad is..." Ella cleared her throat and stared at Dario then shot a pleading look at her mother.

Irena closed her eyes and gave a slight shake of her head. "I'm getting tired. Ella, don't stay up too long. We're having an early start. Dario, get your sparring gear ready. We train tomorrow. Ante, you'll get your wish to see Ella in action."

She headed upstairs. The click of the door indicated she had retreated into Dario's bedroom. Dario glanced at Ella. Her eyes glistened and she blinked fast, averting her gaze. Her sadness yanked his heartstrings. Perhaps his idea to wait for Irena to come forward with her admission wasn't the wisest. Pressuring her into it wouldn't be any better. Still, he must try for his daughter's sake.

"It's okay, sweetheart, I'll take care of the dishes." Dario grabbed the plates from her hand and smiled at Jasmin. "Why don't you show your big cousin the photo albums while I clean up?"

Damn it, why couldn't Irena just let go of her guard and let Ella say it? She should know he understood. It was the circumstances preventing her from letting him know of his child. Yes, the fact had taken him aback. Had she thought him some low life of a man who'd hold that against her? If she had, that would be a low blow and already hurt.

"Sparring gear?" Ante's question pulled him out of the turmoil. His brother already started the cartoon, but no one joined him on the couch. "I wouldn't know where to begin to look for mine. Do you still have yours?"

"Should be in one of the boxes in the basement locker, I kept it after we sold the old shack." Dario picked up Irena's bags and carried them upstairs. He set the bed in his study for Ella. On his way down, he paused by the door of his bedroom. No sound came from within. Could Irena be already asleep? No way, more likely she brooded in there.

"Ella," he called over the railing. The girls joined Ante in front of TV, but his brother had already got comfy and was snoring softly.

Ella turned to him. "Yes, Da—Dario?"

Something snapped inside of him and he couldn't

take another second of this torture. "It's okay, sweetheart. Just call me Dad."

Chapter 9

The door to his room popped open. Irena stormed out, her expression mimicked Ella's, except for the blaze igniting her eyes. She halted, her face relaxed before creases formed between her eyes. She then took a slow step toward him. Fresh tears glistened in her pale-blue eyes, giving them an appearance of two flickering ice crystals. Her hand pressed against her mouth blocked a muffled shriek.

Dario's chest squeezed. He took a step closer and reached out to her. He halted, fighting the urge to pull her into his embrace. One more second and she'd admit Ella was his child. *Come on, babe, you can do it.*

Ella appeared at the top of the stairs, her bare feet soundless on the lush carpet. "Please, Mom. It was hard to call Dad by his name. I never called him Dario. He was always Dad. My daddy."

Irena lowered her hand and cast her daughter smile then turned to him. "Ella's the best thing in my life. I don't know what I'd do if I didn't have her. I'm so proud of her. She is the reason I made it in that hell of a life my parents cooked up for me."

"Babe," Dario said, pulling Irena to him, "every parent would be proud of such a child. I'm proud of you for raising her on your own. Let her call me Dad."

Nodding, Irena swiped her knuckles under her eyes, wiping off tears. After a few broken up sniffles, her voice steadied as she continued. "I wanted to call you the minute I found out I was pregnant. And I dialed your number, but then I put the phone down before the first ring. Fred would know I called you, the number would show up on the bill. Besides, you were somewhere on the seas. How would I get the news to you?" She faced the window and stared at the twinkling city lights spread out beneath his penthouse. Her back straightened and she drew in a loud breath. "You'd jump overboard and swim across the ocean to get to me." Her tone changed to somber one. She tilted her head and locked her gaze with him. "I couldn't have you drop everything and abandon your family. They needed you too. It'd only been a couple of months since our parting, but I'm sure your mom came to depend on the bit of money you sent her."

"You know me, babe." Dario tightened his hold on her and extended one arm to Ella who waited at the top of the stairs.

Ella flew to him, wrapped her arms around his torso and buried her face in his chest. "Daddy."

He huffed at the impact, embracing his girls and pulling them into a tight hug. He kissed Ella's hair. His family was here and his love increased tenfold. "It's okay, baby girl. I wish I was there for you from the day one, but we have lots of time to make up."

A heavy load dropped from his chest. If he'd received the news fourteen years ago that he was about to become a dad, nothing would have stood in his way to be with Irena, but rash actions wouldn't have accomplished anything, only cause more hardships. His impulses and anger had derailed him so many times in the past, but with some hard discipline, he got them under control. His mother would've understood, though the money he'd sent her every month meant the world to her and Dad. As Dario's pay grew, he was able to carve out a bigger portion for his parents. Still, it wasn't enough to buy their health back. Mom's cancer progressed and poorly treated sepsis ate at the stump of Dad's amputated leg. It had taken Dario years to pull his life together after the loss of Irena and later his parents, but now she was here with his child. A new surge of energy swept through him.

"Oh, Dario." Irena sniffed, burying her face in his chest. "I wrote so many letters, explaining my predicament, but I couldn't bring myself to mail them. Besides, Fred had me watched and threatened if I was to leave, Ella would suffer. As years passed, all I wanted was to work and save money so once Fred released me from my obligation, I would come back to you and take care of you and your family. Only he never had any intentions to let me go. Things are different now, and I fear we may not have each other for long."

A heavy stone sank his stomach. He would not allow Fred to take his daughter and his Irena. No matter how many cronies the snake had in his employ. "Don't talk nonsense, babe. We'll have each other for as long as we live."

"I think Mom means we may not live long if Fred…" Ella tightened her lips and her brow furrowed.

"You are not going to lose me. No one's going to hurt us." He hoped that many he'd done favors had not forgotten their promises. But he could be asking for too much. He hadn't risked his life when he made a few phone calls to his connections for their goodwill.

"He's well protected." Irena rubbed his shoulder, her fingers dug deep into his muscles. A bit of his tension released with her pressure.

"How many of his thugs could he bring along with him? If he thinks he can come to my town and get away with his bull..." He bit his tongue before he finished swearing in front of Ella. "I mean his cra..." *Damn, man, not in front of the kid.* "His crime, he'll find out things are not going to work his way. He can't bribe everyone."

"He always travels on the company's jet, so he has any number of his thugs around him at all times. The rest he will get here. He knows people are struggling to survive. Low employment and small salaries, it wouldn't be hard to bribe a few more." Irena gave a lopsided smile at the sight of Ella's tight hold around his torso.

"That may be, but," Dario raised his index finger, "there are those who cannot be bought. I have friends in low places, as well as high."

"I don't want to bring anyone in harm's way." Irena shook her head slowly. "They can be found dead someplace and no one would be able to prove any foul play."

"What foul play?" At Ante's booming voice, all three of them turned to the stairs. He stood in the middle, cradling Jasmin in his arms while she sucked on her thumb and her eyelids drooped, sure sign she was beyond tired. Still, she propped her head up, her known way to fight off sleep. "What's everyone babbling about here? And does anyone feel like filling me in on all this?"

"You were asleep on the couch." Dario leaned

against the railing, his stomach knotting. His brother heard only the last bit of the conversation. He would overreact when he found out the rest.

Irena's face mellowed, and she pulled away from him. "Jasmin looks pooched. Let me put her to bed."

"Yep, missy skipped her nap. Apparently, she was too excited to spend the evening with her daddy." Ante climbed a few remaining steps and stopped in front of Ella. "She wants her big cousin to tuck her in. Would you mind? The couch inside Dario's study is big enough for the two of you to stretch. I often crash in there." He passed Ella the princess bag with Jasmin's things. "Her pajamas and toothbrush are in here."

"Ante slept there every time he was in a dog house, which was often." Dario patted his brother's back. Until today, he was the only family he got, and their teasing helped him keep the sanity over the years.

"Thank you, Uncle. I'll get her ready." She took Jasmin in her arms.

Jasmin popped her thumb out of her mouth. "Why is my daddy sleeping in a dog house?"

"I don't know. Something grownups say." Ella cinched Jasmin higher up her hip.

Ante leaned to give Jasmin a goodnight kiss. "Sweet dreams."

Ella carried Jasmin inside the bedroom but didn't fully close the door. It would take her some time to feel at home. Heck, he could barely wrap his mind around the whole thing. He had a teenage daughter and still wasn't married. This last bit didn't sit right, something he'd have to remedy and fast. The ring he'd bought years ago was still locked inside the safe, tucked in its blue velvet box. Irena would love the band with the three pale-blue aquamarine stones, the color of her eyes. He just had to present it to her at the right moment. A thought occurred. She had left that snob but did not mention whether she divorced him. Must've at least filed for separation, she referred to her nuptial as her obligation.

A loud clap of Ante's hands snapped Dario from his reverie. His brother pointed at the couch. "How about we sit and talk? I like to know what we are facing. Do I need to send Martina and Jasmin someplace safe, away from here?"

Dario wrapped one arm around Irena's shoulder and followed his brother down the stairs. Ante joined them on the couch, plopping a beer on the glass coffee table and opened the other one in his hand.

"You said no one followed you to or from Martina's house." Dario eyed the brown bottle in front of him. His mouth watered, but he opted for the glass of now warm and flat mineral water left there by Irena. Beer could impair him and, given the circumstances, he needed his head clear.

Ante took a long swig from the bottle and smacked his lips. "As far as I can tell, no one did. These men, what are they capable of? Would they kill if Fred ordered them?"

"They are paid well to do what he wants. There'd been suspicious deaths in the past, though no foul play was proven. Witnesses develop sudden memory loss, they couldn't be certain of what they saw. No one would testify and cases were dropped." Irena tucked one leg under her. "The fact Ella and I are still alive means he wants us that way. I think he enjoys this chase." She shrugged. "He thinks he will win, and odds are in his favor."

"Were in his favor." Dario squeezed her shoulders.
"His mistake was following you here. We tolerated him
when he hung out with us, not even his cousin who had
to drag him along liked him. She said the guy was a
nutcase." Now Dario could see why Fred's cousin had
seemed afraid. He'd have a hard time believing her
when she confided how she caught Fred fondling her
younger brother. She was twelve-years-old then and she
didn't know what to do, but pull the pants up over her
brother's hips and stop him from crying. Fred was
sixteen and bigger than her. He scared her, threatening
her if she told of the incident to anyone. Consensual sex
between adult males was not a crime, but forcing a
minor into the act was.

Irena closed her eyes. Her chest heaved with her
loud exhale. "No one is safe in his presence. He was
caught in the sexual act with a teenage son of his
father's business partner. Shortly after the boy was sent
to religious school and his parents suddenly retired, the
father handed his shares in the company to Fred's dad. I
suspect they were silenced. Fred continues his
relationship with, Father Diego. Through the years,
Father grew close to me and he revealed that priesthood
wasn't his choice." She twirled a lock of her short hair
around her finger. A sure sign talking about this made
her nervous. "Poor guy is confused about his sexuality.
He doesn't think he is a gay, but cannot break free from
Fred. He has some strong feelings for him. Fred was his
first partner even if he coerced him into sex."

Ante's arm holding beer froze halfway to his
mouth. "So sending this Diego hombre into priesthood
didn't change a thing. Fred was on him like a flea on a

dog." Lines appeared around his mouth with his frown. "As the saying goes, it takes all kinds to keep the world go round, but Fred... coercing young boys like that... Still, I don't see why Fred is after you and Ella if boys turn him on."

"His company sponsors some high school where they send employee's kids, but in fact, they are selling them to politicians and other bigwigs for sex." Dario held his breath, gauging Ante's reaction. Would his brother connect the dots?

"The company sponsored The Paradise School for many decades. At first, the intentions were noble, after his dad retired Fred replaced the key people. The academy, as he calls it, got a facelift. The campus buildings, the grounds, facilities are amazing. Some new academic programs are introduced. No wonder kids are drawn to it. Ella wanted to go there too until I uncovered the truth." Irena took the glass from Dario's hand and sipped on the water, moistening her lips.

Ante slowly straightened in his seat. "Oh dear God, he wants Ella. Please tell me I'm wrong. The sick, perverted bastard thinks he can have my niece. Over my dead body. I'm gonna give that douchebag what's coming to him."

Dario raised one hand, his palm facing Ante. His brother failed to realize his body may end up dead if Fred wanted. "Keep your voice down, the kids are sleeping upstairs."

"Oh, shee, err, I mean sh-h-shoot." Ante leaned back, couch cushions flattening under him. "How can he get away with all this merde?"

"He does a lot of philanthropic work. So, naturally, he's a saint in public eye. Even some families don't believe their children. He had them all convinced that kids are delusional, none of what they're saying happened." Irena rubbed her hands over her face. By the dark circles and blotchy eyes, her energy was drained. But the strength of her voice convinced Dario, she believed she fought for what was right. "A group of parents asked Father Diego for help. They wanted to sue but had a hard time finding a lawyer that would take the case. He helped them find a good attorney. Then out of the blue, the solicitor returned the retainer fee and said he was too busy to represent them. There's no doubt in my mind Fred found out, threatened the lawyer and got him intimidated into dropping the case."

Silence hung heavy over them. Ante pursed his lips and nodded several times. His way of processing the facts he'd just heard. There was no time to ponder all of this, however hard it was to wrap one's mind around it. "We should get Joe to help us. I hear he's working with Europol."

"Despite the rumors, he's just a small island cop." Dario rubbed his tired eyes. Maybe their friend kept the low profile, not wanting to prove the gossips correct. Still, Dario should make a contact with Joe, get him to do some discreet digging and see what he could come up with. "Will talk more about this tomorrow and come up with a plan. We cannot go against Fred hotheaded. Right now, I think Irena would like to turn in for the night." Dario arched his back, stretching his arms above his head. "I know I can't keep my eyes open and I slept in today."

Irena covered her mouth with her hand and yawned. "I'm tired too and can't wait until my head hits the pillow, but I'm also dying for a bath."

Ante put the empty beer on the table. "Well, I guess that's my cue to leave you two. I'll just get comfy on here." He patted the couch and pulled the cushions on the floor. "I'll get Martina to take Jasmin to her folks on the island."

Ante's plan to escape from the city sounded brilliant. With over one thousand islands, it would take Fred and his cronies some time to find them. But, no, Irena was on the run, they couldn't hide forever. Plus, he couldn't stay away from his restaurant for long. Under no circumstances would he leave his family alone.

"That would be the best. I'd hate to see anyone get hurt." Irena nodded at Ante then turned to Dario and repeated the gesture. "I'd like to take a bath now."

"Yes, ma'am. After you." Dario swept his right arm, and followed Irena up the stairs, admiring her tight, round butt. A part of his body reacted to her in an instant, yet he'd have to curb his desire. She seemed too tired, perhaps more than Jasmin.

She flipped the overhead light in his bedroom then headed straight for the on-suite door. "Your bathroom is stunning. I can't wait to try out the soaker tub." Leaning against the double sink counter, she gazed over the small space, then crouched in front of the white cabinet. "Would bubble bath be in here?"

"I might've put it in there." The only way he'd have any of that stuff would've had to be left behind by his dates who loved to get with him into the tub to soak in essential oils, as they had called those balls they dropped in the water so diligently. By the thick layer of dust on the tub, it's been a while since he had such a date. "I don't take baths and usually forget to clean this tub."

Irena's voice came muffled from inside the cabinet. "My, you've got an array of bubble bath stuff and you said you don't take baths."

"Can't remember last time I took one." He sluiced the clean water over the tub, sending the brown dust down the drain, then plugged the hole and opened the faucet adjusting the temperature.

"This one smells nice." Irena handed him the bottle of strawberry scented bubble bath, her eyes closed while she rubbed the side of her neck. "In fourteen years I learned to sleep with one eye open and jump at the slightest sound."

"Tonight you'll sleep like a baby." He poured two capfuls of thick, pink liquid into the running water. Foamy bubbles formed and the sweet smell of strawberries filled the room.

By the time he turned to her, she had her shirt removed and she worked the belt-buckle of her jeans. The lacy, blush straps of her bra tempted him, he approached her from behind. Her shoulders trembled as he slid the silky fabrics down.

"I hear you girls are dying to take off your bras at the end of the day," he said, unclasping the hooks from the band.

"As if you don't know." She arched her back against him and moaned while he placed soft kisses between her shoulder blades.

"You shouldn't believe everything you hear about me. I had my fair share of girls, but I'm not some Casanova." It wasn't until recent years that girls started to drop at his feet. Coincidentally, around the same time his business took off and money poured into his pockets. Hmm, funny how that worked out.

Pulling the lacy fabric off, he glided his hands until her breasts filled his palms. A long sigh rolled off her lips as his fingers played with her pebbled nipples. Fire in his groin ignited with her citrusy scent. He glanced down her back. Her jeans still covered half her taut buttocks. "You've got too many clothes on you."

"I'm not the only one." She turned to him and captured his lips with hers, while her fingers worked the buttons on his plaid shirt. "The tub is big enough for the both of us."

He swallowed, inhaling next to her lips. His cock tightened. Their almost teenage daughter and his little niece slept on the other side of the wall. If he was to join Irena in the tub, he'd have a hard time remaining quiet. "Are you sure about this, babe? I thought you'd enjoy the bath by yourself."

"Someone has to wash my back." She worked the last button of his shirt through the hole and yanked the cotton fabric off his shoulders. Her sigh of satisfaction as she glided her hands over his torso was his undoing. He scrambled out of his jeans and tore the socks off, then grabbed her waist and peeled her denims down her legs, pulling along her panties. She stood in front of him in all her naked glory. Unbelievable, she was a muse from his dreams and all his.

The foam reached the top of the tub, and he shut the water. Irena tested the temperature by dipping her toes. She was about to step in, when he rolled into the warm bath, splashing the water over the side.

"Come here, you vixen." At his pull, she shrieked and eased her body between his legs, her back pressed to his chest. Suds settled over her leaving swells of her breasts peeking above the waterline, covered in lacy bubbles.

Reaching one arm around her waist, he dipped the sea sponge and glided it along her shoulders and back. She moaned and relaxed against him, swishing foam back and forth over his arm. For a while, only the occasional echo of slow drip from the faucet broke the silence.

Bubbles dissolved, leaving the thin patches on the surface of her skin. Her pink nipples stood erect and a sudden shiver raked her spine with his soft kiss on the base of her neck. She snuggled against him, turning her face halfway to his chest.

"Are you falling asleep on me?" He brushed the wet strands of her hair away from her forehead. Would he ever get used to seeing her with this cropped short dyed brown tone? He missed her natural blonde color.

She peered through her heavy lids. "I'm trying to get in the mood, but I'm drained."

"It's okay, babe. I'm tired too. The water's getting cold. Let's go to bed." He slowly got to his feet and pulled her up with him. "Here," he said, stepping over the tub's edge, gripping his toes on the slippery tiles. "Use this towel."

Her body swayed while he patted her dry then wrapped her in the terry cloth. He took another towel from the rack and dried himself off then folded it around his hips.

Irena's smile and gaze directed at his middle had him pause while tucking the loose end of his towel. "What are you thinking?"

"It seems a shame to let such hardness go to waste. I'm sorry." She covered another jaw-splitting yawn. "I can get into it."

He pressed his index finger to her lips. "Don't be silly. I want you as a willing and equal participant. Besides, it'll get harder next time, after I've rested. We're both baked and some sleep will do us good. Come, I'll give you a nice massage."

"M-m-m, yes massage. I love you." She stepped closer to him and he pulled her into a tight hug.

"I love you too." He placed a soft kiss on her lips, then brushed his lips against hers, taking in her fresh scent. If a tight hug could mend all that was broken inside her, he'd suffocate her in his embrace. Instead, he swiped her into his arms and carried her to his bed.

"Remove that towel," he whispered, pulling on the tucked end. Once again she lay in front of him nude. God almighty, she was beautiful. He watched muscles on her arms and chest twitch as he glided his hand over her skin.

He reached for the bottle of massaging oil on the nightstand. Now he'd try the stuff for what it was intended to instead of rubbing it into his dried and chapped hands after long hours of working in the kitchen. "Turn to your stomach."

The smell of lavender filled the room. She obeyed while he warmed up a dribble of scented oil between his palms. Straddling over her buttocks, he sat on his haunches and kneaded her muscles starting at her lower back.

"M-m-m-m that feels good." She pulled the pillow under her head. "Don't stop."

"Anything for you." He changed kneading motions to gliding his palms over her back and shoulders. By the time he reached her neck, her body loosened up, and her even breathing indicated she was asleep.

He kissed her cheek, got up and pulled the covers over her, then snuggled behind her. She rolled to him and he wrapped his arm around her. The warmth of her body and her closeness relaxed him. She was back where she belonged. Fuzziness filled his head and he drifted off to sleep.

Soft fingers played with his hair, waking him up. He peered through his lashes, his eyelids heavy. Irena's silhouette loomed in the darkened room. Her lips lingered half an inch from his, her breath tickled his nose. He tilted his chin and captured her mouth, wrapping one arm around her shoulders. Their tongues met in a hungry, demanding union, then slowed down to a sensuous dance. Exhilaration sizzled through his every nerve, stirring a fierce ache that demanded more.

She pulled back, wrapped her hand around his stiff cock. "You were right when you said you'd be harder."

A sudden realization struck him. Before she seized his lips again, he managed to get his voice back. "Babe, the kids...ah-h-h." He hissed, throwing his head against the pillow. She made him a slave to her desires.

"Everyone's still asleep. It's barely dawn," she whispered between kisses she rained down his neck, then straddled him.

He wrapped his hand behind her neck and urged her back to his waiting lips. She welcomed his kiss, her palms gliding over his chest, making his skin quiver. His hand brushed the downy hair on her neatly trimmed pubic mound and she gasped a heady breath.

She rose to her knees and shoved her hips backward. His heart raced in his ears while her moist folds teased the tip of his stiff ridge, sending a series of rippling spasms to his core. He seized her hips and she thrust down. Her gasp filled the air and caused him to groan. He pulled his lower lip between his teeth. The last thing he wanted right now was to wake up the whole house. He bucked his pelvis, meeting each of her thrusts. Her body rocked back and forth. A deep ache gathered its strength within him. She arched into him, riding him harder. He ground against her, digging his fingers into her hips, pushing her down while she took the last inch of him. Changing his rhythm, he urged her to ride him faster.

She shuddered on top of him. With his next thrust, she tossed her head back.

"Ah-h-h! Yes!" she cried, bucking.

He held onto her while wave after wave of release pulsed through him. Muffled groans escaped his clenched lips.

The tremors slowly ebbed and she collapsed against him, her arm draped over his shoulders, her cheek nestled in the crook of his neck.

Only their panting broke the silence of the early morning. Sleep crept over him. Another breath and he would doze off. The shrill ring of his cell irked him. Who would call at this hour?

He blinked in the glare of the light on his cell phone's screen. Manager's phone number displayed, stirring Dario's guts. He pressed the talk button. "This better be important if you're waking me up this early."

Fast and loud breathing rasped through the phone. All he could make out was restaurant and fire. He kicked the covers off. "I'll be right there."

Chapter 10

Dario's car rounded the sharp corner, the wide city harbor opened before him. The small vehicle careened dangerously to the edge of the winding road meandering along the coast. Ante grabbed onto the handle above the passenger's window. "Slow down, man. I would like to arrive at our restaurant preferably in one piece."

"I want to get there before the streets fill up with traffic." Dario flipped the blinker on, then canceled it. On the empty roads, no one would care if he turned without signaling. But that would change soon. Pale ripples of light shimmered on the surface of the blue sea, shattering under the hull of a passing ferry that carried people to the city, cutting through the still water and reforming at its bow. The first rays of sun touched the red roofs of the ancient buildings on the peninsula.

Was he truly prepared to lose everything to protect Irena and his daughter? Strange thought, of course, he was. They were his family. Still, if Fred had anything to do with the fire at the Mezzaluna, this could be only the beginning, and his wrath already stung. But The Fates—the spinners of the thread of life and destiny— had determined the course of his future at birth.

Ante stifled yet another yawn. "I'm dying for an espresso."

His brother's inability to take the situation

seriously irked Dario. He gunned the engine. "I thought you'd be the one who'd freak out. How can you think of coffee when our restaurant burnt down?"

"Typical of you to assume the worst. The manager didn't say it burned down. We'll find out the extent of the damage when we get there." Ante pointed at the intersection ahead of them with changing traffic light. "It'll be faster if we cross the footbridge and cut through the Old Town instead of driving around the port."

"You're right." Dario pulled his two-seater into a tight spot between sport utility cars. By the clean tires of the vehicles, he concluded they never drove off road though they had such capabilities. German plates and rental bumper stickers had him raising his eyebrows. In offseason, it was a rare occurrence to come across a foreign car. Irena had made him promise to stay on high alert and not to overlook anything. That was the only way he could convince her to remain in the penthouse and watch Ella and Jasmin. To gain entrance into the building, Fred and his dogs would have to have the code or be buzzed inside. Hopefully, the tenants wouldn't let them in. If the fire had been set deliberately and on Fred's order, it would be the snake's ploy to draw Irena and Ella out in the open and their enemy would expect them at the site of the accident. She must stay out of her husband's reach.

Last night's rainstorm had passed, leaving clean air behind. The sun fully rose and burned off the lingering mist over the water. Dario stepped out of his car. The scent of sea brine filled his lungs. No time to revel in the fresh air when his restaurant could be nothing more than a pile of smoldering ashes by now. He broke into a run. As his lungs squeezed, he fought for every breath and his legs gave up, forcing him to slow down to a brisk walk. The stitch in his right side had him doubling up while gasping for air. There'd be no defending Irena and Ella in such bad condition. Getting his endurance up was his priority and there was no time like now. At the end of the bridge, he tapped Ante's shoulder and broke into a run again, ignoring the red pedestrian light. Thank God for empty streets. "Come on, man. Let's go."

"What? Run again?" Ante's feet pounded the pavement despite his grumbling.

The ancient cobbles of the Old Town met the cement, and Dario slid on the stones polished by centuries of foot traffic, still wet from the morning mist. He swore, but regained his footing and kicked the pace up a notch.

He turned the corner, entering the narrow street. A few more strides and he'd arrive at the restaurant. The stench of heavy smoke replaced the morning freshness. Coughing forced him to change his run to a jog. Covering his nose and mouth with his thin cotton t-shirt did nothing to ease his breathing. The tension in his shoulders eased at the sight of the flashing lights of the small pumper. At least they were able to get the fire truck into this tight ally. A small throng of onlookers gathered around the vehicle. A few people wore their housecoats over pajamas, most likely residents from the apartments above his restaurant. No sight of Fred or burly men always surrounding him, but they could be looking on from afar. Dario scanned the scene, searching for an ambulance. The lack of one didn't mean no one got hurt. He approached the man in firefighter's suit and red helmet, holding a radio communication piece in front of his mouth, and waited until the man stopped talking and turned to him.

"I'm Dario Vitez, the owner of Mezzaluna." He turned to Ante who was still catching his breath, judging by his wide eyes, he was more shocked than breathless. "That is my brother, Ante. He's the manager. Anyone got hurt?"

"No." The man in brown protective gear gave him the once-over, then nodded. "You're lucky, your neighbor spotted smoke pouring out the window or the damage would be a heck of a lot worse and there'd be casualties."

Exhaling, Dario turned in the direction the firefighter pointed. The owner of LaGrotta leaned against the stonewall facade of his restaurant, unlabeled bottle of some kind of hard liquor in his hand.

"Looks like you have more smoke damage than fire, but the fire Marshall will have to investigate of course. You're not permitted inside until the inspection is done." He slipped the clipboard under Dario's nose. "I need you to sign and date this, please fill in the blanks with the contact info."

The fire captain's deep tone had Dario turning his attention back to the man in the red helmet. "Yes, I understand." He took the clipboard in his hand, then glanced at Ante. "You heard that?"

Ante screwed up his face but remained silent. He may not need that coffee he'd been dying for after all, but once he found his tongue there'd be no stopping him.

"Dario!" The shift manager's bewildered face pushed through from the crowd. With only a couple of years away from retirement, he worried about losing his job. "I swear on my son's grave nothing was turned on. I checked it myself after everyone left. I don't understand how this fire could have started."

Dario squeezed the man's bony shoulder. Walter had worked for him since day one when no one would offer an old restaurateur a job. Yet, he had learned the most from this veteran. The manager wouldn't swear on his son's grave lightly, his only child hadn't lost his life in the 90's civil war in vain. "Of course I believe you, Walter. Don't fret, I'll get to the bottom of this."

Worry vanished from the old man's tired eyes. His face relaxed. "I'll inform the staff once we're allowed back in. There'd be lots of cleaning to do, a fresh coat of paint. Hopefully, we'll find a willing soul or two to offer a helping hand."

"Sooner we're ready for business, sooner they'll return to work and start earning money." Ante seemed to find his voice. "God-damn-it. One evening we decide to take off and shit happens. If the fire Marshall finds out this was due to negligence or set deliberately, insurance will not pay out the damages. Money from last night could've burnt too."

"All cash and credit card receipts are deposited in the bank's night depository, so if the register burned there was only some small change," Walter reassured him.

Ante blew out his breath. "Good to know we didn't lose everything."

"See, Walter would do everything right." Dario patted Ante's arm. Hours of toiling shoulder to shoulder with their employees had earned them their respect. He had no doubt in their time of need the workers wouldn't leave them in the lurch. Many bosses strived to work their staff and pay as little as possible. Dario would not have any problems replacing those who wouldn't extend their help. Besides, jobs were scarce in offseason.

Dario took in the sorry exterior of his restaurant. Thin layers of smoke still poured from the broken windows, flattened hose extending from the pumper and disappearing inside the front doors indicated the firefighters stopped blasting the water, but the rivulets drained from the stone steps. How had the fire happened? His gut tightened anew, the fire wasn't an accident. Yes, the inspector had warned him of faulty wiring, but since they opened there hadn't been any incidents.

"I'll start making phone calls." Walter pulled out his cell phone.

Dario nudged his head toward the owner of LaGrotta still leaning against the wall. Only the level of golden liquid in the bottle he was holding had decreased. Something serious was going on. The man loved his booze, but Dario had never known him to drink alone or this early. With heavy steps, Dario approached him. Over the years they were healthy competitors, but never adversaries.

"Hey Frank," Dario said, pointing at the firetruck. "You called them."

Ante pushed on Dario's shoulder for a better view of Frank. "Have you seen anyone snooping around?"

Frank's heavy eyelids rose, revealing anguish in the man's pale green eyes. He pointed the neck of his bottle toward the narrow alley. "A black shadow ran that way when I yelled. It's that man, Dario. I'm telling you. Wish as hell it was my place that burned. I should put a match to it before he gets it."

Dario shook his head, though he suspected who Frank referred to. "What man?"

"I thought he just paid my fine, but he bought me out, Dario. How can he buy something that wasn't for sale? I don't understand. Now he's offering me my restaurant back for twice the amount." Frank pressed the almost empty bottle to his chest and dug into his pants pocket, then produced the crumpled sheet of paper. "I don't have that kind of money. How can I buy something that's rightfully mine?"

Ante emitted a low whistle. "Some nerve he's got."

Dario exchanged the glances with his brother then looked back at Frank. "I know this man. Fred, right?" A glimmer of hope sparked in Frank's drunken eyes. Dario's throat tightened. He was about to crush that hope. "He's a snake. This is how he conducts business everywhere. Takes over small, struggling establishments and incorporates them and replaces owners with his people. What is he offering you if you can't buy it back from him?"

"He says I can stay and work, but he'll place a new manager over me. The hell he will! I'll burn it down." Frank pulled the lighter out of his pocket. "There's plenty of booze in there. He stocked my bar with good stuff. It'll shoot flames thirty feet high."

Rage burned inside Dario. Why would Fred do this? Did he truly need to buy Frank out in such sneaky way? This would not end well. Fred could take his dirty business elsewhere, but he would not succeed in his plan.

Ante clicked his tongue while shaking his head

slowly. "I feel your pain, but don't do anything crazy."

Frank's shouts turned a few heads. Thankfully no one paid much attention to a drunk. Dario pressed his finger to his lips. "First you need to sober up then think hard about it. Fred is like a venomous spider. If you go hotheaded against him, you'll get hurt."

"What am I to do, Dario? This restaurant is all I have." Frank sobbed.

"What were you doing these past months when the Health inspector closed you?"

"Worked, where I could find some, but I'm a restaurateur, not some grunt laborer." Frank drained the last bit of booze from the bottle.

Dario pried the empty flask out of Frank's hand before the drunken guy could do something stupid he'd regret later. Should he offer him the money? Not only to help him but to show Fred his filthy moves did not work in this town. If Frank took him up on the offer, would he agree to his terms? No point dealing business with an inebriated person, especially not before he talked to Ante about his plan. "There's nothing more you can do here now. Get some rest and we'll talk later when you can think straight. Thank you for alerting the firefighters. I can't imagine what would've happened if you hadn't been here."

"It's what the neighbors are for. You'd do the same for me." Frank drew in a long, slow breath then blew it out, blasting Dario with his booze odor.

Dario tapped Frank's shoulder, then turned his head in the direction of the firefighter exiting his establishment, a device of some sort in his blackened hands. "I have to go now. Do you have someone to drive you home?"

"I'll call my daughter." Frank disappeared behind the glass door of LaGrotta.

"Tenants from the apartments above can return to their homes. The carbon monoxide levels are minimal, but make sure you air all rooms well." The crew Captain's dark eyes settled on Dario, his unyielding stare sending shivers down his spine. "The CO2 levels are above normal in your restaurant. We'll have to wait before an official investigation takes place."

Dario cleared his throat, loosening the tightness. "Can you at least tell me where did the fire start?"

The firefighter glanced from the small screen of his handheld and removed his yellow helmet. "Sorry, can't do that. Fire Marshall needs to investigate."

"Darnation. There—"

Dario jabbed his elbow in Ante's ribs before his brother finished talking. "My shift manager says everything was turned off by the time he left."

"Sir," the Captain put his hand up. "We already took his statement, and we have your contact info on file. You'll be sent an official report once the inquiry is done. Understand that we're not at liberty to disclose any information." He pointed at the idling truck where his crew gathered. "We're done here." Touching the brim of his helmet, he tilted his head. "Have a good day."

The Captain climbed into the cabin, and the gathered crowd parted to let the pumper pass.

"A good day?" Ante's tone reached a new high as he thrust his arms in the direction the fire truck left. "He wants us to have a good day after all of this. He's kidding, right?"

"I'm afraid he's not." Dario stared at the back of

the truck until its square rear rounded the corner.

"Ante! Oh, my God. Are you okay?" Martina's distressed voice pierced through the hubbub. By her runny makeup, mussed up hair, and wrinkled clothes, she ran straight from the friend's couch where she'd crashed. She threw her arms around Ante's neck and kissed him. "Oh, baby, I didn't want to believe it's Mezzaluna, so I had to see it for myself. How could this have happened?"

Ante returned her kisses and hugs. "Yeah, it's bad. Most important no one's hurt."

Martina halted and pulled back, scanning the thinning crowd. "Wait, where's Jasmin?"

"She slept so peacefully, I didn't want to wake her." Ante flashed a sheepish grin, knowing Martina would freak out in next second.

"What?" She shrieked. "You left her alone in Dario's penthouse?" Martina slapped her purse on Ante's arm, her voice rising in pitch and volume. "How can you be so irresponsible? What if she walks out on the balcony?"

Ante cowered under her continuous blows. "She's not, hey, stop it."

Dario stepped in, then put his hands on Martina's shoulders. This has got to be a new record for the two of them to break into a fight. "Relax. She's in good hands."

Martina halted, her arm poised high, ready to strike Ante again with her purse. "Err…whose hands?"

"I can't tell you here, come with us." Under Dario's firm hold, Martina's rigid posture loosened and her shoulders slouched.

"Why can't you say it? Are you lying? You'd

better not." Her tone was uncompromising as she stepped away from Dario and sent a narrow-eyed glance to Ante, shoving her index finger in his face. "This time you've really done it."

"You got to be mad to think I'd do anything to endanger our little princess." Ante strengthened, pulling on the sleeve cuffs of his jacket.

"Come, you lovebirds, we're wasting time standing here." The mocking tone in Dario's voice came out despite his half efforts to hide it. When would the two of them figure out this was love? It didn't always run smooth, no matter how hard they tried. It was life, not their incompatibilities, but as long as they work at it, their differences would complete them not cause a further rift.

Martina's heels clicked on the cobbles of the ancient streets and urged Dario to speed up his steps to his car. At least she kept quiet, only huffed now and then, shaking her head at Ante.

The two muscle cars were gone by the time they returned to his Boxster. Ante opened the passenger door of Dario's two-seater. She flashed him a puzzled look.

"You go on with Dario. I'll grab a cab." Ante shrugged.

"Don't be silly. I can squeeze in the back." She flipped the backrest of the front seat forward. "It's tight, but I'll fit."

Ante wrapped his arm around her waist. "No, no. You take a comfy seat, and I'll take the back. You're worth a bit of discomfort."

"Fine." She stepped away, allowing him to the back of the car, then slid into the front seat. "I don't get you. In one moment you're the sweetest guy, and in the next, you piss me off."

Dario slipped behind the wheel. The last thing he was in the mood for was to listen to his brother and his woman bicker. "If you two don't stop getting on one another's case, you'll be fetching a ride in a cab."

"I'll stay quiet." Ante stretched his lips and made a zip-it motion with his fingers.

Good choice. Dario started the engine and pulled from the parking spot.

Martina squirmed. "Can you tell me now in whose capable hands did you leave my baby? You know she doesn't take well to strangers."

Ante leaned forward. "Jasmin is not with strangers. In fact, she took quite well to Ella. The two are like sisters."

"The girl you brought along last night? She called you her uncle, but I thought it must be one of Dario's hussies' kids."

"Ah," Ante sighed then shifted his position to the middle of the seat, his head filling the rear-view mirror. Dario clenched his teeth and grinned at Martina. She of all people in town should know he hadn't been with any of *his hussies* in a long time.

Martina flipped the visor down and inspected her makeup. "God, I look like sea spit me out. Blah." She pushed the visor up and turned to Dario. "I have to say, Jasmin was taken by Ella. Who is she?"

Dario tilted the mirror, but couldn't adjust it to capture the full rear windshield. "Slouch down some more, Ante. Your big head's preventing me from seeing what's behind us." He glanced at Martina from the corner of his eye. "Ella's my daughter."

Martina choked on her snort. "No, really, who is

Ella?"

"I'm not joking. She's mine. Be patient. You'll discover everything in a minute."

Martina dug into her purse and pulled out her cell. "This is rich."

Ante reached from behind and grabbed the phone out of her hand before she could call any of her gossip loving friends.

"Hey!" She twisted in his direction. "Give it back."

Ante held her phone in his open palm. "I know you're about to start calling around. We must keep this fact under the wraps for now. Once Dario gives you his go ahead, spread it all you want."

The sun was high by the time Dario parked in front of his building. Fluffy clouds on a blue sky reflected in a few remaining puddles from last night's storm. Ante and Martina fell in step with him on the way to the main entrance.

Neighbour Stan huffed under the weight of the black garbage bags in his hands. "Oh, hi, Dario. I heard about your restaurant on the radio. How had it happened?"

Ante and Martina meandered around nosey Stan and headed for the elevator, but Dario couldn't squeeze his body between the wall and the large bags.

Dario ran his hand over his jaw, stubbles prickling his palm. What he needed were a shower and a shave. If only Stan would move to the side. Since he trapped him in, perhaps a bit of prodding would be in order. After all, his neighbor saw everything and knew as much. "We won't know until the Fire Marshall investigates. Listen, on the off topic, have you noticed any new faces in the building?"

Stan lowered the garbage bags to the high sheen floor of the foyer. "Now that you mentioned it, yesterday two guys dressed all in black, dark glasses pocked around the building. I asked if they needed help." He shrugged. "Thought they were lost. But they asked about you."

Shivers raced down Dario's spine. Fred's dogs were on the prowl and had picked up his scent. Maybe he wasn't the hero he thought he was.

"I told them there's no one in this building with that name." Stan slouched to grab the ties of the bags, then halted and tilted his head up toward Dario. "Should I have told them differently?"

"No, you did great. Thank you. Where did they go after that?"

"They got into a car, big SUV with German plates and rental sticker on the rear bumper and drove off." Stan finally moved out of Dario's way, giving him access to the elevator.

Black SUV with German plates and rental sticker. What were the odds the cars he'd parked next to and the one Stan had seen the men drove off were two different vehicles? The brass door chimed and the door slid open. "Thanks again, Stan. I owe you one."

"Saw your woman and her daughter teach Ante's girl some karate moves in the rec room." Stan pursed his lips, nodding fast. "Maybe you can get that girl to teach my son some of those moves. Man, she's good. I bet no one messes up with her."

Dario pressed door button on the panel, not allowing them to slide out. "I'll ask her."

He let go of the button, the elevator doors closed and slowly climbed to his penthouse.

Jasmin stood in the middle of the living room, the coffee table pushed against the wall. She demonstrated some awkward karate moves to her mom and dad. "Watch this. Ella taught me."

Martina clapped but flashed an angry look at Ante. "Excellent."

"She's a fast learner." Ella turned to Jasmin and extended her hand. "Now, show me Dario's pictures."

"Don't get mad about this. It's good for Jasmin to know a few of these moves. With a bit I've taught her, she'd remember how to break free if…" Ante cleared his throat and squeezed Martina's shoulder. "I meant to ask you if you could stay with your folks on the island for a few days. Or weeks."

"Why?" Her scowl drew her eyebrows together. "What about my work?"

"I'll talk to your boss. The fire in our restaurant, we believe it was set deliberately."

She leaned backward. "Who'd do such thing? What the hell is going on here?"

Irena sat on the armrest of the chair opposite Martina. "The man who is after me and Ella doesn't care who he'll have to destroy to get to us. It would be wise if you disappeared from the city."

Martina chewed on her lower lip while rubbing her chin. "I remember you from the high school. You and Dario were the most popular couple. Then you vanished and left him broken in spirit. He boarded the ship to forget you. Did you come back to destroy him again? I took care of these boys after their parents died. They were lost."

"It wasn't like that. You're making a terrible assumption." Ante pulled her close to him. "Take

Jasmin and go. For the safety of both of you."

Martina's face paled. She glared at Irena. "Look what dragged here behind you. It's a big world. Couldn't you go someplace else?"

Her words stung Dario's core and at the same time rooted him to the spot. Damn it, Martina could lash out some harsh words. "It's—"

"Martina!" Ante snapped before Dario could finish. "Apologize. Irena has every right to be here. This is her home."

Irena got to her feet and approached "It's okay. No need for apologies." She smiled at Martina. "Ante is right. It's the safest if you leave for a while. Let us deal with this. Ella and I are trained in martial arts and can protect ourselves...for now."

Dario's cell vibrated in his pocket. He pulled it out and frowned at the unknown caller ID, but he recognized Irena's old number. He handed the phone to her. "This may be for you. Do you want to answer it?"

She stared at the ringing phone in his hand. "You answer it."

Dario pressed the talk button and placed the mobile to his ear. "Hello."

A woman's sobbing came through, coupled with the heavy breathing.

"Is that you, Mrs. Novak?" A premonition knotted Dario's guts.

"I know Irena's there. Let me talk to her." Mrs. Novak's teary voice cut his hope that the caller had called a wrong number.

"It's your mother." He passed the cell to Irena, shaking his head at her raised eyebrows.

She took it and, in slow-motion, raised the device

to her ear. "How did you get this number?" She tapped her foot on the floor. "Ana? No, she was never my friend. Why are you calling?"

Ana, the traitor. Anger flared in Dario. What did Fred buy her for this?

"I told you this moment would come the day the two of you tore me from Dario for good. Still, you think I'd care, after everything he's done." Irena pressed the end button, lowered her arm even slower, and her face went blank. "My dad was rushed to the hospital, again. This time, I'm afraid, he won't come out alive."

## Chapter 11

Dario stared at Irena. A war of emotions showed in her darkened eyes. He nodded, and Ella flashed a slight smile. She joined her mother, giving her a comforting hug. His gaze shifted to Martina, who lowered her lashes and played with a loose thread on her sleeve cuff. Ante seated next to her. Jasmin flipped through an old photo album on the floor by the bookcase.

Irena placed Dario's cellphone on the coffee table.

Damn, would anyone broach the subject of Irena's dad on his deathbed? Dario's mind raced, searching for a few appropriate words. He swallowed and stepped toward Irena, placing his hand on her shoulder. "If you want to see your dad, we'll take you to the hospital if you think it's safe."

Ella faced Dario. "Mom and I went to see Grandpa in the nursing home. He barely opened his eyes, and I doubt he knew who we were."

"He made eye contact for a split second. I'll never forget that look, like he should know me, but couldn't quite place me." Irena's voice trembled. What emotions could be battling inside her? "Before we left his room, I said my goodbyes. In truth, I wanted to make peace with him. I knew that would be last time I'd see him."

Though Irena's father wouldn't win a Dad of the Year award, he was still her dad, and perhaps seeing him at the end of his life was hard on her no matter all the hardships he'd put her through.

Dario kissed her palm. "We'll call the hospital tomorrow."

"Mom's going to see him today." Irena shook her head. The initial tremor in her voice vanished, and the sadness in her eyes replaced by steely determination, easing the tightness in his chest.

Dario understood her turmoil. If this was his dad, he'd be confused about what to do too. On one hand, she should be sad for her dad, yet on the other...only God knew. Her parents should've protected her. To add to it, she grew up never hearing a nice word from them. Her extended family thought her an airhead, incapable of anything. Marrying her off to that snake had meant getting rid of a problem. Without a man to take care of her, her father believed she'd live on streets, earning her living as a prostitute high on drugs. The sad part was, almost everyone believed him. Many tried to convince Dario of same, but he had always known she was nothing like what they said. She went along with her parents' wishes all her life, mostly to avoid getting beaten if she didn't comply. Now the destiny in the Gypsy amulet called them to fulfill their heart's desires.

Martina drew in a long breath, turned to Ante and threaded her arm around his. "Fine, we'll go to Sylba. Will you stay with me? It gets pretty boring on the island in offseason. There's nothing to do there but watch TV and eat."

Ante wrapped his finger around the coils of her dark hair. "I'm not going to get on your nerves?"

"You will, but it'll break the monotony so I don't die of boredom." She squeezed his hand. "Now, take me and Jasmin home. I have to pack."

Ante stood, pulling Martina up with him. He wrapped his arm around her waist and drew her to him. "Have I told you that I love you?"

"No need to tell me. I know you do. And I love you too." Martina faced Irena. "I'm so sorry about your dad and...forgive my harsh words. Your situation is bad enough without me adding to it. Come to the island. The house on Sylba is big enough for all of us."

"I'd love to visit you, but not when danger follows me everywhere." Irena glanced at Ella. "Our short presence here already caused plenty of grief to you all."

"Nonsense. We'll beat this and send Fred packing for good." Dario's throat tightened at the sadness in his daughter's eyes while she stared at Jasmin. He pulled Ella closer. "Don't worry. Jasmin and her mom won't stay on the island for too long and if they do, we'll go for a visit. Commuter boats can take us there in the afternoon and we'll return to the city the next morning."

"That would be great. Mom talked about the islands. I've seen videos and pictures, but I'm dying to experience them for real. She said they are peaceful at this time of year."

Martina shook her head, then stepped to the coat closet and pulled out Jasmin's jacket. "Peaceful? I'd say dead. Just a bunch of retirees live there. They barely poke their heads out in the winter afraid cold winds would cause them all kinds of illnesses. You'd have to feel for your own pulse to check that you're still alive." She waved a hand to her daughter. "Come on, girl. Let's go home. Tomorrow we're going to Grandma and Grandpa's."

Ante stretched and yawned. "If you decide to come to the island, don't take public transportation, movements could be easily tracked. Call me and I'll bring my boat to the city." He rubbed his eyes. "We all had an early start today. I could go for a nap."

A thought sprouted in Dario's head. They could all use a getaway if only for a day. There was nothing he or Ante could do in the restaurant until the fire marshal was through with the investigation. The condition of Irena's father prevented them from leaving. Though she'd stated she'd made her peace and said her goodbyes, her tone and deep creases between her eyes told him she had forgiven her father, but she had not forgotten. She would want to attend the funeral.

Little hands wrapping around his snapped him out of his thoughts. "Uncle Dario," Jasmin said, "You didn't hear me saying bye."

"Bye, sweetheart." He bent down to kiss her forehead. "You'll see Ella again soon, I promise."

Jasmin ran to her dad and he picked her up in his arms. Dario's chest squeezed. Knowing Fred could send his men after anyone who helped Irena, each time a member of a family left through the door could be the last time he'd see them. Dario would fight and do the right thing, no matter the consequences.

He waited until Martina went outside before he raised his hand, making his brother halt. "Ante, keep your eyes open. Call if you suspect the slightest thing wrong. No one's safe."

Ante nodded. "If Martina packs for the trip, I'll take her today and stay there. Her brother is between jobs, so he's on the island too. If he's away, I'd stay with her longer, but...he could get a bit pushy."

"Right, you're lucky he hasn't broken your nose yet." A silent shiver shot up Dario's back at the memory of Ante's swollen lip when he first met Martina. As their relationship progressed, her brother eased off his control of his sister's date nights and quit shadowing Ante.

"You're a funny guy." Ante hitched Jasmin higher on his hip, stepped out and closed the door.

"God, I feel awful." Irena pulled her feet closer to her and leaned her forehead on her bent knees. "People must leave their homes, because of us."

Dario wrapped his arms around his girls, who sat on either side of him. Now would be the perfect time to bring up his plan. "Don't worry. Martina speaks her mind without thinking. The fact she wants Ante around is a good sign. Time alone will do them good." He tickled Irena's neck, making her squirm. "I've been thinking, how about we all get away to the island for a bit?"

Ella pivoted toward him, her eyes big and round. "Can we really?"

"Honey," Irena said, wrinkling her forehead. "Not before we find out how Grandpa is doing. If he…" She cleared her throat. "If he…it wouldn't look nice if we didn't attend his funeral."

"Irena, babe, how can you be sure that would happen?" Dario slid his hand down her arm, pulling her to him. "You said he's been in and out of the hospital for the past two years. He may recover."

"Not this time. His eyes were empty. His soul's gone." She drew in a long breath then let it out slowly. "Hard to believe, but he too had a soul. Not a good one, but a soul nonetheless."

Dario frowned. Since when did Irena become so spiritual? Martial arts, yoga, and meditation must've steered her toward Zen. "Did your mother say which unit he's at? If you want, I can go in alone and maybe have a talk with the doctor."

"He's in the Internal Medicine ward. They are running tests, but cannot pinpoint why he's coughing up blood."

Irena caressed Ella's arm. "Grandpa—"

"Right, Grandpa." Ella's sarcastic tone, followed by a long snort, stung Dario. "...they never sent me a gift or card, or anything."

"Whatever the case, honey, let's show them we're better than stooping to their level." Irena pointed to the photo album left open in the middle of the floor. "I'd like to have a look at those."

Ella got to her feet, picked up the album off the floor and handed it to her. "You're avoiding the issue now, Mom."

Dario harrumphed. That was Irena, all right. Once she decided she had enough, she'd change the subject and the matter was no longer open for discussion.

Irena treated her daughter with a soft smile. "You know me, honey." She flipped through the pages of the old photos and stopped by the picture of Dario on the deck of the tanker. "What sea are you on here?"

"The Northern Atlantic. The ship was tossed on the huge waves of a bad storm all through the night. You can see I'm not clean shaven and my stomach hadn't returned to its rightful place."

"Was it scary, Dad?" Ella pointed at the cresting waves of the ocean surrounding the ship.

"You bet, especially when you experience it for the first time. Though it wasn't the first time I was on the stormy sea. Our Adriatic can get turbulent, but nothing like the ocean. You think these are your last moments, but it gets easier. Our captain was an old sea dog. He laughed at us green faced novices." He chuckled at the memory. "It's the night I won't forget. Spent it hugging the toilet in my cabin."

Leaning over the album in Ella's hands, Irena piped in, "The Adriatic Sea is a puddle comparing to the Atlantic."

"Wow, you're brave. We crossed the ocean on a ship but thankfully didn't encounter any storms. The ship rocked one day. It was so cold. I couldn't stay for long on deck, but the icebergs like distant mountain tops shimmered in the sun." Ella shivered as if she remembered the trip, then tapped her mother's hand, urging her to turn the page.

"Not unusual for northern Atlantic in February. I'm glad your voyage was calm." Dario studied Irena's face as her gaze locked on the last picture in the album. It was the only photo of the two of them, taken during their last summer together.

"I didn't know you had this picture. We were so young, so carefree then." She glided her finger over their smiling faces. "Oh, God, where did the years go? If we could turn back time and take what's ours."

"I wish we could." He slapped his thigh, brightening the mood in the room. "Anyone hungry? I can whip up something."

Ella pushed on his shoulders, preventing him from rising. "Can I take care of the lunch?"

"Be my guest." He arched an inquisitive eyebrow at Irena.

"She's quite a master chef. Guess she took after you." A proud smile lit Irena's face for the first time since her mother's unexpected phone call.

He climbed the two steps to the kitchen where Ella stood in front of the wide open fridge. The appliance emitted soft chimes, indicating the door stood opened for too long and the temperature inside would rise. "What culinary wonder would you like to prepare?"

"Mom and I love omelets, I hope you do too." She pulled the milk carton out and shuffled the items on the shelf.

"Not something I eat often, but I love them." He stepped to the window sill above the sink and checked on the herbs in his terrarium. The sorry state of the plants reminded him he neglected to water them in a while.

Ella inspected his kitchen cabinets. "Where are your mixing bowls?" She appeared next to him. "Wow, Dad. Are you a gardener too? Mom always says she ends up with plants with no will to live."

"I can hardly call myself a gardener. This box of herbs is all I have growing." The scent of rosemary wafted from the terrarium as he bent the branches to check the moisture of the soil. "But if you could've seen my mother's orchard, she could plant a stick in the dry ground and it would bloom into a tree full of fruit."

Ella nodded. "My mom told me. Too bad I didn't get to meet her."

"She would've been crazy happy to have you." His eyes burned. The conversation was entering the emotional territory and he needed to change the subject. He focused on Ella who returned to rummaging through the cupboards. "Mixing bowls are here." He pulled out a deep drawer under the stove. "Are you sure you don't need any help?"

"No, Dad. Go sit down and relax. I'll call you both to the table when it's ready." She pointed her chin toward Irena seated on the couch, flipping through the photo album. "Can I get another bowl?"

"One isn't enough for an omelet?" he asked, but pulled a smaller bowl out of the drawer.

Ella broke the egg and dropped the yolks in a bigger bowl. "Mom can only eat egg white omelet. Would you have any spray on oil? It's for Mom."

Irena's dietary restrictions returned to his mind. He'd meant to ask her about it, but with everything that had happened, the long list of foods she couldn't consume slipped from his mind. Now the worry had returned. She must have some condition, but she may not want to open up to him. Perhaps he could test the subject with Ella.

He checked the cabinet opposite the stove, the last time he'd seen a can of spray on stuff was in there. "Here," he said, handing her the yellow cylinder. "You're lucky. I meant to throw it out. Why can't Mom have regular oil?"

"This oil has less fat and Mom...um...she was sick." Ella sucked her lower lip, not meeting his gaze. "She must be careful or she'll get sick again."

Irena couldn't digest fats? His insides twisted. There were many conditions that could cause such inability. Each worsened with time if the affected person continued with their eating habits. Ella's reluctance to talk about her mother's condition was a clue not to prod deeper. He'd have to get the rest from Irena. He took a step down, halted and turned to her. "Holler if you need any help."

"Oh, Dad, I'm fine. Trust me." She didn't spare

him a glance while beating the mixture with a wire whisk.

He lowered to the couch next to Irena. "So, I hear, you didn't have much luck with plants."

Irena huffed. "Fred had us living in a one bedroom basement flat meant for a maid. There were two small windows. Little daylight came inside. It's a miracle we survived, much less plants. His neighbors actually thought him gracious for taking in a single mother and her kid as his house cleaner."

Wrapping his arm around her, Dario pulled her closer and inhaled her citrus scent. "Now you live in a beautiful penthouse with huge windows and plenty of light. I'm thinking it's a bit small for the three of us. We'll look for a house. What do you think?"

Her face fell and she let out a desperate breath. "Our love was doomed from the start. Please, don't set your hopes up. I'd hate to see you get disappointed again. If we could start with a clean slate…"

"We can't, and don't need to." Keeping his eyes on Ella who had her back to them, he placed a kiss to Irena's neck, then trailed his lips down the soft skin. He gave a small bite to her shoulder exposed by the low cut neckline, making her flinch. That should shift her mind from her worries and to more pleasant things. Questions about her dietary restrictions burned on his tongue, but he didn't want to dampen her mood. Still, he couldn't resist. "Why are there so many things off your menu?"

She sat straight and drew in a long breath. "Life in Canada is hectic," she said, keeping her voice low. "Rarely people sit down to eat meals. It's easier to gobble up fast food on the go." Reaching for her purse next to the couch, she retracted a photo. "I kept this as a constant reminder of what such lifestyle did to me. I never knew I could get like this." After a long sigh, she handed the picture to him. "See for yourself."

He took the photo from her. His eyes widened. No, this couldn't be right. The woman in the picture was twice the size of Irena seated next to him.

"No matter how hard I worked out, the pounds kept piling. I had no idea my digestive system couldn't handle it. Pain in my upper abdomen bothered me for days, but it was manageable, at first. Then I collapsed in the karate class." She plucked the picture from his hand so fast the corner caused him a paper cut. "Forget you ever saw this. Ella was six years old. Poor thing, she was so scared she'd lose me. Since then she kept me on track. Always reminding me that I should watch what I'm eating. I know she's sacrificing food she loves not to tempt me."

After some uncomfortable silence, Irena continued, "I'm afraid your cooking will be wasted on me. God, Dario, this is not how I imagined I'd come back to you, damaged and tired. I'm amazed you still want me."

"You're talking nonsense again. If I didn't want you, I would've settled with someone else years ago." Dario took her hand and brushed her knuckles on his lips. His insides melted. Not only that she had to deal with Fred, but she also pushed through scary time with the support of their daughter. Small wonders Ella acted older than her peers. He too had taken care of ill parents, dealt with the ugliness of disease no child should ever see. Stuff like that would force any kid to grow up fast and take responsibility. "If eating less fat is all you require that's doable. God knows I could eat healthier. Many nights I reached for food I shouldn't, and paid the price."

Irena smiled. "Thank you for understanding. Many thought I put this into my head."

"Dad," Ella called over her shoulder, panic rising in her voice. "Everything's sticking to the pan."

Dario pulled away from Irena and rushed to his daughter. "Add more oil and lower the heat."

Smoke billowed from the stovetop. Ella's fingers fumbling with the knobs. The flame under the frying pan burst out. Ella shrieked and dropped the pan from her hand. "Oh, God, it's ruined."

"No love. There was oil on the bottom of the pan. But your omelets are still salvageable. Let me." He grabbed the pan's long handle and removed the metal container from the heat source, then scraped away the burnt egg mixture stuck to the bottom. "We'll just use another pan and I'll let this one soak in soapy water."

"I wanted to surprise you. It's not my best work." Ella wrung a tea towel in her hands.

"Don't worry, love. Nothing's ruined." He kissed her and pulled another frying pan out of the same drawer. "The first time it's always the hardest. Here," he said, his hand hovering over the pan until the surface reached the right temperature, then stepped away. "Take a deep breath and try again."

"Thanks, Dad, you're the best." Ella took over, pouring the thick mixture onto the pan. The sweet smells of rosemary and oregano filled up the kitchen. He stayed close by in case he needed to prevent another disaster, but she had calmed down and seemed to have it under control.

In a few moments she turned to him, a perfect golden omelet next to the egg white one for her mother, on the plate and a beaming face. "The brunch is served."

"Good, I'm starving." Irena already set the table and was pouring orange juice into tall glasses.

"Did you guys eat yet? I meant to tell you to help yourselves with anything you find." In the rush to get to his restaurant, he'd totally forgotten about their breakfast. How stupid of him.

"Your neighbor, Stan, brought some sweets and coffee while we trained. He stayed to watch and even attempted a few moves." Irena chuckled, awkwardly chopping air with her hands. "It was fun watching him."

"I'll have to thank him for his generosity." Dario shoved a forkful of food into his mouth. "This is fantastic, sweetheart. Who taught you to cook?"

"I did. But she took it to another level." Irena drowned her portion in ketchup. She shrugged at his appalled look. "Got hooked on the stuff."

"That's an insult to the chef." Her second half shrug and goofy smile made him chuckle. He turned to Ella. "Have you thought of becoming a chef?"

Her smile vanished and she shook her head, twirling the fork between her fingers. "I haven't given my career any thought."

How stupid of him to ask her about her future, knowing it seemed grim. No certainty that they'd come out of the predicament as winners, but they would not go down without a fight. "If you want to become a chef, I can help."

"I'm more inclined toward nutrition, I'm thinking a dietitian. You know, help people eat healthy like those with special dietary needs." Her glance directed at

Irena. Ella's enthusiasm brought a smile to his face. The need to help others was also his trait and Irena's. Perhaps coming from both parents, the desire was doubled in Ella.

He washed the last mouthful down with a big gulp of juice, cleared his throat and slid the empty plate away from him. "You're right. People would eat healthier if the health food was more appealing. Thank you for the lunch. I haven't had anyone cook for me in a long time. Now it's my turn to treat you. What can I do for my girls?"

"I'm tired, and Ella must be too. We were all up early and need to rest." The chair scraped the floor at Irena's push and she got to her feet.

"But, Mom—" Ella stretched the syllable.

"Maybe later when it gets dark. I know you're dying to see the city." Irena gave Ella a stern look, closing the subject for further discussion.

"Don't worry about the dishes. You cooked, I'll clean. Go get your rest. I too can use a nap." Dario kissed Ella's head, then watched her dragging her feet up the stairs to her room. Could this sudden sternness be Irena's way of not wanting to venture outside due to her fear? He could use the quiet time to make a few phone calls and inquire about her father.

Almost forty-five minutes of waiting he was transferred to yet another person and he had to explain all over again who he was and which patient he was inquiring about. He got put on hold again. Damn it, enough was enough. He pressed the end talk button and groaned. Irena and Ella still slept, but he couldn't settle down. The car keys on the counter beckoned him. He scribbled a note for Irena, grabbed the keys and headed out.

Pulling in front of the hospital parking lot entrance, an idling taxi blocked his way. He tapped the steering wheel. An elderly woman leaned heavily on the walker and approached the passenger's side. His eyes widened at the sight of Anna following behind. The woman was none other than Mrs. Novak. He barely recognized her out of her faded housecoat and slippers. But what was Anna doing here? She helped Mrs. Novak into the cab, slipped some bills to the driver and waved to the woman at the back seat.

He honked his horn, gaining Ana's attention, then rolled his window down at her approach. "What are you doing here?"

She bent, lowering her face to level with his. "I can ask you the same."

"I asked first."

"I was helping Mrs. Novak visit her husband since her daughter is hiding behind your back." Ana's accusatory tone grew louder and turned to yelling by the end. A sign she was under pressure.

Dario wrapped his hands tighter around the steering wheel. "Fred put you up to this, didn't he?"

"So what? Her husband wants to help. She's delusional, stares and talks for hours at some amulet. She's mentally ill, Dario. What are you doing with a psycho?"

Ana's words infuriated him. If anyone was ill, it was Fred. The slithering snake was spreading lies about his wife to discredit her. "And what are you doing with a married man?"

"And what are you doing with a married woman?" Ana crossed her arms over her chest and twitched one eyebrow.

He clamped his mouth tight. Ana was right, damn it. The intent to ask Irena about her marital status slipped off his mind. Whenever the topic came about, she referred to her marriage as her obligation. "It doesn't change the fact that Fred is dangerous, but you're blinded by his money. Ana, he cannot be trusted alone with young boys. Where's your son?"

For a split second, panic flashed in her pale blue eyes he'd once mistook for Irena's and made a big blunder. She snorted. "That's preposterous. Fred wouldn't hurt anyone. He's like a brother to Nicky. The two played an Xbox game when I left his house. Fred bought the system just for Nick."

Dario's stomach dropped. "You left your child with a pedophile. God, Ana! Get in."

"But my car is parked here." She pointed in the general direction of the parking lot. "And Fred wants me to see a plastic surgeon—"

"For Christ's sake, Ana, you can come back for your car. First, make sure your son is safe." He pushed the passenger's door open. "What plastic surgeon? Don't fall for that crap."

She skirted around the hood and almost threw her body into the passenger seat. "Nicky is at Fred's house in White Hill. Drive and don't spare the gas. I'll get a good laugh out of this when I prove you wrong."

He floored the gas pedal, springing the small car into a jerky start. White Hill, on the outskirts of the city, meant at least half hour's drive from the hospital, providing the traffic stayed light. People jumped out of his way. Some uttered loud curses or flipped him the bird, but he didn't care.

For a stretch of several minutes, Ana chewed her fingernail. "Can you go faster?"

He glanced at the speedometer, already doing twenty over the speed limit. "Not unless you want me to get pulled over."

"Oh God, what have I done? I'll never forgive myself if anything happens to Nick. Shit, his dad will kill me first, then Fred if he touched Nicky in a wrong way." Ana's voice trembled. She couldn't steady her hands to unclasp her purse buckle and pulled out her cell phone. "I hope you're wrong and make a big ass of yourself when you find out nothing's happened." She pressed the phone to her ear. Several long tones, her face paled. "Shit, Fred's not answering his phone."

"I'd rather end up looking like an ass than be right." Dario focused on the road ahead. The light at the intersection changed to red and he stepped on the brake. At least the seriousness of the situation seeped into her head, still, her nervousness made him wish his car would fly. Maybe a slight change of subject would ease her mind until their destination. "What did you find out about Irena's dad?"

Ana shook her head slowly. "His doctor told Mrs. Novak her husband will be fine, but his patient is gray and can barely breathe." She grabbed the handle above the window and faced him. "Funny, the nursing home sent him to the hospital without any medical records. Mrs. Novak was appalled that the doc didn't know her husband was asthmatic." Metal bracelets on her wrist clunked as she pointed. "Turn left here. This is the street."

Perhaps Irena had seen death's shadow hanging over her father. Had Fred anything to do with sending

Mr. Novak to the hospital without medical history? Possible, the snake had paid everyone to play his dirty game. Dario made a sharp left turn, almost missing the street Ana pointed.

Ana indicated the house, but it wasn't hard to guess which one belonged to Fred. The biggest three-story surrounded by a low red brick fence. Dario brought the car to a screeching halt in front of the mansion. The curtain on the second-floor window moved then fell back into place. "I'll wait for you here."

Her chest heaved with her loud breaths. She stared at the black front door. "Please come in with me?"

Chapter 12

Urgency pressed on Dario's shoulders while Ana fumbled with the keys to Fred's mansion. He had hoped she wouldn't ask him to accompany her inside Fred's house, but fear reflected in her wide eyes. Only a coward would send her in there alone.

He squinted to make out shapes through the frosty glass decorating the door. The twining cast-iron vine ran through the amber glass obstructed his view. She grabbed the golden knob, slid the metal inside the keyhole, then exhaled a shaky breath.

"Doubt this key will work." She stared at her hand. "I think Fred gave me a fake key to shut me up. He made it abundantly clear I'm just his guest. Though I feel more like his maid."

Dario gave her shoulder a gentle squeeze. Hell, he'd be frantic to rescue a child if he found out he'd left him with a pedophile. "Please hurry. You may prevent the disaster. Gosh, Ana, I hope I'm wrong. Wait." He grabbed her wrist, halting her. "Are his cronies staying here?"

She nodded. "There are five guys in the other half of the house. It has a separate entrance." She finally turned the key, making the loud click of the bolt. At her push, the door silently slid open. "It worked!" Surprise laced her voice.

Dario followed her inside the spacious foyer. Fred

had five guys guarding him. The number of his bodyguards seemed low, there had to be more of those who would fall for his money, local, unemployed, desperate men who had nothing left to lose.

A large bouquet of fresh white roses decorated the round mahogany table. Music drifted from the monstrous size television in the room adjacent to the open concept living room. She cast him a worried glance. "When I left, they'd played their gruesome killing game."

Dario glanced at the screen as they slipped past it. Okay, so he wasn't much of the gamer, but the split screen indicated two-shooter game. From the low score and EvilNoob profile name of the gamer, he figured it had to belong to Fred. Nickelodeon was the name Ana's son picked for himself ever since he discovered the cartoon channel, so the higher score belonged to the kid. Had Fred tried to lose on purpose to get some brownie points with the lad or was he really that bad at these shooting games? He had to be, as Irena had said, his killing methods would include poison, freak accidents, sudden illness, not firearms. All executed by cronies on his payroll. Fred's involvement could never be proven. No, the snake wouldn't besmirch his name.

"Nicky, Fred." Ana's voice trembled as she called from the bottom of the stairs. "Where are you guys?"

Silence hung like a heavy curtain. A faint sound of running water drifted from the upstairs. She swallowed and put one foot on the bottom step. "Come on, guys. This is not funny. Where are you?"

The shower stopped, a moment later fast feet thumped on the carpeted floor, and a door on the other side of the hallway slammed shut. She gasped and turned to Dario, her eyes wide and mouth agape. "Someone ran into Nicky's room."

"Let's go upstairs." Dario took her by her elbow, nudging her forward.

She halted. "Wait here. Fred will be pissed at me for bringing you to his house. I can't accuse him of molesting."

"Go see what's going on. If it'll make you feel better, I'll stay put."

She ran up the stairs, her bare feet soundless on the thick carpet.

"The floor here's wet and I can see small feet imprints." She held the banister, one foot hung over the top step. Casting him a glance over her shoulder, she heaved a heavy sigh.

Dario gave her encouraging nod. "Just hurry."

He tapped his fingers on the dark wood of the banister. All he could do was to speculate what happened while Ana was gone, but how was he to prove any of it? As all abusers, Fred befriended the boy, bought him stuff his parents couldn't afford and gain his trust. Dario had to hand it to him, the man only knew the boy for a few days. Ana, gullible as she was, trusted the man mostly for the stuff his money could buy and therefore Nicky had no reason to doubt Fred. He must've taken the boy in his room and coerced him to shower together, but Ana and Dario's unexpected arrival spoiled Fred's plans. Still, the man had enough time to inflict some damage on the youngster.

A door popped open on the upper level. Fred strolled out of the room, a white towel wrapped around his neck while he pulled the white t-shirt down his pale, skinny torso and pudgy stomach. At least his trousers were done up and in place.

Like a liquid shadow, the man slid down the stairs. "What the hell? What are you doing...did Ana bring a knight without his shiny armor? Tell me, is your white horse tied to my fence?"

"Ana asked me to come in." Dario scowled, saliva gathered in his mouth. Spit—his secret ammo he hadn't used since his childhood—proved useful in gaining the upper hand in many fist fights. When Fred leaned his back on the wall of the hallway, Dario swallowed.

"I remember the summers. How I hated every minute I hang out with your dumb friends and your even dumber jokes, laughing at my expense, calling me nasty names, like Koschei or something."

Dario chuckled, he had forgotten about the moniker. The dummy still hadn't figured out the meaning of the name Koschei the Deathless, a Slavic legend of immortality, and a snatcher of hero's wife. It suited him and not just because of the skeleton like appearance. According to the ancient tale, the creature hid his soul in a needle, that's inside an egg, carried by the duck, existing within a rabbit, stored inside the iron chest, buried under an oak tree on an island protected by three winds. Those who held the egg controlled the being. Not an easy feat. Whether or not the Fates weaved into his life to win over Fred, Dario would fight with all he's got. "Why did you tag along if you hated us that much?"

"You know why." Fred lowered his gaze at Dario's hips and moaned. "I always admired your tight little ass."

Dario suppressed a gag. So the burning desire in Fred's stares had not been a product of his imagination.

Fourteen years ago he'd dismissed Fred as no more than a quiet, shy, guy with affection for younger boys, but despite the stories that circled, he dismissed him as harmless. Proof how wrong he'd been. Seemed as time passed Fred only grew more unstable. Someday soon Dario hoped to wrap his fingers around Fred's neck and squeeze the living daylight out of him. Unfortunately, the bastard wasn't worth the prison sentence if he'd killed him, so he'd have to release him before Fred breathed his last. "Touch my ass and I'll break your hands and your face. Need I remind you that butt isn't on a teenager anymore?" *Change the subject and quick.* "Your parents can thank me for 'their' granddaughter. What would you have done if I didn't do you the honors?

"Your ass is the one that got away, and nothing gets away from me." Fred scoffed. "As for the grandkid, well, there are other ways to get my seed into her, besides sex." He scowled as if the mere thought of having an intercourse with a woman churned his stomach. "Cunning that she is, she weaseled her way out of it. Miscarried my ass, she never kept her appointment at insemination clinic." Fred's seething snapped a tight bend in Dario's guts and restraining to punch the snake's face became unbearable. "You think I don't know Irena's hiding at your place. She must return and continue her therapy. The amulet she obsessed over drove her to insanity."

Damn Fred and his lies. Did he know the story behind the Gypsy amulet? Irena could deliver some deadly blows, every black belt person could, but she didn't have a sense of a killer. How much had Fred known of her martial arts training? Dario laughed, but there was no humor in it. "Some trinket drove her crazy? Come on, man. Do you hear what you're saying? It's you who sounds insane."

"I only want what's best for her." Fred ran his long, bony fingers through his receding hairline. His faltering voice indicated he didn't believe his own lies.

A door at the end of the hallway opened and two burly men in white t-shirts and tight jeans stepped inside, taking their place in front of Fred.

Fred's arrogant chuckles echoed among the twelve feet high walls. "As you can see, your time's up. Leave now before I lose the rest of my patience."

Dario widened his stance, trying to recall what he'd learn in karate classes. Two against one, it didn't take a genius to figure out the odds weren't stacked in his favor. Had he kept up with his skills the burly guys wouldn't stand a chance. "I see you called up your dogs. However, I'm afraid I can't leave before I make sure your guests are not in danger."

As on cue, Ana stormed down the stairs, her hand gripped Nicky's arm. "Why is his hair wet? And where are the clothes he wore earlier?"

Fred turned his head slowly, his stern gaze fixed on the boy behind his mother. The boy shivered and gave a slight shake of his head. Poor thing got scared into submission. If anything had happened, Nicky would never tell.

"He reeked. I told him to take a shower. And I tossed his worn out, cheap knock-offs rags in the garbage. He's got decent jeans and shirts now. No one will make fun of him in the schoolyard." Fred leaned toward Nicky. "Isn't that right, boy?"

Ana eyed the wet towel draped around Fred's neck.

"Did you shower with him?"

"Please," Fred's face contorted. "Who do you take me for? I would never hurt a child." Fred pressed his thin fingers to his narrow chest. His tone bordered with hurt at Ana's insinuation. "There's more than one shower in this house."

Dario studied Fred's slumped posture. No, he would never hurt a child, but he would coerce him into a disgusting act as a repayment of expensive things he'd gifted. Then he'd made the victim promise to keep their special game a top secret or he'd take the gifts away. Most pedophiles worked the same way and Fred was no different.

She tapped her foot and crossed her arms over her chest, a tell-tale sign she was thinking hard. "Nicky," she called not breaking her eye contact with Fred, "get your stuff. We're leaving."

"But, Mom," Nicky tugged Ana's arm. "Fred didn't do anything."

"He did something, I'm sure." Ana glared at Fred, then pulled out the keys from her jeans pocket. "The car's parked at the hospital, you can collect it yourself." She threw the pendant holding the key at Fred, but one of his dogs caught it in his hand.

She nudged Nicky toward the dark door. "Let's go. Nothing he gave you is worth this."

Dario reached for the knob and opened the front door. Everything he knew about Ana had overturned. Irena had it right, Ana cared about her son. At the threshold, Fred's voice stopped them.

"As I recall, the jeans you both are wearing were bought with my money. So are the rest of your clothes."

Ana turned and faced him. "I'll send everything

back."

"You're not leaving this house with a single thing gifted by me."

She stood frozen for a few moments. Dario took a couple of steps closer to Fred, but his men pushed him back. He steadied his footing, ready to fight when Ana placed her hand on his forearm. "It's fine, Dario. Fred can have it all back."

She unbuckled the belt of her pants and slipped them down her hips and legs, then over her feet and tossed them in Fred's direction, catching one of the bodyguards with the belt buckle. After she yanked the shirt over her head, she did the same, but the garment was light and landed at the foot of the table.

"I can live without your stupid stuff." She pulled on Nicky's shirt and pants. "Take them off. We don't need Fred's charity."

"That bra is also my gift." Fred cocked his head, a mocking grin on his face. "I did say you're not to take anything with you, but I'm feeling generous today. Keep the panties."

Ana's mouth hung open. She took a step closer to Fred. "You wouldn't." She squared her shoulders and huffed. "Of course you would. Fine," she sneered, unclasping the hooks at the back, then threw the bra on the floor. Her naked bosom bounced as the turned and directed her glare at the bodyguards. "Have a good look, boys." She pointed her chin at Fred, then threw her heels at him one at the time. Too bad her aim was terrible, making the guards snicker when the shoes landed way off the desired target. "You want to take my teeth while you at it? You paid for them."

Fred waved his hand. "Those you can keep, they

are temporary crowns."

"Jerk." Dario removed his jacket and draped it over Ana's shoulders. "I'm proud of her. She showed you she's not going to stand for your bullshit."

Ana marched out the front door, head held high and dragged her son behind her.

"Sure, Mr. Vitez the knight comes to the rescue. Know this, I always get the last laugh. This is far from over."

"Later, Koschei." Dario slammed the front door shut cutting off the last of Fred's shaming words and empty threats, hoping the old nickname further infuriate Fred.

Ana, self-proclaimed queen of heels, stumbled barefoot over the interlocking in front of Fred's house to Dario's car. He pulled away from the curb. She sat in silence, her chest heaved, but at least she seemed to keep her temper at bay. "Can I borrow your phone? God, look at me. I left with nothing from that place."

"You left in time, with your pride and dignity. Most importantly, you saved your son." Dario handed her his cell from the cup holder and glanced in the rear-view mirror. Ana's boy stared out the window and crossed his arms over his naked chest. Dario wished he had another jacket to give to the boy. Still, the youngster witnessed his mother's humiliation and only he knew what else that monster could have done to him. With some elaborate twisting, Dario managed to pull his t-shirt over his shoulders and head, then handed it to Nicky. "Are you cold? I don't have anything else to give you."

The boy reached for the offered shirt and murmured his thanks. Dario returned his hand to the steering wheel and leaned closer to Ana, lowering his voice. "Don't try to force Nicky into talking about this. He could start to confuse things and say something that didn't really happen."

She nodded, pressing the phone to her ear. "Hi, Tom. Can you come get Nicky? In about an hour. Yes, I understand it's not your custody day, but I need some alone time. Err...really? You want me to come too? I...I don't know...I have to think about it. Bye."

She placed the phone back in the same cup holder and sank against the backrest. Blowing her breath out, she set the loose strands hanging over her forehead to flutter. "I'm so confused. What should I do now?"

Dario squeezed her hand. "Don't sit home alone. I know Tom hasn't got a single romantic bone in him, but his heart is in the right place. He can be militant, he's breeding and training those watchdogs and they are vicious, but he would never hurt you or his son. And he's overprotective of you both."

Fred getting on Tom's bad side and hurting his child and Ana might just aid in Dario and Irena's case. Tom would go ballistic if he suspected any foul play with his son.

Ana sighed and shook her head then sighed again. "Tom will gut me. He would gather his men from his security company and declare war on Fred. I guess once a man gets a taste of battle, he can't break free from the combat." She rubbed her forehead. "And he's stingy with his money. God forbid I'd buy a thing he didn't approve of, yet he wants me to be pretty for him. Though he said he'd pay for my nursing school."

"See, he wants to invest in you. Why don't you take him up on his offer? Schooling is important. You'll set a great example for Nicky." Dario pulled in front of Ana's apartment building. "You can give me my jacket and shirt later."

"Thankfully my sister's working. If she sees me coming home wearing no clothes, she'd never stop bitching. Ah, she'll bitch regardless, there's nothing I can do right in her mind. My mom's hopefully playing cards at her friend's house. I can sneak in and pack things for Nicky." Ana turned and took her son's hand. "I'm so sorry, baby. I was selfish and only thought of me. I should've listened to Dario when he warned me about Fred. Come now, your dad will be here soon."

"Come with us, Mom." The pleading in Nicky's voice pulled at Dario's heartstrings. Damn these broken families where children suffered and parents used them against one another. He and his brother grew up poor, but compared to today's family's values, they had riches of the loving parents all the time.

"I don't know, love. Your dad can be..." she lowered her gaze.

"He promised he wouldn't get mad at you anymore." Nicky gave her an awkward hug, wrapping his arms around the backrest of the seat.

Ana made an eye contact with Nicky. "He made such a promise before and the last time he got mad, he scared me."

Nicky tapped his mother's shoulder. "He's sorry, and he's learning to be cool."

Dario leaned in his seat. "Things will work out if you give them a chance."

Ana swallowed. "I don't know, Dario, I said some pretty awful things and he got mad like never before."

"Maybe you both needed time apart to cool your

heads off. You learn to curb your tongue, and he'll put a lid on his temper." Dario frowned at the thought of Nicky witnessing the fights between his parents.

"Thank you, Dario. I needed to hear that." She turned to the window and pointed at the weather-beaten door of her building. "Let's go, Nicky."

Ana stepped out of the car, her son squeezed through from the back seat. She leaned in and smiled. "Tom may help in your battle with Fred."

"Thanks, Ana, I may hold you up on the offer. Fred may be armed. Did you see if they handled any weapons?"

"I didn't, but be careful." She closed the door and hurried toward the building, wrapping her arm around Nicky's shoulders and pulling him closer.

Dario shifted gears and reversed from the parking spot. The neighborhood hadn't changed one bit. New graffiti covered the dumpster and the facades of the buildings surrounding the parking area.

No sooner than he turned onto the main road, his cell phone buzzed. Unknown caller displayed on the screen. He pressed the talk button and slowed down to pull safely onto the side. "Dario Vitez."

"Yes, Mr. Vitez." The deep man's tone filled Dario's ear. "It's the fire marshal. The investigation into the fire incident has been concluded. I'll be sending you an official report, but wanted to tell you that the blaze started inside the dishwasher."

Damnation, he feared as much but other than the staff, who else would know of this hazard? "My manager confirmed the machine was emptied and turned off, he ensured that everything was off before he left for the night."

"That is why this fire is suspicious. There was nothing in the dishwasher but a butter knife stuck to the bottom preventing the appliance to take in the water. So the motor overheated and burned out. The greasy rug hanging off the handle caught the blaze." The fire marshal coughed. "I will keep in touch. Have a good day."

Dario pressed the end talk button and hugged the steering wheel, easing onto the road. His harping at the staff had proven effective. The boy working the dish pit always checked the bottom of the dishwasher for any cutlery before running the appliance. Would the insurance company see the incident as negligence or foul play?

Dario pulled in front of the barrier gate of the underground parking of his condo building. Before he could lower the window and flash his access card at the barcode reader, he turned in the direction of screeching tires and engine revving. In the round, corner mirror, he spotted a dark SUV. The vehicle bolting for the road bore a striking resemblance to the one he'd parked next to the day before. Could Fred's dogs have followed him? He hadn't paid too much attention to the cars around him.

The parking arm lifted and he continued down the slope, then eased his car into his designated spot. Cold air hit his bare torso as he got out of his car. When he'd left his place, he'd never anticipated he'd be handing half of his outfit to Ana and her son. Only a snake like Fred could strip a woman and her child of their clothes because he'd paid for them. Dario pressed the lock button on the pendant and a click indicated his car was secured. He took the side exit for the condo lobby.

Dressed in her white gi, Ella stormed toward the elevator. Her arms folded over her chest, a deep crease marred her petite face, her chin shook and she blinked fast.

Irena trailed behind her. "Ella, honey, please be reasonable."

"What's going on?" Dario stepped between mother and daughter. Not the best place to be, but someone should mediate the situation.

"Mom promised we'd go out tonight and see the city, then she changed her mind." Ella's deep voice quivered and she swiped at a tear running down her cheek.

"I like to see the city as much as you." Irena attempted to hug her daughter, but Ella pulled back. "Honey, the car I saw through the binoculars circled the building for hours."

Dario's chest squeezed. "Was it a big, black SUV with German plates?"

Irena scowled at his torso. "Yes, did you see it too? And why are you half naked?"

"Long story. Let's go to my place and I'll tell you everything." He pressed the elevator button. At least Ella seemed to calm down. "Don't be mad at Mom. We must be extra careful. I know you're dying to explore the city, but there'd be days for that."

Chapter 13

Irena brushed her fingers over the weather-beaten stones of the remaining walls of the ancient Roman Forum. A slow smile crept onto Dario's lips as fond memories flooded him. As many evenings during their teenage courtship, they ended their stroll through the old city huddled in this secluded corner of the long forgotten world. It had taken a week of hard training and promising they'd be safe until he convinced her to step outside. She'd put him through some tough workout sessions, in the rec room and bedroom, but his skills were returning in both. And after two days of stiff muscles, he would never scoff at yoga again.

Though he had not seen anything out of the ordinary during their sightseeing, he stayed vigilant and suspected anyone they cross paths with. Damn Fred, this was how fear-mongering turned people against their friends and neighbors.

She turned her head, longing reflected in her gaze. "Our little nook hasn't changed one bit. As if time hadn't passed and we're here to carry on as always."

He wrapped his arms around her waist and she snuggled her back against his chest. Her citrusy scent overtook his senses and the flawless skin on her neck beckoned him to kiss her. A cold wind whipped at his back and he lowered onto the slab of stone carved with Roman numerals, pulling Irena onto his lap. "Time doesn't seem to touch this spot."

She shifted to face him and wrapped her arms around his neck, kissing him. Shivering, she sat up straight and scanned the walls covering the square. "Ella is having fun jumping on the walls, I don't have the heart to pull her away from here, but I'm frozen and my feet are killing me. Can't remember the last time I walked this much."

Ella's careless laughter bounced off the high walls of the nearby church. Dario's insides melted. It had been hard, but over the week he'd pulled her out of her brooding over Irena's cancellation to explore the city. "She was worried you would never change your mind."

"I disappointed her, but she understood it was necessary. Growing up, she's had so little to be happy about. We had each other, and that was enough." Irena lowered her gaze to her gloved hands. "My mother thinks our lives in Canada were grand, but that's a lie. I thought of running away from Fred and back to you all the time."

"I know, babe..." He squeezed her hand and placed a kiss on her knuckles, taking a hard swallow against the lump forming in his throat. "You've been through a lot."

"So have you." She cupped his face and tilted his head back, then her pale-blue eyes locked with his and sucked him into her world. In a slow motion, he seized her full lips. Her mouth opened and their tongues met.

"I thought I lost you for good." He slid his hand under her short jacket and fumbled with her shirt tucked into her jeans. When the heat of her skin met his fingers, he let out a throaty groan craving more.

"No." She whispered against his lips and he pulled

back. Her smile and saucy wink reflected a promise of a rain check. "We shouldn't get carried away with Ella around or in public."

Ella jumped from the shoulder-high wall to their left. "Wow, Mom, this is great."

He ran his hand over his mouth, making sure to wipe all traces of Irena's lipstick. "Told you, you'd love it, didn't I? But I think your mom is getting cold and tired, and so am I. Hungry too."

"And cranky." Irena tapped his shoulder, then rose. "My feet are so sore. Ella, honey, did you have enough skipping over the stones of the Roman Forum?"

"How can anyone have enough of it? Ancient Romans built this, Mom. Their hands chiseled and carved and laid these stones, paved this street in front of the shops they kept. I wish there was a replica of what the Forum looked like back then. No, I don't think I can ever have enough of this."

"Ella, honey," Dario intercepted. "Forum's been here for over thousand years, it'll be here tomorrow. We'll come back. If you're so fascinated with Ancient Rome, we should visit Pula's Arena or Diocletian's Palace." At Ella's widening eyes, Dario continued. "He was an Emperor who retired in the town today called Split."

"I know who he was." Ella threaded her arm around his. "I haven't heard of the arena. Was it built for gladiatorial fights?"

"Originally, yes, until Honorius banned them in the early fifth century. Since then the arena was used for theatrical performances." He laced his fingers of his free hand with Irena's and nudged his girl forward. "Do you know which Emperor banned women from competing in gladiator games?"

"Septimius Severus." She giggled. "Funny name sounds like a fancy name for sewage."

Dario nodded, joining in her chuckles. "Mom said you're smart and I see you've got a sense of humor. There's so much to see in this country even the biggest history enthusiast such as you would get sick of sightseeing. Come, it's getting late and I don't feel like cooking tonight. So. Your choice, pick up a pizza on our way home or stop and eat at a restaurant."

"Pizza." Irena and Ella said in unison.

"You don't want to stop by Mezzaluna to see the damage?" Irena's distraught tone stung his core. She still blamed the incident on herself, despite his reassurance.

"Not without Ante. He'll be back tomorrow and I'll need him to record everything. The damage is estimated at about fifty thousand euros." He pulled them toward the nook in the wall. The smells of fresh oregano and baked dough set his stomach on a rumble. "It doesn't look like much, but trust me, this is the best pizza you'll taste. They make everything from scratch here. What kind of toppings would you like?"

Irena chewed on her bottom lip, staring at the assortment of vegetables behind the glass, but going by her fast blinking she was fighting to keep tears at bay. He wrapped his hands around her shoulders and turned her to face him. "Babe, if getting my restaurant burned down is the price to have you back in my life, then so be it."

She shook her head slowly. "Yes, the fact you have to go through that makes me upset. I'm so sorry. Don't let him get your money too."

"My money is deposited in a reputable bank outside the country. I wouldn't trust these banks or their corrupt managers. I've learned from those who lost their life savings." He nodded to the pizzeria's staff who greeted him with a typical head nod to indicate it was his turn to be served. "Have you decided on toppings? I think the man's waiting and we are holding up the line."

"Any vegetables are good for me, whole wheat, extra thin crust and no cheese." She turned to Ella, her eyebrow arched. Their daughter shrugged before her gaze returned to the panoramic photo of the olive tree covered island above the entrance.

Not his kind of pizza, but he'd agreed to eat lean to not to tempt her into consuming something that would upset her digestion. Not so easy to stick by to, he found reading labels and calculating fat contests tedious. The effort paid off, he noticed his waistline trimming down. He paid for their order and picked it up from the counter next to the cash register. Heat from the freshly baked pizza radiated through the bottom of the cardboard box. He lifted the corner of the lid and inhaled deeply.

The drive to his building on the outskirts of the city passed in relative silence. Irena kept checking side and rear view mirrors and set his nerves jangling. "No one's following us?"

She exhaled loudly. "Fred couldn't risk too many witnessing our demise if he couldn't make it look like an accident."

"Babe," Dario lowered his voice to a soft whisper and checked Ella in rear view mirror. The girl stared out the window at the passing surroundings. "He could've cut my brake lines, run me off the road, pay a waiter to poison my food…"

She waved her hand in dismissal of his assumptions. "No, he'd have to come up with something new and unexpected. And I'm sure he's planning out something."

"I'm not asking you to let your guard down, but maybe you can relax for one evening." Dario placed his hand over her fidgeting fingers.

"This is not the time to relax." Her words deprived him of happiness but also deepened his determination to fight Fred and his cronies.

Silence fell over the three of them and Dario concentrated on the winding road ahead. But a worm of fear gnawed at his mind. Should he ask the question that had eaten at him for some time now? At least it would ease his fears and confirm his beliefs. "Did Fred ever try to buy Ella's attention with expensive stuff?"

"No." Irena's firm voice told him she was sure of the fact. "He likes young boys. He wouldn't pay for her basic needs just because I didn't 'gift him a son.' The first year was hard. I often visited the Food Bank." Irena gave his hand a reassuring and firm squeeze. "Thank God Ella turned out to be a girl or who knows what he would…" Irena glanced away and fell silent.

He clicked his tongue and felt his rage burn in his heavy exhale. Ella must've sensed his irate state and she slid behind his seat and rubbed his arm. "No point getting angry."

"You mentioned you find out something about my dad?" Irena changed the subject in time or he would've turned the car around and drove up to Fred's mansion to beat the crap out of the worm.

"Ana said he was sent to the hospital without his medical records. Do you think Fred could have anything to do with that?"

Irena shrugged. "I wouldn't be surprised if he does. The more I think about his parents' deaths, the more I'm convinced he's got something to do with it. Both battled high blood pressure. For years Fred told them to ignore the doctor's warnings all while bringing them a copious amount of food they should've stayed away from."

From the corner of his eye, Dario gauged Irena. He drew in a long breath. "I don't know what you're feeling inside, I guess I should say that I'm sorry about your dad, but I'd be lying."

Irena swallowed, once again facing the darkness outside the passenger's window. "I don't know. I always believed when the time came I'd feel something, but I don't. There is no goodness in him. And he was bitter, bitter man."

"Don't be too hard on yourself. It's understandable you don't feel much for your father." Dario wanted to pull her into his embrace, but the gear shift and having to concentrate on the road prevented him.

"You'd think Grandma would want me and mom near her during these moments, but she told my mom to stay away and not disturb her." Ella's harsh tone pulled on Dario's heart. No child deserved to be shunned by grandparents. Small wonders his daughter was disappointed.

"People deal with grief in their own way. Maybe Grandma prefers to be alone." He hoped his explanation would ease Ella's hard emotions, but he knew Mrs. Novak's real reason for not wanting Irena and Ella around. For such a God fearing woman, she couldn't see her actions were sinful. "How about we change the subject? The smell of pizza is making my mouth water." Dario drove slowly through the parking lot of his building, looking for any unknown cars. Nothing seemed out of the ordinary. Damnation, he was turning into a nervous wreck. Even his sleep had suffered. The Gypsy woman appeared in his bad dreams that woke him every hour. He and Irena should come with a plan not just become sitting ducks.

He pulled up in front of the metal arm blocking the entrance into the underground parking of his building and made an eye contact with Ella in the rear-view mirror. "We'll make it a movie night."

"You know how to make every day perfect." Irena ran her fingers through his hair, a gentleness he could never get tired of, then she turned to her daughter and smiled.

"There'll be plenty of perfect, ordinary days." He eased his car into his designated parking spot. "Today was just a little taste of it."

He wrapped each of his girls in his arms and led them toward the blue, metal door into the empty building's lobby. The elevator carried them to the top floor while the smell from the pizza box wafted and made Dario wish they could move faster.

"You girls get comfy. I'm bringing plates and...would anyone need cutlery?" He kicked off his shoes and headed for the kitchen cabinets that stored the dishes.

Irena lowered onto the couch with a long sigh and slid the cushion behind her back. "No cutlery for me, but be sure you bring napkins. Oh, and I think I'll have a beer with the pizza."

Ella perused the DVD cases on the shelf, then pulled out a colorful box depicting a horse and its rider in a golden gladiator's armor.

Irena reached for the box and pulled two slices on her plate. She popped the corner of her first slice into her mouth and chewed slowly. Her little moans as she continued eating her food, licking the sauce off her fingers, drove him wild as he imagined making those sounds during sex. God, how had the family dinner turned into some kind of foreplay with Irena's murmurs and smacking of lips?

He popped the DVD disk into the player, shifting his mind out from the gutter. Though his dick still stood erect, he backed up to the couch, keeping his tented pants from Ella's view.

With his legs crossed, he lowered to the couch. Irena sucked her bottom lip between her teeth and patted her mouth with a napkin. But her shaking shoulders told him she fought laughter and lost.

Ella snuggled up to him, pulling the blanket over her knees. About one-third into the movie, Ella's head drooped and her breathing evened.

Irena moved up closer and worked the buttons of his shirt. "I think we lost Ella and I have no interest in this movie." She got on her feet and closed the distance to the TV, then shut off the set, the screen turned black. "Prop the pillow under her head, she'll be good here for the night."

He pulled out the spare pillow stored inside the deep drawer of the wall unit and lowered his daughter to the couch, then kissed her forehead. "Sweet dreams, honey."

Her lips stretched into a half smile, but she didn't open her eyes. Irena waited at the foot of the stairs. A box of mint mouth strips in her hand. "I want to try something tonight."

The longing in her voice and fire in her eyes caused him to gulp audibly. "What do you have in mind?"

She stepped closer to him, molding her toned body to his, wrapped one leg around his hips, and whispered with lust in his ear. "What's the one thing we both wanted but never could achieve?"

He cupped her firm buttocks and ground his pelvis against her hips. "If you mean—"

"Shh." She pressed her index finger to his lips. Then she released her hold on his hips and took him by his hand, starting up the stairs. "Let's take this nice and slow in the bedroom."

## Chapter 14

Dario's body stiffened. Irena flashed him a seductive smile, running the tip of her index finger over her bottom lip. In a few slow, sexy strides, she closed what little space remained between them and his bed. She grasped his arms while he nipped and sucked her lips. He caressed her hair, dotting kisses at the corner of her mouth. She parted her lips under his and their tongues tangled.

She pressed her palms flat on his chest and backed him against the wall. His fervor reached a new high, stiffening his cock. His hands roamed freely down her arms, skipping to her hips and around to her butt. Her lower belly was pressed up against him, rubbing his erection.

"Babe, the suspense is killing me." He lowered his head and softly kissed a trail to her ear. "What is that thing you wanted to try tonight?"

"Ah, patience is the virtue." She hugged him tighter and he drowned in the heat of her embrace.

He chuckled, then snagged her hand from around his neck and circled her palm with the tip of his thumb. "I'm a patient man, but this moment is taking its toll."

She smiled. Her hand snuck under the fabric of his shirt. "In that case, let's not prolong your suffering."

He swept his lips back and forth over her wrist. Her citrusy perfume sent a shiver through him and warmed his stomach. "My God, I can never get enough of you."

Her hands slid down his chest, stopping at his hips. One hand grabbed his butt, the other traveled to the front of his trousers. "Can't wait to see what you're hiding here."

Her hoarse whisper cascaded a thrill through his body. He groaned, pushing his pelvis forward while she worked his belt buckle.

He glided the zipper down on her jeans and slipped his hand inside. Her warmth seeped into his palm through her silky panties. Tucking his fingers under the elastic band, he inched toward the folds of her sex. Her laughter turned into moans and whimpers as he lavished attention to her hardened nub.

His pants and boxers slid down his hips. At her push on his chest, he took a backward step toward the bed, freeing his legs out of his crumpled jeans and underwear. He pulled his T-shirt over his head, glanced down his stomach and grinned. No other woman could turn him on like this and, darn it, it'd been a while since he had this kind of erection.

His calves hit the footboard and Irena pushed harder. Though her thrust wasn't hard enough to send him flying flat on the bed, he got the idea and fell to the mattress. Her gaze skimmed over his wide chest and slim waist to admire his dick standing at attention.

Their eyes met and he waggled his eyebrows as he smiled. "Like what you see?"

"Absolutely." Swaying her body to some tune she hummed, she removed her clothes, except her panties. Then starting at his feet, she slinked like a feline stalking her pray until she came upon his arousal. She licked her lips and smiled as her fist closed around his cock, and she rubbed him from tip to the base. "My, you're hard."

She popped a minty mouth strip on her tongue and gave him no chance to react, as the warmth of her mouth replaced her hand.

"Oh-h-h." His quiet moan seemed to spur her on and she increased the tempo, giving the head a light tease with her tongue, then taking his whole length in her mouth. Holly shi… He pushed the back of his head into the mattress while his hips took a rhythm of their own and thrust inside her mouth. That mint strip on her tongue gave an added tingling sensation along his shaft, intensifying the wild experience.

"Babe," he cried, wanting to stay in this suspended state of euphoria forever. His stomach fluttered on his inhale and the spasms jerked his hips beneath her mouth, hurtling toward his orgasm. An intense release rippled through his body, seizing every muscle in reaction. He cupped her face, trying to pull her head away, but before he could withdraw, he exploded inside her mouth.

Judging by the increased pressure of her lips on his cock, she seemed to enjoy the experience.

Kissing her way up his torso, she pressed the blue plastic container of mints on his chest. "Your turn."

Sliding lower and lower along her body, he nipped on the smooth curve of her belly and rubbed his cheek on the sensitive skin of her side. His stubble evoked a sweet sigh. He tucked his fingers inside the elastic band of her panties, snapped them against her skin to make her yelp, and tugged them down her hips. She grabbed the corners of the pillow underneath her head and raised her pelvis. In one fluid motion, he took off her undergarment and tossed it over his shoulder. She cried at their swift removal, but given her lust, he decided to forgo the sweet torture.

He sat on his heels and shimmied down the bed on his knees, planting kisses around the triangle of her trimmed hair. After kissing the small, round mole on the inside of her thigh, he popped a mint strip on his tongue, moved up her leg and settled between her folds.

In an instant, her body danced to the rhythm of his tongue, cavorting, and his mouth sucking. Her female scent intoxicated his head and stiffened him. Giving her a break when her body trembled, he blew on her moist, heated skin, evoking spasms. She was seconds from climaxing, though he wanted to prolong her yearning. Already, he was hard again and craving her.

Kissing his way up to her torso, he pushed her knees wider apart and slid his stiffened cock inside her heat. Meeting him thrust for thrust, she writhed and bucked against him. They rocked, his fingers grasping her shoulders, keeping her firmly in place while he plunged deep inside her.

"I'm coming, Dario," she cried, her voice strained.

A second, stronger orgasm hurled through his pelvis and claimed his body. Euphoria rushed through him, making him toss his head back as waves of release pulsated inside.

Their sweaty bodies lay tangled, motionless while they gasped for breath like marathon runners who just crossed over the finish line. He planted soft kisses on her neck and jawline, coaxing a deep, throaty laughter from her.

"Sweet mother," he said, rolling off her. "Where or how did you discover that neat trick with a mouth strip?"

She glided her hand over his torso. "Girls talk and I listened."

Her bite on her lower lip indicated she had more to tell. He kissed her brow, chuckling. "You were always a good listener. What else did you learn?"

She uttered a long, deep moan, drawing the tip of her finger around his nipple. "Many things, you'll find out soon."

"How soon?" Propping his head on his bent elbow, he waited for her to elaborate. Instead, she yawned and regarded him with a smile.

He expelled a frustrated breath. "During our years apart...you must've had...you know... the urge for sex."

"Of course I did, silly. For your loving and no one else's. So I got creative...and perfected the game. I'll show you." She flung her long legs over the bed's edge and got on her feet. For a few moments, she rummaged through her suitcase and pulled out a small cosmetic bag. Crawling on all fours over the mattress, she rejoined him.

"What's in there?" Curiosity stirred inside him, but by her slight blush, he guessed what treasures hid inside.

"This is my naughty bag, for my toys."

He reached for the pouch, but she grabbed his wrist and placed his hand on his lap. "God, you're impatient tonight."

He flicked his eyebrows and nodded at the bag. "Let's see."

She unzipped the small case but didn't open it. "Promise you won't laugh."

Leaning closer, he cupped her neck and whispered, "You have my word."

"See for yourself. I stayed true to you." She passed the bag to him.

"I never doubted you." He sat straight and peeked inside. His eyes widened at the sight of several dildos of different size and shape. Why did this surprise him? Must be that he couldn't picture her venturing inside an adult shop, let alone purchasing these things, but she had changed from the shy girl. He must've been staring at the pleasure toys for a tad too long. Irena's snickering pulled him back. "So, do you have a favorite?"

She blushed deeper but pulled out a mid-sized, slightly curved vibrator. "This one."

He arched an eyebrow. "Why?"

"Um...I...well it hits my g-spot with every thrust. Just like yours." She pointed at his pelvis.

He blinked a couple of times, but then burst out laughing. Her scornful expression made him stop, but laughter still rumbled in his chest. "Sorry, I couldn't help it. This is a great collection. Do I get to use some of this on you?"

"I hoped you would ask that." She leaned against him and stroked his arm. "There are things we both can use during lovemaking."

He pulled out a small u-shaped device. "And what's this?"

"Dual stimulator." At his arched eyebrow, she continued, "It stimulates g-spot and clit together, a wicked little toy with remote control and several different vibration settings." Her sudden casual tone surprised him. The blush from her face had gone too.

She grabbed the bag from him and zipped it, then scrambled out of bed and returned the pouch to her suitcase. "We can play with it some other time." Picking up her crumpled clothes off the floor, she tossed his boxers at him. "Throw something on. I hear Ella's footsteps on the stairs."

"I don't hear anything." He scrambled into his briefs and pulled on his track pants and a t-shirt, just in case. Tenderness tickled his insides with her confession. "Perhaps I spoiled you, knowing exactly what you need to make you wet and wild."

Irena chuckled and disappeared into the en-suite bathroom, then closed the door.

A second later, a soft knock and Ella's voice resonated behind the bedroom door. "Can I come in?"

"Ah, give me a second." He straightened the bedcovers in haste. The piquant smell of the arousal still hung in the air. Would a thirteen-year-old girl suspect what had happened here if she saw tangled sheets? He hoped not, but better to play it safe.

In two long strides, he approached the door and opened it. "Sorry honey, I hope we didn't wake you."

"No, Dad. This did." She waved her hand, holding his cell phone. "You left it on the coffee table. Must've rung for a while before I heard it. It's Grandma Novak. She's crying and I can't understand what she's saying. Where's Mom? I think she'd better get this."

"She's in the bathroom." He took the phone from Ella, who seemed uncertain what to do with it. Before he could knock, the on-suite door opened a crack and Irena reached her hand through. Her fingers brushed against his as he placed the cell in her palm. The sound of the running water from the sink faucet replaced the buzzing of the toothbrush.

The door closed and he turned to Ella. "Sorry, I never expected your grandma to call at this hour." He glanced at the clock on the nightstand. The red, digital numbers flashed 2:45. Wow, their lovemaking session lasted that long, but then again, he'd lost track of time after Irena's suggestion. Suddenly, tiredness claimed his mind and body and he covered a yawn.

"Do you think my grandma is calling about Grandpa?" Ella wrung the hem of her t-shirt and took a step closer, fear in her wide eyes. "It was bad when Fred's parents died. He held one of his all-nighters. On those two occasions, the parties lasted several nights. Each day Mom and I would clean the house and every night Fred's friends would trash the place." She scowled as if she was seeing the messy house in front of her. "Drunken people passed out naked all over the floor and around the pool. We had to clean their puke, collect empty booze bottles and crushed beer cans, and used con...um." Her breath hitched. "Condoms," she whispered.

Damn Fred, he'd pay for forcing Ella and Irena to live as his maids. He, of all people, could've afforded to hire a few full-time servants. Dario hugged his daughter and she wrapped her arms around him. "Don't worry, love. If grandpa Novak passed away, there'll be no parties."

The man's death deserved a celebration, but Dario would put a solemn appearance for Irena's and Ella's sake. Only, how would they take the news? Ella barely knew her maternal grandfather and from what she'd volunteered there'd be no love lost. And Irena...? Her feelings must be as confused as hell.

The bathroom door opened fully and Irena emerged dressed in her casual, beige pajamas. Though the top was low cut, lace encircling her bosom. His cell still pressed to her ear, she shifted through her neatly folded things in her luggage. Dario arched one eyebrow. Why hadn't she unpacked yet? He'd given her half of his closet and she still lived as if she'd have to scamper. His previous dates had brought in their belongings on their second date and attempted to redecorate his bachelor pad, but Irena wouldn't take the space he'd freed for her. Perhaps she got used to living out of her suitcase.

"Mom," Irena's snapped. "I said I'll come over, no matter the time of the night...fine, so you have your sister with you, but wouldn't you want your daughter and your granddaughter there?" She pulled a black skirt out of the luggage and held it in her outstretched arms, clicked her tongue and shook her head. "As you wish, but don't change your story later and complain to anyone who wants to listen, saying I didn't want to be with you. Okay...fine...Mom...just get the details of the funeral and we'll see you at the cemetery."

She huffed, tapping the end talk button. In a slow motion, she lowered to the mattress. "That's it, he's gone." She drew in a long breath and shook her head. "Even now, my mother doesn't want me near." Her chin trembled and she turned to him, her eyes wide and shiny. "Why?"

He joined her on the bed and pulled her into his embrace. "She'll take the answer to that question to her grave. If you wish, I'll drive you to her apartment, but I hope you'd rather stay here."

Ella kneeled on the floor in front of her mother.

"What can I do to help, Mom? I don't know what to say, but I don't want to go to Grandma's."

"It's okay, sweetheart," Irena whispered, smoothing Ella's hair. "Just a thought of my parents' place churns my stomach. No, I don't wish to go there. We'll face her at the funeral and we must be civil no matter how rude she turns, and she'll turn unpleasant, don't doubt that."

Dario leaned and pulled Ella closer to him. These were his girls and it was up to him to give them comfort in their time of need. "I must admit, words left me. I should be sorry for your loss, but..."

"I should be sorry too, and I believed when the time came I would be, but I feel nothing." Irena stared at the space, still smoothing Ella's hair. "People say grief doesn't always hit you right away. I don't think it ever will."

Dario gave her shoulder a light squeeze. "Are you okay?"

She nodded fast. "Yeah, I'm fine."

"I can see you're not." He kissed her cheek and her trembling eased. "You're strong, but sometimes even the strongest people need comforting. It's okay to show weakness."

"You're right, I'm not okay. I'm angry at myself for not being able to feel a thing. They say there's something good in everyone. I'd beg to differ. My mother wasn't better. As long as he beat me and left her alone, she didn't care. She should've taken me away from him, but she was always on his side, no matter what he did."

"Don't fret over that. It's past." Dario rubbed the back of Irena's neck, hoping to ease the stiffness. How could a man raise his hand at his own child? And for the mother not to protect her baby with her own life, he would never understand.

"It still hurts." Irena's heavy whisper sliced his chest.

"And it will continue to hurt until you let it go." He stared at her unmoving form, hoping his words were sinking in, then nudged her with his elbow. "Maybe we can salvage what's left of what was a beautiful night and get some rest. Tomorrow we'll deal with everything that is in store."

"Do I have to sleep alone?" Ella turned to him, pleading in her eyes. "I don't want to be alone tonight."

"No one is going to hurt you, honey. You don't have to be alone, this bed is big enough. I can crash on the floor or on the couch. Mom and you can sleep together." He'd hoped to snuggle up with Irena after such a great sex, but his daughter's fear had him give up the comfort of his bed and warmth of Irena's body.

"No, don't be silly." Irena squeezed his hand. "The three of us can share the bed. It'll be tight, but tonight I need you all close. I'll be the monkey in the middle."

He stared at Irena then at Ella. Once or twice he'd woken up between two girls after a wild party, but that had been a whole different ballgame. Would he be able to keep his hands off Irena with Ella sleeping in the same bed? *Oh, grow up, man. You have thirteen years of fathering to make up to Ella.* "Are you sure about this?"

"Positive. Come, the night's wasting and I'm tired." Irena stepped away from him and flipped the bedcovers. "I'd sleep better knowing I have you both close."

"If it'll make you feel better." Dario took one end of the bed, fluffed the pillow and turned off the light on the nightstand.

The mattress sank even farther when Ella climbed into the bed. A moment later tug on the cover indicated she had settled in. "Goodnight everyone."

"Goodnight, honey." He cleared his throat, tucking one arm under the pillow and searched for the appropriate place for his other. Irena grabbed his wrist and draped his arm around her waist.

A thought occupied his mind, but he hesitated to ask. He shouldn't discredit his gut instinct. His body picked up bad vibes, telling him something could go wrong with the situation. "Do you think Fred will attend your father's funeral?"

Irena inhaled and snuggled closer to him. "My dad was his father-in-law after all, even if he couldn't stand him, but that's not the reason for his attendance. He counts on the fact that we'll be there and he won't come alone."

## Chapter 15

Raindrops ticked against the canopy of the large umbrella in Dario's hand. Had someone bet him he'd attend Mr. Novak's funeral someday, he'd have lost all his money. Yet fourteen years later, he accompanied the deceased closest family members, but they were the ones watching the service from the sidelines, away from the crowd. Irena's fingers in black, leather gloves squeezed his elbow, making him grip the brolly's handle tighter. She leaned the bouquet of long-stem, white chrysanthemums over her left arm.

Standing to his other side, Ella laced her fingers with his. She cupped her hand around her mouth and whispered in his ear. "Thank you for this beautiful dress and the coat and all the other stuff you bought. I love my cell phone, so does Mom, but she won't admit it."

"You already thanked me, many times. I love splurging on you guys," he whispered back. Switching to a family plan with additional two phones had jacked up his phone bill, but he'd sleep sounder knowing they could reach one another in an emergency. "Those cheap prepaid phones you had wouldn't do."

Dario took in a small crowd of people clad in black, covered with the mournful umbrellas, gathered around the open grave. An arrangement of white roses and baby breaths stood stark against the polished, dark wood of the casket. Mrs. Novak's wails drowned the priest's reading. The man of the cloth ceased his intonations and cast the widow a pitiful glance. She pressed the lacy handkerchief to her lips, her muffled weeps sounding like a begging pooch. The cleric then returned to his task at hand, speeding up his words and flipping through the Bible's pages in haste.

Dario barked a tight cough to suppress a snort. Not even the priest bought Mrs. Novak's overly dramatic grief.

Irena squeezed his fingers and caused him to turn to her. She pointed her chin at the tall, balding man walking in front of two robust guys. Black umbrella covered most of his face, but his gait identified him. Judging by the light gray suit, Fred Penne couldn't find enough decency to wear a full mourning color. Dark, reflective sunglasses on the three men's faces covered their eyes, but couldn't hide their malice. The large flower wreath the two bodyguards carted behind Fred made them look like they were going to a parade of a sort, not a funeral.

Dario scanned the parking lot beyond the low wall encircling the consecrated ground. Fred's shiny rental SUV was the biggest car on the lot. Dario turned to Irena. "Looks like he bought all the flowers in the shop."

She snorted, then jabbed her elbow in his ribs. "People will talk for days how he bought the monster of all wreaths, but that's what he does to present himself in the public eye."

Dario harrumphed. People were fickle, easily fooled by outside appearances. Men like Fred could manipulate them and they wouldn't see past the money he flashed in their faces, like dangling a carrot on the stick in front of a donkey. For many, the true malicious nature of such men was impossible to accept or comprehend. Those who tried to expose them were quickly silenced, often kept in contempt for telling *lies* about the benevolent acts of the philanthropist.

Dario cleared his throat and straightened, passing the umbrella to Irena and wrapping his arm around her shoulders. Let people think he was comforting her, rather than hiding her giggles.

"Disgusting." Ella piped in, but her narrowed gaze, scrunched up nose, and upturned mouth was fixed on Fred hugging Mrs. Novak.

At last, the priest sprinkled holy water over the casket, made a sign of the cross over it, and clapped the Bible closed. He turned and nodded to the two caretakers in their muddied navy-blue coveralls and they sprang into action, lowering the casket into the grave. Mrs. Novak's laments echoed through the cemetery. Ella leaned closer to Dario and whispered. "Is she for real?"

"It's hard to tell. Your grandpa wasn't nice to her, but she loved him regardless." He tilted his head to the top of Ella's, raindrops glistened in her hair. Wrapping his arm around her shoulders, he pulled her under the canopy of the umbrella.

"Love shouldn't hurt." Ella shook her head in slow motion.

"She was from a different time, honey." Irena hitched the bouquet of white chrysanthemums up her arm. "To young women of her generation, a husband was everything. They married straight out of the high school and devoted their lives to their families."

"But Grandma was a teacher." Ella's surprise

turned her voice to a high pitch.

Irena straightened the collar of Ella's coat. "Teaching was regarded a woman's profession." Irena leaned into him, tilting umbrella over the two heads. "My flowers are getting soaked."

"Who is that bouquet for?" Dario asked, stepping behind Irena so she could be in the middle. "I thought the flower arrangements were sent directly from the shop."

"I wanted this one especially for your parents' grave."

"Nice of you, babe." He hugged her and kissed her cheek. "I'm sure they'd love the bouquet, but they were laid to rest on the island, in the serene cemetery surrounded by centuries-old pines. They'd curse us for eternity if we buried them here. Where the dead wouldn't find any rest from all the traffic on the highway." He stared into the distance and the relentless coming and going on the roadway. His parents choose wisely, there was no peace here for the living or the departed.

"Oh, I'm sorry. I guess I should've asked you before I bought them. I'd hate to throw them out and my dad's grave got plenty already. See." She pointed with the bouquet. "With that monstrous wreath, the show off brought, the other wreaths are piled up to the top of the tombstone."

"They could survive for a few days in a vase, couldn't they?" Ella shook the water beads from the long stem sticking out of the cellophane wrapper. "I think you can close the umbrella now, Mom. The rain is slowing down."

A smile crept across Dario's lips, along with the

idea and the perfect opportunity to present it. Ella would jump on it, and would not stop bugging her mother until she caved in and agreed. "If your mom would like to put them on your grandparents' grave, we could head for the island tomorrow."

Ella snapped her head toward him, her jaw dropped. "Mom, please, please, can we go? Oh, please." She stretched the syllable for the dramatic effect.

"What do you think, babe?" Dario winked. "It doesn't appear like your mom needs you to spend some time with her. I promised to take you to the place where the stargazing is the best."

"I don't think my mom's going to turn around and crave my company. I'm disgusted at her, a wilting violet. She thrives when attention's on her." Irena heaved a sigh, closing the umbrella, her gaze at the group of friends and relatives expressing their deepest sympathy to the widow. "How many of them will offer their hand to me or Ella? I'd be surprised if anyone even steps up in our direction. Brace yourselves for some scowls and scorns, they are about to leave and have to pass by us on their way out of the cemetery."

The first few people passed them by with only a nod; a couple flashed leery glances as if they wondered who the people standing aside were. A soft smile lingered on Irena's lips, while she returned nods and thanked them by their names for attending her father's funeral. Disgraceful Novak family, they knew full well who she was, but not one bothered to extend a hand to Irena.

A short man waddled over to Irena, preceded by his round belly, thrusting his meaty hand to her. "My deepest condolences. You lost a good father."

Dario choked on a snort, but this time had trouble masking it with an awkward cough. The man must be mad, or the sins of the dead were quickly forgotten. One must not speak evil of the deceased, after all.

Irena's hand disappeared inside the man's large one. "Thank you, uncle Drago. "

The man she addressed as her uncle gave Dario and Ella a once over then addressed Irena again. "I better go warm up the car. Your mom and Aunt Davina are wet and cold."

It wasn't until he mentioned his wife that Dario's light blinked. How could he forget uncle Drago, the only man who tried to talk some reason into Irena's parents? Well, over the years uncle's girth got bigger and his face rounder, but the concern in his eyes seemed increased. Perhaps he knew the truth about Fred and real danger Irena and Ella faced.

"Ella, my child, what's your mother doing to you? Making you look like a boy." Fred's sneer jerked Dario from a moment of serenity.

Dario's blood boiled. He stepped in front of Fred, tightening his fists. The bodyguards lunged forward. "Call your dogs off. This is neither the place nor time."

Fred waved his hand and they took their posts on either side of him.

Ella stepped forward, her chin jutted out, her narrowed gaze full of defiance. "You can see the hem of my dress under my coat."

"A dress?" Fred's ridiculed tone echoed over the vast area of the city's cemetery, causing people to stop in their tracks and turn to him. "A dress doesn't make you a lady."

"And a suit doesn't make you a gentleman." Ella's witty comeback prompted some oohs from the passersby and pride filled Dario's chest. No need to fear teenage boys knocking his door down to get to his daughter with such quick wits and her fighting skills she could handle any pushy boy. But teenagers weren't the threat, grown middle-aged men lusting after prepubescent girls were.

Fred's face reddened and he took a threatening step toward Ella. Dario pulled her back and assumed her place in front of the raging man. "Ella is my daughter. If she wants to shave her hair off, that's her right."

A sly smile stretched Fred's thin lips. "You fathered her, but whose name is on her birth certificate?"

Dario snapped his glance at Irena. She stepped forward and placed her hand flat on his shoulder, calming him in an instant. "Dario's."

"What?" Fred gasped, his color draining.

"The nurse came back with the forms, said the father's info was not filled. I told her you must've forgotten, you were in a hurry. So I filled it, with Dario's name." Irena gave a nonchalant shrug of one shoulder. "No one ever questioned it."

Fred's beady eyes settled on Dario, hatred showing in those pale-brown, lifeless pools. "In that case, teach her to behave. Soon, she'll be at the disposal of a very powerful man and he wants his bitches obedient." He signaled his men toward the cemetery's exit, a narrow break in the waist-high wall, but he halted and turned to Dario. "You might've fathered her, but I raised her and the little cunt didn't come cheap." He pulled the box out of his jacket inner pocket and waved it in front of

Ella. "I've got you a nice cell phone, but someone else won't mind having it."

Ella cocked her head, a mocking grin danced on her lips. Then she took out her phone and waved it in front of Fred's face. "Shouldn't have bothered, my dad already got me one."

Dario reached for the wallet inside his suit pocket. "I'm not buying your B. S. about raising Ella, but whatever, I'll pay you for your efforts right now. Just leave them, leave us the hell alone."

Fred took a couple of slow steps toward him, his snotty chuckles shaking his thin shoulders. "So you think you can buy me out?" One corner of his mouth dipped. "Maybe you are not that destitute teenager anymore, but there's no way in hell you can match my worth. And I told you already, Irena is sick, a compulsive liar. Could be that amulet made her tell so many lies she doesn't know the truth anymore."

"Ha!" Irena's shout had Dario turning his head to her. "You're still trying to push that theory? No one believed you months ago. What makes you think anyone would buy your crap now?"

"You're the liar." Ella lunged forward, but Irena pulled her back and gave her daughter one of those steely gazes. Ella nodded in some silent agreement and stuck her tongue out at Fred.

Fred hissed, left the cemetery. His bodyguards fell in behind him.

"Irena?" Her mother's flabbergasted voice had Dario snapping his head at Mrs. Novak heavily leaning over the walker. "How did you raise your child? Is this the respect she shows to her father?"

"Fred's not my father, Grandma." Ella propped her

201

hands on her waist and leaned forward.

Mrs. Novak's face drained of little remaining color. "Irena, is this the truth? Fred says you're a liar and you were caught lying before, many times, but I thought Fred's firm hand cured you of that."

Irena scrutinized her mother through her narrowed eyes. "It's the first time you're meeting your granddaughter in person and this is all you have to say?" When Mrs. Novak fell silent, Irena raised her hand and shook her head. "Yes, I lied, out of necessity. You wouldn't believe the truth anyway. It was easier to eat the bullshit I served you. Besides, who could keep up with lies you told, by omission or otherwise? I taught Ella there is never a need for lies. She always speaks the truth."

Mrs. Novak's face fell and she lowered onto the seat of her walker. "I should've known. After all, you're not that much different from me."

Irena's brows drew closer. "What are you saying, Mother? And did you know that dad was sent to the hospital without his medical records? Does Fred have anything to do with it?"

"No, he doesn't." Aunt Davina placed her hand on Mrs. Novak's shoulder. "Oh for heaven's sake, Anna-Maria, we just buried Lorenzo. He can't hurt you anymore. Irena can be told."

Irena took a step closer to her mother. Her tensed face awaited an answer. "What can I be told?"

"They say God will never put you through more than you can take. Twenty-three years of Lorenzo's tyranny was more than I could bear. It was me who never submitted his records to the nursing home." Mrs. Novak patted her sister's hand on her shoulder and nodded. "You take her. I'll wait here."

Dario emitted a low whistle. Thankfully, no one seemed to hear him. *Well, Mrs. Novak, I didn't think you had it in you to seize the opportunity.* He couldn't blame the woman, she had suffered enough.

Davina took Irena's elbow and pointed down the row of graves. "Come with me. There's something you should know."

Irena jerked her arm out of her aunt's hold and swallowed hard. "Whatever it is, Dario and Ella must come with me. They are my family and there are no secrets among us. Secrets only destroy trust."

"Very well. Come along then." Davina waved at Dario and Ella.

Crushed gravel crunched under their feet to the place Davina led them. She stopped in front of the dark granite grave with only one name in golden letters on the headstone.

"You must not be hard on your mother. She begged her husband to let her visit you when Ella was born, but he forbid her. Told her to forget you."

"I still don't understand why you brought us here." Irena's gaze froze on the name of the person lying in the grave. "I didn't know professor Vlahos died."

Dario shrugged. "Me neither." He pointed at the year of death. "I would've been on the sea in two thousand and seven." Man, he loved their math teacher, why hadn't anyone bothered to tell him?

Irena puffed, gliding her hand over the smooth stone. "He was the only one who showed some compassion when everyone else turned away from me. For that, he suffered. The twisted minds of bored house moms said I seduced him, and that he lost his head.

Damn people, I know he fell ill during my senior year."

"He cared about you because..." Davina swallowed, saggy skin on her neck bounced. "Not because he had some crush on you, but because, he's, well..." Her gaze wavered from Irena to her feet and back to Irena again. "Please understand, there was so much sadness in your mother's life...and yours, I don't doubt. She wanted the best for you."

"Come on, Aunt, you know all she wanted was money and we all see how well that turned out. Now, who was professor Vlahos?"

"Your father."

A rolling thunder swallowed her last words, but they echoed louder than the brewing storm. Irena stood rooted, her gaze fixated on the black and white photograph of the man resting eternally beneath the dark granite slab.

Davina continued to spit words out as if she was afraid Irena would run away. "He was married when your mother met him, but childless. She fell in love with him, got all giddy, thought he'd divorce his wife. When he broke her heart, our parents found Mr. Novak who was willing to marry her with a child out of wedlock. Then the professor's wife died and he followed your mother here, but it was too late. She was already married. He got a job in the same school, he pursued her despite the warnings to back off, he—"

"This explains why Fred never loved me." Irena's voice came out deep and foreign to Dario.

Davina dabbed the tissue at the corner of her eye and stuffed the crumpled napkin back into her black purse. "Oh darling, he fooled us all. He got us all to believe he'd be a wonderful dad to you, then bruises started appearing and Ana-Maria blamed them on your tripping feet and clumsiness. She would run to us in the middle of the night with you in her arms to get away from his wrath, but she'd always return to him after he begged and wooed her back with presents."

Irena placed the bouquet on the professor's grave, took a step back and squeezed Dario's fingers. "Do you mind?"

"Not at all, babe. He deserved those flowers." Dario took Ella's hand and for a long moment, all four of them stood silent. Mr. Novak was buried today, but in the single day, Irena and Ella found and lost their real father and grandfather. If there was justice, Mr. Novak would not enter Heaven. The man had a temper on him yet Mrs. Novak would rather stay married than suffer the societal scrutiny reserved for the disgraceful divorced women.

Davina rummaged through her purse again. "I kept this for years."

"What?" Irena asked, not glancing away from the professor's grave.

"Ah, here." Davina pulled a yellowed business card, its corners crumpled. "A man contacted me shortly after the professor died. I wanted to send this to you earlier, but was afraid Fred was opening your mail." She handed the card to Irena. "He said to give this to you only. The Professor was a smart investor. You're his beneficiary. His investment portfolio is worth millions of Euros and still gaining interest. They are expecting your call."

Irena's mouth stood agape. "Whoa, this is unbelievable. You're smart. I didn't get much of the mail, but yes, Fred opened every letter, even my credit

Zrinka Jelic

card statements to berate me about my spending."

"I hope he leaves you alone once and for all, never liked that man." Davina pulled the collar of her coat tighter as if a shiver raced through her at the thought of Fred.

Irena's eyes darkened. Her face hardened.

"What was in it for my dad, or I guess it's Mr. Novak?" She kept her gaze on the business card in her hand.

Corners of Davina's lips dipped. "What do you mean, child?"

"Come on, Aunt Davina. Don't give me half the story." Irena's uncompromising tone cut deep inside Dario's chest. "He would marry a disgraced woman with a child out of wedlock out of the goodness of his heart? No, he must've worked up some kind of a deal with your father."

Davina drew in a long breath, then let it out slowly. She turned to stare at the grave in front of her. "Just be thankful your mother struck a deal with Fred's parents and they insisted his wife be a virgin."

## Chapter 16

Dario eased his foot off the gas pedal and took the sharp turn on the road hugging the coastline. Ella stared out the passenger window. Since they'd left his condo she hadn't uttered a single word. He tapped his hand on the steering wheel in beat with a song from the radio. At Irena's insisting, and with a ton of reluctance, he and Ella headed to meet Ante at the Mezzaluna. Irena had agreed to keep her phone on her at all times. She needed some alone time to take out her anger on a punching bag in the rec room.

With one hand on the steering, and his attention on the road, he squeezed Ella's hand and her tense muscles relaxed. "You're awfully quiet. What are you thinking about?"

She slowly turned toward him. "Mom. She's beyond mad. Her whole life she thought Mr. Novak was her dad. It explains why he was never nice to her."

"Honey." He gave Ella's hand another reassuring squeeze. "I know you're worried about her, give her time, she'll snap out of it. She's entitled to vent her anger. Though she's right, your grandpa, I mean, Mr. Novak, ruined her childhood." He swallowed hard, trying to remember Mr. Novak wasn't related to Irena or Ella by blood. Up until today, the man who had caused them all greatest hardships was Irena's father by nurture, if one could call it that, but not by blood. "And if he had it his way, he would've ruined her entire life, but your mom is the smartest, toughest woman I know. Nothing can bring her down, at least not for long."

"Wish Grandma left him and went to the Professor. What was my real grandfather like?" A battle of emotions showed in her quivering voice and knotted his gut.

"Your grandma is worn down by bitterness and regret. She's afraid she'd become a topic of gossip." He thought as the town grew the nasty rumors might end, but it seemed they were only getting worse. Dario scowled at the small city mentality and continued, "The Professor Vlahos was a good man, too smart for this place. He would've loved you, I'm sure. His pupils loved him. He lived for teaching." Dario's knuckles whitened with his grip on the steering wheel. The poor child had grown up surrounded by selfish and indifferent people she called her grandparents, while her real, loving grandparents never knew she existed, except for Irena's mother, but the woman was emotionally unapproachable.

Ella nodded slowly and faced the window again. "Still, I never saw Mom this angry before. Not even when I lost her shiny amulet."

He glanced in her direction, but quickly returned his gaze to the road ahead, looking for a spot to pull over. This new revelation from Ella required his full attention and he couldn't concentrate on the winding payment and her at the same time. "Shiny amulet?"

"You know it, Dad. Mom told me how you got the amulet from a gypsy woman at the fair. When I was little, I loved playing with Mom's gem, but I had to return the pebble in the special box when I was done, and I always did. The lines in the rock would glow in my hand, that's why I called it shiny amulet. I don't know why but it never happened in Mom's hand. She said it's because I'm special." Ella licked her lips before continuing. "Mom would find her amulet around the basement and yell at me. Then one day…it disappeared. We upturned the whole house and nothing. Mom got angry."

He brought the car to a safe stop and cut the engine. His poor daughter sat with her head hung low and her shoulders slumped. "Hey, look at me." At the caress on her cheek, she snapped her gaze at him. Good, he got her attention. "How long since you last saw it?"

"Over two years now." She pursed her lips and glanced away. "I didn't lose it, Dad. Mom had nightmares. After the amulet got lost, her bad dreams became more frequent."

"Did she ever speak of her nightmares?" His chest squeezed. By his recon, the nightmares that had plagued his dreams increased in frequency some two years ago.

"They would start with the dream of you, but after a while, the gypsy woman's face would replace yours. The woman's mouth opened as if she was trying to say something, but no sound would come out. Mom would wake up screaming and drenched in sweat. Thank God she didn't have a nightmare since we arrived in Zadar, her screams scared me." Ella's voice faltered. "I hope they don't come back. My theory is that the two pieces are close to one another and soon the amulet will become whole again. Let's not talk about that anymore. Can I see your half of the amulet?"

He swallowed against his tightening throat. Irena's

nightmares were identical to his, save for her face becoming Gypsy woman's. If only he hadn't been so damn scared of the image and listened what was she wanted to say. Perhaps there was some secret mystery she wanted them to know. To his defense, the woman's appearance wasn't for the faint of heart. Thinking back, he too hadn't had that particular dream since Irena returned. The amulet would become whole again. How?

"Of course, love. I keep the second half on my desk as a paperweight and only saw it glow once. The night your mom returned to me." Hopefully, the fire had not spread to his office. God, he'd barely stepped his foot out of his restaurant since that night. His family was worth the sacrifice. In recent years he'd cursed the very establishment he bled for and built from the ground up. While being immersed in work helped him not to think of Irena, at the same time he envied those who lived normal lives.

The restaurant owner was no longer a noble profession. With countless establishments in the city, competing for the drop of the business from an ever drying well, restaurateurs turned ugly. Gone were healthy coexistence side by side, replaced with only bitterness. That kind of foulness repulsed and disturbed him.

To his surprise, lately, he caught himself pondering of folding the business and perhaps opening something else with not such a large overhead. A topic he needed to discuss with Ante. After all, he was his equal partner and half owner of Mezzaluna.

Ella shifted, making the leather on the seat creak, and faced him. "How did the gypsy woman break that amulet?"

"With some magic chant and a weird finger symbol she drew in the air above the rock. But gypsies are tricksters."

Ella's sad expression sent heaviness to his chest. He needed to cheer her up and make her forget her mother's tumulus angry state. With Ella's fascination of the history, there was no shortage of things to show her that would take her mind off her troubles. "Hey, did you know this city has a sphinx?"

She shot him a wide-eyed look. "A real sphinx? Where?"

"Yeah, it's right there." He pointed at the wide open intricate cast iron gate nestled between waist high garden walls running along the other side of the road. "Want to go see?"

"Are we allowed in there?" She craned her neck, peering through the driver's side window.

"It's a private house, but the owners don't mind as long as you respect their property. All the villas along the coast here are from Belle Époque period. In spring and summer, their gardens are beautiful." He opened his door. "Come, you'll love it."

She reached for her nun-chucks under the car seat, but he stopped her. He'd opposed her having the wood sticks concealed under her coat during the funeral. However, had things turned ugly when Fred approached them, he'd have been glad she didn't heed his protests. "You can leave your weapon. We won't be long."

He stepped onto the sidewalk, and Ella eagerly skirted the hood of his car, joining him. The northerly wind brought brisk air and pushed the dark clouds away, leaving clear skies. On the open sea, white crests formed on the waves. Hopefully, the wind would die by tomorrow or their speedboat would get some trashing on the churned waters.

She wrapped her arms around her torso and shrunk deeper into her jacket. "This wind is freezing. Is this what Mom called the Bura weather? She said it's usually not this bad."

"Yes, this wind is called Bura from Greek mythological figure Boreas." He checked both ways for traffic and waited for the few cars to drive by. "Our city's protected by the mountain ridge to the north and on rare occasions, we feel the blast as bad as today. However, up the coast, in a channel between mainland and islands, the wind speed in the winter exceeds two hundred kilometers per hour daily. No wonder pirates set their stronghold there. The coast was unapproachable most of the time. They were quite skilled sailors."

Holding onto her elbow, he ran across the street and entered the large garden. "Here's the city's sphinx. It's not as big or as old as Egypt's Sphinx, but it's the largest in the Europe."

Much work still waited for the new owners who strived to restore once the professionally landscaped area that had been left to deteriorate after the nationalization of the Villa Attilia and its grounds after the World War II.

"The sphinx was built in 1918 by Giovanni, the man who originally owned this villa in memory of his dead wife, Attilia. The villa bears her name too." He pointed at the three-story building to the right of the Sphinx with its white window frames accented by the mustard yellow walls. His plan to give Ella a quick history lesson on the Zadar's almost forgotten part of the past fell through as she saw the Sphinx and dashed ahead before he could finish.

"It's concrete, but that somehow enhances its beauty. Look, Dad, she has fingers instead of paws." Ella pointed at the ground between the Sphynx's hands where a few green blades of grass marked the first sign of spring. "These bricks suggest there was something here?"

"A fish pond stood there as if the Sphinx's hands protected it by a dagger and a shell she held. Those deteriorated as well. The grounds and the villa stood neglected for years. Some stories circled of buried treasure under the Sphinx and no one ever deciphered the hieroglyphic inscription on her hair, it spurred some wild imagination." He pointed at the top of the Sphinx's head with strange engravings. "Giovanni and Attilia dabbled in the occult."

She inspected every nook and cranny of the concrete structure and stepped closer to trace her hand over the face. "Was the treasure ever found?"

"There was never any treasure." He pulled the zipper of his bomber jacket as far as it would go, but the collar provided little protection from the bitter wind. "People came sniffling with metal detectors and aside from a few beer caps, found nothing."

He waited until she snapped a few pictures. His quick plan worked and, judging by her grin, she must've forgotten her mother's anger. "Well, shall we go? I don't want to overstate the owner's welcome, and Uncle Ante is waiting for us."

"Sure." She pocketed her cell and cast one last glance at the Sphinx. "Her face shows sadness and happiness at the same time." Ella pivoted in his direction and threaded her arm through his. "Thanks for showing me this."

"I love to stop here sometimes to enjoy the peacefulness of the sea among the tall pines surrounding the property." With one last glance at the sphinx, he vowed to give Irena the same kind of contended life Mistress Attilia had with her husband. Their marriage had been blessed with five children, and hopefully, Irena would want a big family too.

He turned to Ella and wrapped his arm around her shoulders. "Promise me one thing?"

"Sure, Dad. What?"

"Slow down and don't be in such hurry to grow up. You get to be a child only for a little while." He nudged his forehead against hers, coaxing her laugh.

"Okay, Dad. I promise."

Once he was seated in the car, the warmth caressed his face and replaced the brisk, biting wind. He fastened his seat belt and turned on the engine.

Ella placed her reddened hands over the vent on the dashboard. "It's great to have a heat in the car."

"It is?" He gave her a quick glance. "Heat in Mom's car didn't work?"

"Mom only turned the heat on to defrost the windshield. We had to be frugal. Every penny we saved helped us to run from Fred. Last year I was the most sought after babysitter and kept two paper routes." Ella turned toward the passenger's window. She could revert to her subdued state, he should keep her talking.

Now would be a perfect time to ask his burning question. "Would you live here?"

The corners of Ella's mouth dipped. "There's so much history to see, but I don't think I'd want to move to this country. The few times I've got to see the city, I noticed many beggars and people seem generally unhappy. The service we received at the stores and restaurants was without smiles. On top, I think the younger kids are kind of punky."

Dario smiled despite her accurate observation. "Yes, youngsters are turning aggressive." He pulled into an empty parking spot by the footbridge.

She grabbed her weapon from under the passenger's seat and stuffed inside her short jacket.

He opened the driver's side door and put one foot out. "I hope you didn't bring those to your school."

"I did in my last year, but no one knew." She eased out of the car and joined him. "It's tricky to hide them under my jersey during the gym."

He harrumphed but refrained from commenting. No child should feel unsafe to the point that they need to carry a weapon of any kind. Yet, the naïve ones became easy victims to the predators. Perhaps he should be glad his daughter knew better and could take care of herself. At the top of the footbridge where the wind gusts were felt the most, she moved closer to him, and he wrapped his arm around her shoulders. "Once we enter the old city it won't feel this cold. The Medieval high walls offer great protection against the wind. Unfortunately, we have to walk back this way to get to the car."

Only a few souls braved the cold day and mingled the streets of the ancient town. The establishments had their front door shut tight, and a few didn't bother to open, knowing the business would be scarce. The charred walls of Mezzaluna's interior squeezed his heart. Ante stood slouched over his laptop, his expression sour.

Dario scanned the smoke damage inside the restaurant's dining room.

Ante raised his head from the computer screen. "Hi Ella didn't know you were coming. Is Irena with you? Poor thing, I heard what happened at the funeral. By now that's pretty much the talk of the day. "

"Something to amuse the people. We left Irena to beat the punching bag to a pulp. She's quite upset." Dario lowered the lid of Ante's laptop.

"I wish I could've been there to get into that craven's face too. Knowing Irena, she is not shocked by the gossip, but the secrets her mother kept all these years." Ante turned his attention to the papers next to his laptop and dangled his copy of the insurance report in front of Dario's face "How did the bill get so astronomical? For the most part, it was the smoke and water damage."

Dario snatched the papers from his brother's hand and slammed them on the dirty counter. "The fire marshal fined us for faulty wiring and plumbing."

Ante snorted. "Load of crap. The building owner wouldn't cut us a deal on the lease. We would've gladly upgraded his wiring to bring it up to the code. If we were to fold the business, we can't take the work put into the building with us."

"That's what I wanted to talk to you about."

"What? Upgrading the electrical and plumbing in this place?" Ante tiled his head toward the overhead light. "The building is old and getting it up to the code will require some serious cash. I'd sooner move the business somewhere on the outskirts of the town where we're bound to find a newly built location. That would also mean less visibility."

"I thought about it myself and came to the same conclusion." Dario gauged his brother's reaction. Ante's continuous frown and furrowed brow made him finally give up. It was obvious he wasn't getting Dario's hint. "There's no way of winning this, bro. The only solution is we cut our losses while we can. The sales are going down no matter of our location and frankly..." He glanced at Ella. She smiled at the phone in her hand and her thumbs flickered over the screen. Who could she be texting with, other than Irena? "Well, I'm also tired of putting up with people who cheat us on deliveries, patrons who want freebies, dealing with employees who can't pull their weight and we had to cut loose. Who's to say one of them didn't sell his soul to Fred and told him the best way to start the fire in the restaurant?"

"That's only a beginning." Ante put his index finger up, stopping Dario from continuing. "Half of our employees took jobs elsewhere and other half left the country. We'll have to start from scratch and hire and train new staff." Ante pursed his lips and crossed his arms over his wide chest. "It's possible someone sold us out, but what do you have in mind?"

*Here goes nothing.* Dario took in a long breath, bracing for Ante's reaction, but had to voice out his plan. "We give Frank the place to manage and drive Fred's out of business, then Frank gets his own restaurant back and if he wants he can buy Mezzaluna from us."

Ante scratched his thumb back and forth over his jaw. "How's Frank gonna come up with the cash to fix this place? He couldn't buy his own place from Fred."

"He's got money. Not as much as Fred wanted for the LaGrotta, but he'd do fine leasing our restaurant. Anyway, we'll have to sell for less. He can have the place, but not our recipes."

"Of course. Recipes are our best-kept secret." Ante cocked his head. "Not a bad plan, but what do we do?"

Dario relaxed his shoulders. Ante took the news better than he anticipated. "I haven't discussed this with Irena yet, but if she agrees, I'll go with her to Canada. She's already established there, so it would be easier for her and Ella. I get set there and send you and your family a one-way ticket." At Ante's raised eyebrow, Dario continued. "How are things with Martina? Good, I hope."

A wide grin bloomed on his brother's face, suggesting things with his woman were better than good. "Fantastic, I think this time we'll make it. Jasmin is happy too to see her parents together and not arguing." Bouncing on his feet, he continued, "I'll have a talk with Martina. She'd have a hard time leaving, but I can persuade her." He waved his hand back and forth between Dario and him. "We've seen the big scary world out there. Our minds have opened and expanded and can't ever shrink back again. That is why we didn't really fit with these people back home. Most of them never step their foot outside of this small country."

A knock on the open front door had them pivoting in the direction of a tall, hulking man standing in the threshold. "Have you forgotten me, Dario? It's Tom. Ana's ex, or rather current again, thanks to you, and hoping to stay that way."

Dario's chest constricted and he drew in a slow and deep breath. Tom's presence here meant only one thing.

His teeth were about to meet the man's hard knuckles for treating Ana as a sex object. Instead, Tom's features relaxed and he put one hand up. "As you were, gentlemen. I wanted to ask you about that low life called Fred. Where can I find him? He'll pay for what he's done to my boy and my woman."

"I know where he's staying, but I need to warn you, the man doesn't work alone, and he's got some big brutes guarding him. They may be armed and I'm sure they are dangerous."

Tom's deep chuckles reverberated against the stone walls. "I wasn't born yesterday, and I can come up with more men than he can think of. If it was your child, wouldn't you beat the living daylight out of the pervert? My boy's having nightmares but still, won't talk about what that man did to him. Only confessed he got into the shower with him, naked and washed him down. Truth be told, I'm not sure I want to know the rest. There's no doubt he touched him inappropriately, but damn it, not knowing keeps me up at night."

Dario shivered. What horrors could the poor boy experienced while in Fred's care? "Oh man, sorry to hear that." Dario shook his head. Having Tom and his buddies on his side would make for one powerful ally. He should play his next card carefully to not to risk and blatantly ask for Tom's help. "I hope Nicky gets better soon."

"Yeah, the damn shrink told us to give the boy plenty of love and assure him he's safe. We're doing that, but it's not working." Tom punched his fist into his open palm. "I want that man's head on a plate."

Silence followed while Dario's mind raced to how to fulfill Tom's request. Ella cleared her throat and snapped him from his musing.

Tom turned his head to her. "Your daughter? She's a real beauty, like her mama." He grinned, turning to Dario. "I remember Irena." Tom dusted his hand off the soot after the touched the counter. "So, where do I find this low life? From what I heard, that man runs some dirty business. While a few say he's a saint. He offered them schooling abroad for their children, but I see the fear in their eyes." Tom reached into his jeans back pocket and retrieved his wallet.

"You heard right. One of my buddies works with Europol. He promised to check Fred out." Dario squared his jaw. Despite Irena's urgency not to involve police, he'd promised her his friend would stay discreet. Things may be getting out of hand, and if it came to that, they would all have hard questions to answer if they hadn't alerted the law enforcement sooner.

"Ah, no use talking to them, the scumbag most likely has the city police on his payroll. They won't do a thing unless you have some hard evidence. Here, take my business card." He scribbled on the back of the card. "This is my private cell number. If in need, call me. I and my men are on your side." Passing the card in one hand, he raised his other for a high-five salute.

Dario slapped his palm against Tom's and they shook their hands. A silent nod and understanding passed between them. With Tom on his side, Fred had little chance of succeeding.

After Tom left, Ante stored the number in his mobile's contacts. "I spoke with Joe while on the island. He told me not to do something dumb. He didn't say much, but I've got a feeling he knows about Fred and his child prostitution ring."

Dario pocketed the card and tapped his brother's arm. If their buddy wasn't saying much, it meant only one thing, he wanted to stay low and not come under Fred's radar. "Bring the boat to the pier at first light tomorrow."

Ante nodded, and Dario set off in search for Ella. Where had she slipped to while he spoke with Tom? He found her in his office. The small room stood untouched by smoke, but judging by the upturned contents of the cabinets and drawers, someone had to have been looking for something. Water soaked paperwork covered his desk and the tossed invoices and purchase orders littered the floor. He snapped a couple of pictures for the insurance claim purpose and pocketed his phone. "Come love. We should head back."

"It's not here, Dad. I can't find it." She didn't spare him a glance as she turned the items on his work station.

"What are you looking for?"

She popped her head up and looked him square in his eyes. "Your half of the shiny amulet. It's gone. Someone out there knows the amulet's secret. Mom said only in the right hand it will become whole again. Her half glowed in my hand. I think my hands are the right hands."

Chapter 17

At the tip of the wharf, Dario waited for Ante to guide their boat alongside the stone structure jutting into the sea. Small waves lapped around the corner while the ribbons of early morning mist slowly evaporated in the low sun, salty brine of the sea tickled his nostrils. Dario caught the line Ante threw at him from the stern and wrapped the rope around the rusty bollard.

Ella approached him with slow steps, her hands shoved in her tweed jacket pockets. Her gaze focused on his hands twisting the cord into an intricate knot ensuring the movement of the boat wouldn't loosen the coil.

He tilted his head toward his daughter and winked. The corners of her lips dipped into a tight smile. "Looks complicated."

"It's quite simple. I'll show you." Wiggling his index finger, he indicated for her to come closer.

She crouched next to him, curiosity in her wide eyes. "How long will it take us to reach the island?"

"About two hours if the weather holds." He cast his glance over the sea. The ruffles on the open water increased their speed and size. If he was right, the wind out there and churned waters would trash their boat. They would have to hug the coast. "We won't be able to go at full tilt, but the journey will be a bit more pleasant than getting tossed on the waves." Her face paled, and he wrapped her in a tight hug. "Don't worry, uncle Ante is a skilled sailor." Another cast over the horizon confirmed the wind was picking up strength. It also meant a spectacular sunset.

"Okay, Dad." She straightened and yanked her cell phone out of her jacket pocket. After glancing at the screen, she grinned and stepped away from him.

Turning to Irena, he hoped to find her with her phone in her hand. Mother and daughter had found some silly game on their phones and played against each other. But Irena sat on top of her big suitcase and yawned into her hand while holding her travel coffee mug in the other. Large, dark sunglasses covered her eyes. Okay, it was obvious Ella was texting with someone else. He picked up the tan duffle bag from the ground, next to Ella's feet, and cast a curious glance at the screen of her mobile in some off chance to catch the name of the person with whom she exchanged messages. She touched the send button so fast all he got was an A.

"Mind me asking who are you texting with?" He didn't mean to pry, but he blurted the question before he realized.

"It's Andy." She threw the words over her shoulder and picked up another bag from the ground.

He stood rooted. Andy? Andy? Why did that sound familiar?

"You promised to talk to Mom about letting me go out with him." She cocked an inquisitive eyebrow as if to find out if he broached the subject with Irena.

"Oh, now I remember. The receptionist at the Bastion hotel. Ah, I…" When he made that promise he had vaguely suspected Ella could be his daughter. Well, the things were different now. "With everything that happened, I forgot. Mom lets you text with him? How old did she say you have to be before she'd let you date?"

Of course, Irena had let her daughter text with a boy. There was a mutual respect between mother and daughter, and lying or hiding the truth and their action from one another was not how they rolled. Irena raised her child well. They had accepted him into their small circle of trust and he wouldn't do anything to jeopardize that.

"Fifteen, but—"

"Uh-uh, no buts." Seeing Ella's face souring, he took a step closer to her. By her pouty lips, he concluded she must like this boy. He may have almost fourteen years of fathering to catch up on, but damn it, his daughter should not get banned from life like her mother was. "But if we call it hang out together instead of a date, then she can't say no. Four of us could go to movies or invite him to dinner. What do you say?"

A huge smile bloomed on her face, and she kissed his cheek. "You know how to make me happy. "

He cast another glance at Irena. She slouched and propped her chin on her curled fingers. "Your mom is still upset."

"I guess." Ella shrugged. "She's also troubled with both pieces of amulet missing. Maybe someday they'll turn up someplace we least expected."

"You two look a tad too relaxed. Can one of you help me with this suitcase?" Irena called from the road side end of the wharf, tugging on the handle of the luggage.

"Ante and I will get that," Dario said, strutting up to her. "Why don't you take Ella on board?"

She nodded and picked up her travel mug from the ground. He wrapped his hand around her arm, stopping her. "Hey, we don't need any amulet, Gypsy, shiny or otherwise. Our love survived because of who we are, not some infused magic. And we're stronger than ever before."

She nodded, then rewarded him with a tiny smile. He placed a quick kiss on her soft lips. "There, much better." After a playful pat on her firm behind, he turned toward the heavy suitcase. "If you want to stretch, there's a nice bed under the prow. What time was it when you finally calmed down and fell asleep?"

"Sorry I kept you up, but my mind wouldn't settle and sleep wasn't coming to me last night. I could snooze now, so I'll take you up on your offer." She raised her travel mug to her lips and winked. "This coffee isn't doing its job. If you snuggle up next to me..."

She bit her lower lip and cocked her head, coaxing chuckles from him. "I'll join you after I see that Ella's comfortable and wears a lifejacket. We'll hit some rough seas once we are out of the harbor."

Shaking her head, she turned toward the bay's wide exit and peered over the rim of her dark sunglasses. "Looks wavy out there, but your boat is not that small as you described it."

"Well, it's not a raft, but it's a speck on the vast water." Holding onto her elbow, he helped her over the side and onto the deck. She waved before ducking to go down below. He turned to Ella and extended his hand to her. "Ready to sail?"

"More than ready." She slid her hand inside his and hopped over the side, headed for the slanted roof of the boat's cabin.

"Don't sit there, the deck will get wet and slippery. I don't want you falling in. The waters will be calmer when we enter the narrow passage between islands. You can perch yourself on the roof of the cabin then."

"Then I can swim with a mermaid."

"You'd be the first one." Ante huffed and grunted under the weight of Irena's big suitcase. He glared at Dario. "Didn't you say we'd get this in together? How come I always end up schlepping this valise alone?"

"All right, stop your bi…bickering." Dario picked up the corner of the luggage and grunted as he pushed his arm muscles to raise the bloody thing over the side.

Stepping backward, Ante managed to get one end and together they slid the bag onto the deck. Ante puffed and cursed, picked up the bottom of his t-shirt and wiped his face. "Feels heavier than I remember."

"Mom stuffed a few more things inside." Ella took the seat on the wide bench at the stern.

"Must be more than just a few." Ante nodded, taking his seat at the cockpit. "If you get brave enough I'll let you drive for a few minutes. Don't worry I'll be right next to you."

"I'm not too sure about that." She gave a nervous smile.

The engine roared to life, the sea foamed around the stern, white puff of smoke floated in the early morning air. Dario untied the lines and tossed the ropes on the prow. He pushed the boat away from the quay and jumped onboard, then retrieved the fenders off the side.

Mile, by a slow mile, they crept out of the harbor and picked up the speed. Dario stared at the sinking city line. This was his home. Over the years, the town he grew up in seemed less and less familiar. Even the country appeared foreign, unrecognizable, fragile and small. He often wondered its fate. The economy hadn't recovered much in over twenty years since the breakup from the Yugoslavian federation that ultimately led to senseless and bloody civil war. It seemed the population lived in a constant recession, while the corrupt government only cared how to stuff more into their pockets.

God knew he tried to do the right thing, go out of his way to help out whenever he could. He must leave and start over elsewhere. Irena was aware of the helpless situation. Would she want to settle here? She loved him of that much he was sure. The last thing he wanted was for her to think he'd use her as means to move to the new world.

The spray of the cold water on his face brought him back to the moment, and he sought the shelter under the cover at the stern. Ella pulled the hood over her head and recorded the passing scenery. He sat next to her and craned his neck to look at the screen of her cell phone.

"You don't take selfies?" Another stupid question, Dario. His daughter was not a typical teenager. Life's little things excited her, like the jet of water left behind the boat.

She snorted. "Only vain girls take selfies. Besides, why ruin a perfect picture with me in it?"

"Don't be silly. You'd make the picture better." He pulled his phone from the jacket's pocket and snapped a photo of her. "There, now I have a picture of you." He then slid next to her and took another photo of both of them. "And now we took a selfie."

She yawned, and he pulled her into a hug. "Are you cold? Gets pretty chilly on the water. I'll get you a blanket. Or you can go down below and join your mom. Be prepared for your stomach contents to be tossed."

"I'll sit here and enjoy the view."

"Another ten or fifteen minutes and we'll get between the islands. The sea there is always calmer." Ante yelled over his shoulder to be heard above the roar of the engine and the hauling of the wind.

They sat in silence and yawns plagued him. The thoughts drifted again and his eyelids grew heavy with the roll of the boat. Why was he freezing here when he could snuggle up next to Irena's warm body? He stretched his arms and got on his feet. "Will you be okay here with Ante?"

Ella nodded, holding onto his hand she inched toward the cockpit and dropped into the white chair next to his brother.

Dario cocked one eyebrow, his gaze on the gas gauge pointing at below quarter of a tank. "You didn't fill up?"

"Forgot. Relax, I made it to and from the island before on fumes. We have plenty of fuel." Ante dismissed him with a wave of his hand.

Well, with Ante in control, what could possibly go wrong? Dario slipped into the cabin and found Irena fast asleep under the blankets. He raised the corner of the covers and slipped next to her. As if sensing his closeness, she pressed her warm body to his and he spooned up with her, inhaling her signature citrusy scent. All his doubts disappeared, replaced by his body's instant reaction. Tonight, he would take her to his secret spot where they could stargaze and make love under the open sky.

The steady and monotone drone of the engine lulled him. The door to the cabin burst open. Dario jerked up to a seated position. Ante stood at the threshold. In his extended hand, he held a green tube with the black cube on one end. "What the hell is this?"

Dario took the small device in his hand. "A camera. Where did you find it?"

"Tucked under the steering. I can't believe I didn't see it sooner." Ante pivoted toward the deck, then back at Dario. "We're accelerating. How? I left the auto-pilot at the comfortable cruising speed."

Irena rubbed her eyes and rose on her elbows. "What's going on?"

"Dad! Uncle!" Ella's shrieks raised hairs on Dario's neck. "I didn't touch anything. I swear. The speed went crazy after Uncle ripped that thing out."

Dario followed Ante to the deck, Irena in tow. He peered over Ante's shoulder to take a better look at the control panel. The needle was reaching red fields on the speedometer. Ante yanked on the accelerator and held the stick down, clenching his teeth. Dario pressed his hand over Ante's and grabbed the steering with his other. With some quick reactions and maneuvers, he was able to avoid getting the yacht into the shallow waters. Good thing it wasn't in the middle of the tourist season, crafts of all sizes and types would pack this channel.

"If we don't slow down, we'll burn off the fuel in a few minutes." Ante roared over the engine's clamor.

For once, Dario was glad his brother forgot to top up the tank, however, once the gasoline was consumed, they would be dead in the water.

Chapter 18

Dario clutched the steering wheel, fighting to keep his boat on course. He glanced at the gas gauge. For the past several moments the needle pointed at E. He begged every deity for the last drop of fuel to burn and the craft to slow down.

The engine sputtered, coughed, and then shut off. The prow lowered and the momentum propelled them some ten yards. He swallowed hard and pressed his hand on his chest. His heart raced.

Ante exhaled loudly, pulling his cell phone out of his jacket pocket. "We're just below our island. Let's hope we're within the reach of the service."

He dialed, while everyone stared at him. Finally, he pumped his fist in the air. "Yes, it's ringing."

"Oh, thank God." Irena's shoulders lowered and she eased the grip on Ella's wrist.

Ante scooted toward the prow. "Can you hear me better now?"

"We're fine." Dario pulled Irena into a hug, then reached one arm to Ella. "Don't be scared, Ante is calling for help."

Ella exhaled loudly and buried her face in his shoulder. "What was that thing Uncle pulled out? Why did boat accelerate after he ripped it?"

Dario kissed the top of Ella's head. Damn it, her first sea voyage in his craft had to be scary. "I don't know, love. Somehow the camera was wired into the navigation system and messed things up."

Their boat had been tampered with. First chance he got, he'd have the craft dry docked and the mechanic check everything. This wasn't some amateurish job. If Fred's goons had done this, the man had pros working for him.

Ante returned to the stern, tucking his phone into his pocket. "Ana's brother is on his way." Ante examined the small spy camera he'd ripped from the cockpit. "Where could this transmit to?"

"Who knows?" Dario took the device in his hand. "I hoped they enjoyed watching snow on the screen. The Wi-Fi signal drops a few meters outside the harbor."

"Kris is on his way." Ante pointed at the speck on the water leaving the harbor. Dario squinted at the fast approaching boat. Several meters away, Ana's brother waved from the prow, his friend steering toward their vessel.

Dario squeezed Irena's shoulder. "Doubtful Fred got our location by spying with this device. Once we're sure, I want to take you to the secluded spot I told you about. Let's spend one night alone. Just the two of us lost to the world."

She nodded, but uncertainty flashed across her steely gaze. Damn Fred. Now they'd have to play it safe for days. Dario had planned to take her to his favorite stargazing spot tonight.

****

Dario pounded the stubborn peg into the ground between the rocks. The clinking of the hammer on the metal head eased his angst. Hard to believe two weeks since their wild speed experience and his nerves hadn't settled. The slightest noise made him jump. His favorite spot never failed to relax him and since he tied his boat to the rock about an hour ago, the therapy worked and his head cooled.

He checked the rope connecting the fly of the tent, satisfied with the tightness, he straightened and shook the stiffness from his legs. "Our chamber awaits, my lady."

Irena stood on the highest point of the rock overlooking the islet, a pair of binoculars pressed to her eyes.

"The stars won't be out yet." He glanced at the sun. The burning ball had sunk low, washing the sea in the golden twinkling light.

"I'm not looking at the sky." She didn't spare him a glance, scanning the horizon.

"Anything?"

"Not a soul out there." She lowered the glasses. "Looks like we're alone in this wilderness."

"It's a nice change from the crowded house. Though Ante's in-laws love to have people around." Passion pulled into his pelvis with the anticipation of nightfall. The two times they'd snuck into the attic for a quickie only fueled his desire more. Tonight wasn't meant just for observing the night sky.

Irena raised the binoculars to her eyes again, turned another few inches, scanning over the vast sea surrounding the rock they stood on, the larger island Sylba a hazy mass in the distance. In a moment, she strutted toward him and sat on the ground. "Ante's in-laws remind me of your parents. Gracious hosts, ready to feed you, still, I feel like we're overstaying our welcome. Otherwise, I wouldn't have agreed to leave Ella and come here. Not that we could pry her away from Jasmin. On the other hand, we are overdue for some time alone."

"We sure are." He groaned at the thought of the pleasure he planned to give her tonight. Better to change the subject or he wouldn't last until the dark. "The two girls are like sisters. They are becoming inseparable. Perhaps it's time we start looking for a house." He stepped over the sparse bushes growing among the rocks and inspected the back side of the tent.

"I can't start planning our future. The enemy is cunning. It won't take them long to figure out lights in your condo are on a timer. They'll find us." The sight of the tent seemed to pull her out of the temporary gloom. "Oh, I'm such a lousy helper. Anything else left to do?"

"You can bring the basket of food from the boat. Or you can stay here and pump up this mattress since you don't want to sleep on the boat." He waved at the foot pump then pointed at the blue box storing a double size bed, folded until the next use.

"It's cramped and stuffy in there. I rather stargaze from here than through an open hatch." She glared at the box and scowled. "Ugh, I think I'll get the food and leave you to pump it up."

"I'm kidding." He chuckled at her fast retreat. "The mattress has a built-in pump. The manual is for emergencies."

"Happy pumping, then." She called over her shoulder, pulling on the boat's lines, tied to a peg he'd chiseled out of a rock first time he found this place. Whenever the life asked too much, and his longing for her became unbearable, he'd escaped here. While sailing around the world, he had taken many mental trips to this islet.

With their bed ready in a few minutes, he slid the mattress inside. It took most of the tent space, but it was comfier than the hard bed on the boat. He tossed the sleeping bags in the corners to spread them later. Before he joined Irena at the small pebble beach, he unzipped the window at the top of the tent. Perfect view of the sky appeared. A slow descend down the steep rock face, he found the food basket left on the small pebbled beach. Next to it lay Irena's clothes, her lavender silky panties and bra held by the weight of a large round stone on top of her jeans and sweater.

Had she gone swimming? The sea water was freezing. Her head broke the surface, answering his question.

"Come in, it's beautiful." She splashed water in his direction.

"Have you lost your mind?" He backed up as far as the face of the rock allowed. A shiver rushed down his spine. "You want to get sick? It's middle of February."

"And have you lost all track of time? It's now the end of March."

Had it truly been over a month since she returned to him? Yeah, he had lost the track of time, and his heart. When he loved someone, time didn't matter. He reached for the belt buckle on his jeans and kicked off his hiking boots.

"I can't believe I'm about to do this." Peeling his socks off, he pulled his hoodie over his head, then slid his pants and boxers off. The icy water hit his toes, he drew a sharp breath through his teeth and shrugged clenching his arms to his chest. "Do you have any idea what cold water does to a man?"

She blew bubbles on the surface. "If you're referring to the shrinkage, I think the cold is having an opposite effect on you."

"Just wait until I'm in up to my hips." He took another step forward, searching for the flat stone on the bottom to set his foot.

She flipped onto her back, her breasts bobbing on the surface. Like a tantalizing mermaid, she wiggled her index finger for him to come closer. It would be hard to lose his erection with such a pretty picture in front of him, cold water or not. He took another step forward, sucked in his stomach as coldness wrapped around his mid-thighs. It was now or never. In one swift move, he took a plunge and dove in, pulling her under with him.

He kicked his feet toward the surface and splashed Irena. "Woohoo! Brr...liar, you said the water's beautiful."

"Give it a couple of minutes. You'll warm up." She splashed him back. "I checked the sea temperature before we left. It's balmy ten degrees."

Her naked body brushed his, making him forget the coldness and giving him the idea to challenge her to a race in order to loosen his stiff limbs. He wrapped his arm around her waist and pulled her to him.

In an instant, her legs closed around his hips, and he slid his hands down her back to cup her butt.

"My," she gasped, rubbing the heat between her thighs on his hard cock. "And you were afraid of shrinkage."

"I was wrong," he whispered before seizing her lips with his. Her velvety tongue teasing his, her body fusing with his, all spinning in his mind and he gave her the control. He was in her hands. His plan to take her to the stars tonight was instantly forgotten. Then again, why wait? He would be good and ready again by the nightfall.

"Shall we continue inside the tent? We have a nice, comfy, warm bed there." He brushed his thumb over her hardened nipple, applying enough pressure to tease, but not to satisfy, and coaxed a heady breath from her.

"No, I want you here and now." Her hand wrapped around his cock, massaging his already aching shaft.

Stepping backward until the water again reached his ankles, he lowered on the flat stone wide enough to help him hold her on his lap. Her boobs bounced in front of him. He seized them, then with a soft pull, drew her nipple into his mouth, sending her hips into jerky spasms. Slowly he trailed his hand between the valley of her breasts, down her firm stomach, stopping at soft curls of her mound. She raised her feet on his shoulders and he cradled her back in his arms. She angled her hips to shimmy with the slow building rhythm. The need to taste, touch and smell her salty skin urged him to trail his tongue from her neck to her collarbone. Bending his knees to position her on his thighs freed his arms. Instantly his hand searched for the heat between her legs. Pressing his thumb on the hardened nub, he increased the pressure and speed of the teasing finger deep inside her.

"Oh, yes-s-s," she whispered, tightening her hold around his neck.

"You're beautiful," he murmured, burying his face on the swells of her breasts. Her heart beat fast under his ear.

After years of spending his lowest days on this desolate rock and fantasizing about making love to her, he finally got to realize his wildest imaginings.

"Dario..." Her strained whisper was barely audible. "I need you, now. Inside me."

Yes! He raised her hips and poised her at the tip of his cock. "All for you, babe."

Lowering her, he slid deep into her moist center. She was his for taking and he was hers for giving. She bent her knees and pushed against his chest to shift her hips closer to him and pull him in deeper. Leaning on his elbows allowed him to tilt his pelvis higher, and meet her strong thrusts. Her cries grew louder, spurring him to grunt. Here in the wilderness, they could be truly free. He let go of all inhibitions and released his voice, as hers reached a near scream. With his hand dipped between her legs, he rubbed her clit. She clenched her thighs. Her back arched and each spasm of her orgasm propelled her voice higher.

With one last thrust into the final tremors of her climax, he let out a guttural cry and collapsed on the pebbles, pulling her to his chest. His hand cradled her neck, he panted until he could speak again. "Holy shi...you're putting me through some tough workout."

"I do, don't I?" She kissed his neck, then cuddled against him.

"Hey, I'm not complaining." He ran his hand through her wet hair. "Between workouts at Martina's brother gym and the bedroom, my hip bones reappeared. I thought I'd never see them again."

"They look so sexy on you. I lose my control when you drop your pants." A shiver stiffened her body. "I'm getting cold."

He wrapped her in his arms and rubbed her back. "We should go back to the tent and dry off. I'll build us a nice fire."

"Let's go." She pushed away from him and got on her feet. With her shoulders hunched and arms folded over her stomach, she headed for the tent. The skin on her ass still showed his red hand prints from his hard squeezing. He'd never get enough of her sexy little tush.

He stood and rubbed his rump beneath his tailbone, where a rock dug in during their lovemaking. He scooped up their clothes and the basket of food, then followed her up the steep rock. At the top, he turned and gazed toward the small pebbled beach. In all his fantasies he made love to her inside his tent on the comfy mattress, instead, she had surprised him with her skinny dipping. Going for a swim in mid-March, crazy for sure, but there was a first time for everything. He stared at the tent on top of the flat rock and lust slammed into his pelvis. Well, the day wasn't over yet.

He found her shivering and pulling the sleeping bags out of their drawstring sacks. "Did we bring any towels?"

"Right here." Reaching into his duffel, he grabbed a large, fluffy terry cloth, snugged it around her then pulled her to him. Cradled in his arms against his chest, he rubbed her back with one hand and caressed her head with the other. "You'll be warm in a few seconds."

She took one corner of the towel and rubbed his hair. "Sorry I made you go for a swim. I must've been delusional, but water just beckoned me to take a plunge."

"I'm not sorry at all. Here, finish drying your body and join me." He handed her the ends of the towel and set to zip the sleeping bags together. Had he known the day would take such wild twist, he would've gotten their sleeping nest ready.

"Your bed, my lady," he said, flipping the corner of the covers.

She dropped the towel and crawled across the mattress on all fours, her firm butt swayed before she flipped onto her back and rolled into a ball. He lay next to her and pulled the covers over them then scooped her in his arms. Gasp by long gasp, her shivering ceased and even breathing continued. Her body relaxed, but his tightened all over again, holding her now warm, nude snuggled against his.

Sleep wasn't coming to him as his erection grew. He kicked off the covers, but the chilly air did nothing to soothe him. Placing her head on the pillow, she murmured in her slumber and rolled onto her side. With a soft kiss to her temple, he left her to rest and in two strides approached the stone circle where he'd stacked the driftwood, and crumpled, old newspaper for kindling. She wouldn't sleep for too long, as usual, only a quick power nap to recharge after achieving such a powerful orgasm. A smile stretched his lips. Lately, she'd been hornier than usual, probably making up for the fourteen years of drought in the love department. Or maybe staying at the full house limited their freedom and they weren't always able to act on their urges.

He lit the paper and the flames licked the dry wood, sending embers high into the darkness. If this timber burned as fast, the fire would be out before Irena's nap. That would not do.

He headed for the tent and grabbed the flashlight from his bag. Irena stirred at his rummaging and he slipped out before she awoke. His hasty search for anything burnable produced some dry moss and grass, and several pieces of wet plywood that would no doubt smoke, but would extend the life of their little bonfire.

Back at the stone circle, he threw kindling on the embers and poked the stick at the dying fire. The wet plywood hissed at the contact with the heat. As he'd predicted wisps of white smoke curled from the pyre.

Irena emerged from the tent. Sleeping bag wrapped tightly around her while her bare feet poked out with every step she took.

She plopped down next to him and ran her fingers through her hair. "I'm having a major case of bed head. I never should've fallen asleep with wet hair."

"You look fine, babe. Besides, who'll see you out here?" He nudged her with his shoulder.

"You are looking at me, right now." She worked her fingers through her hair faster and then scrunched her face.

"That's because you're beautiful, even when you don't think so." He reached for the basket behind him and placed the wicker case on his lap. "Hungry?"

"Starving." Leaning over his bent knee, she inspected the contents of the bin. "M-m-m you packed my favorite. Ooh, I love these canapé sandwiches. Oh, my! Fruit and dessert, and of course..." She pulled the bottle out and waved it in front of him. "A good wine."

"I'm not sure about *good* wine." She snatched the basket from his lap. He raised his hands in surrender. It must be the fresh sea air that opened up her appetite lately. "You weren't kidding when you said you were starving.'

She stuffed her mount with cheese slices and crackers. "We skipped lunch and then we got busy with, well...I don't need to remind you."

"After such a huge breakfast, I never thought I could eat again." He poured wine into two glasses and handed her one. "Cheers."

Their glasses touched with a dull thud. He gave her a sheepish smile. "Plastic cups. Maybe we should forgo them and just drink from the bottle. After all, we are pretending to be castaways."

"Who's pretending?" She took a sip from her glass, then coughed up, placing her hand on her chest. Her voice strained when she spoke. "I'm sorry, but it's too sour."

He handed her a bottle of water. "It's okay, babe. The choice in the store is small. I thought this Chablis would be sweet. Oh well, we won't be getting drunk tonight then."

She brought the bottle to her mouth and took a long pull. "This is better. It's safe."

He pointed at the basket. "Left me any food?"

"Oh, sorry." She placed the basket between them. "Don't think I'm being selfish."

He reached inside and pulled out a container with bite-size sandwiches. "You'll love these."

Taking one between her forefinger and thumb, she inspected the contents. "Prosciutto and thinly sliced cantaloupe. Worth a risk." Then she popped the food into her mouth and chewed slowly. "M-m-m another delicacy. I'm afraid I'll gain weight if you keep feeding me like this."

"Ah, you got nothing to worry about. I made sure

the meat is extra lean. Your tummy shouldn't complain." He munched on a slice of baguette. The food she loved hated her in return and after the two times he got to witness the ugliness of her suffering, he vowed he'd be more careful in selecting and preparing meals.

She stopped eating and fell silent, shook her head and glanced away. He wrapped his arm around her shoulders. "Look, I know you're worried about your future...but—" Her silence troubled him. "You can't put your life on hold because your future is uncertain, and nothing good will come out worrying about it. Live for the moment."

"I wish I could." She toyed with the bottle's cap but didn't meet his gaze.

"We gained some powerful allies. No matter how many lowlifes Fred can buy, when things heat up, they'll all scramble. I'd bet on that." Dario kissed her temple, coaxing a shy smile from her. She would worry he involved a cop in the case. His buddy, Joe, had only repeated what he said to Ante, giving Dario a feeling Joe knew more. "I wanted to talk to you about something else."

"Yes?" She perked up and reached for more food.

"Ella gave me an idea, and I already touched on it with Ante. I guess I should've asked you first before I talked to everyone else, but it just kind of worked out that way. Hope you won't get upset with me."

"What's up? Just spit it out." Her eyebrows drew closer as she picked another grape from the stem.

"We decided not to renovate the restaurant. It's too much money and we're leasing the space. Instead, we'll rent it out to our neighbor. He can manage it and drive

Fred out of business."

"The same neighbor Fred bailed out of the fine? Then promptly bought him out without him knowing it?"

"The same." Dario tugged on the sleeping bag wrapped around her when the night breeze picked up and blew through his shirt. "Care to share?"

"Sure." She stretched her arm out, inviting him to her warm, naked body under the blanket.

He sat her on his lap and enveloped them in the thick cover. "So, if you agree, I'll come to Canada with you." He paused, waiting for her reaction. A half smile tugged on her lips and encouraged him to continue. "Don't worry about money. There'll be enough until I get something going."

She pressed her finger to his lips, quieting him. "I'm a rich girl now. My biological father bequeathed me his investor's portfolio." Her gaze wandered off toward the sky. "Only wish I could thank him for everything."

"You already did and I'm sure professor Vlahos watches over you." Dario gave her a reassuring squeeze. "What do you think of my suggestion?"

She returned her gaze to him. "Babe, the fastest way for you to get a visa would be if we marry. And it'll take years to divorce Fred. Father Diego is helping me out with this, but so far I haven't heard a thing from him."

"I want to marry you the moment your marriage with Fred gets annulled. But until that time, I'm not letting you go." Dario swallowed a lump in his throat. No matter what the future held, they belonged together. The Gypsy's amulet predicted so, even if for a long time he lost the faith in the prophecy. She placed her hand in his and the old pipe cleaner he'd wrapped around her finger all those years ago came into his focus. Reaching into the folds of the basket, he pulled out the small, blue velvet box he saved for over a decade.

"I've waited fourteen years. It's time I replace this," he said, sliding the pipe-cleaner off her finger.

"I don't get five minutes of freedom?" Her teasing tone caused him to chuckle.

Her eyes widened at the sight of the box in his hand. But when he opened the box, revealing the three diamond ring set in white gold, her jaw dropped. He'd envisioned going down on one knee when he proposed to her, but she sat comfortably on his lap and he didn't want to move her to live out some fantasy. Funny how life worked out differently.

He poised the ring at the tip of her finger. "Will you marry me?"

She closed her eyes and her lips trembled, hovering between a smile and a frown. After a long exhale she nodded fast. A single tear ran down her cheek. "Babe...I...you know my situation. It's not saf—"

He stifled her protest with a deep kiss. "I won't take no for an answer."

"I was afraid of that."

"Marry me then."

A single tear raced down her cheek and she licked her lips. Then nodded again. "Yes, I'll be your wife. It was our destiny and still is."

With one hand cupping her cheek and his thumb wiping the droplet, he slid the ring on her finger. "I hope this is a happy tear because you've made me the happiest man alive. Look, the ring is a perfect fit."

"Of course it was a happy tear," she whispered, pressing her forehead to his. For a few precious moments, time stopped and the world consisted of the islet surrounded by the blue sea and the two of them.

She straightened and extended her arm, flexing her wrist. Flames of the fire reflected in the diamonds of her ring. "It's as beautiful as the stars above us." With her head tilted toward the sky, she swiped her fingers under her eyes. "Wow. You were right. They look so low you could reach out and grab them." Wrapping her arm around him, she turned her face to him and kissed his lips, then again and again, until her tongue probed his mouth and tangled with his. Breaking the kiss, she licked her lips and whispered, "Make love to me in the tent."

He scooped her into his arms and carried her to their love nest. They dropped on the bed and he proceeded to kiss her senseless. "Did you bring your naughty bag? I'm dying to try that dual stimulator on you."

"Oh, yes, it's in my rucksack." She wriggled under him while he left a trail of kisses from her abdomen to her neck. The next moment she froze. The fire extinguished from her eyes, replaced by fear. She placed palms firmly on his chest, and her breathing seemed to cease.

"What's wrong?" he asked, not able to shake away a feeling of dread. Her sudden unease wasn't just a mother's intuition and he should not dismiss it lightly. He checked his phone. No missed calls or messages. Ante would have contacted him if something bad happened...if he could.

She shot out of the bed and pulled her clothes on in haste. "Something's happened. We must go back to the island. No time to fold the camp."

Chapter 19

The wisps of mist hovered low over the sea, shrouding the sleepy fishing village in eerie foreboding. Knots inside Dario's guts twisted tighter. Inside the port, he cut off the engine and steered the boat toward the wharf. Irena stood on the prow, holding the thick rope and ready to pounce out as soon as the distance between the glider and quay decreased.

Irena leaped off the prow and silently landed on the stone waterfront, tying the boat's line in haste. He cast the anchor into the sea, then wound the rope around the cleat until the line stood rigid, not allowing the boat to drift on the water.

He jumped onto the land and kicked his legs into the run to catch up with Irena. After the fourth unanswered call to his brother, Dario had given up on dialing Ante's number and turned his efforts to reach the house they resided on the island of Sylba.

She halted, panting in front of the two-story stone house. Its stillness and the closed door didn't instill confidence. He squeezed her shoulder to gain her attention. "You wait here. I'll go in first, make sure it's safe."

"Like hell I'll wait." She broke into a run again and reached the front door, her hand wrapped around the knob. Her shoulders rose and fell with each long breath, and she pushed the door open.

A strange chemical odor filled the hallway. Ante lay on the tiled floor, in nothing but his boxers, which he put on backward. He moaned and swiped the back of his hand over his mouth. At the foot of the stairs, wearing her blush negligee, Martina stirred and winced, then rolled onto her side and cradled her head in her arms.

Dario rushed to his brother and tapped his hand on Ante's cheek. "Wake up. Are you okay? What happened?"

Ante rubbed his eyes, sighed and coughed. His grogginess suggested he'd been poisoned by some kind of sleep chemical. "We were just getting down to business when I heard a loud thud and then a second one I threw on my underwear, in case I ran into Martina's mom or dad." A new fit of hacking broke his words. When he could speak again he continued, "I was afraid old folks tumbled down the stairs. Martina followed me, despite my insisting she stayed put. Then I saw gas was coming from a canister and the last thing I remember…ah…passing out here."

Irena checked on Martina. Martina nodded to some quiet question and slowly sat up, propped by the banister. Irena ran up the stairs leading to the second-floor bedrooms. Dario dialed the island's emergency, then his childhood friend, Joe.

"Dario!" Irena called from the top of the stairs. "Martina's parents are in their bed, in deep sleep. I opened the window in their bedroom." She fixed him with a grievous stare knots formed in the pits of his guts. "Can you please come here?"

"Sure." Dario's heart sank to his stomach. The tremble in Irena's voice gave him a bad feeling.

She entered the girls' room. He followed her. Two empty beds greeted him. Twisted sheets and covers suggested the struggle. A white rag tossed on each pillow. He picked one up to smell, but before he put it to his nose, the pungent lemony scent like too much wood polish stung his nostrils. Anesthesia gas—he'd remember the smell ever since Ante's sixth-grade trip to the ER to have his broken arm set in a cast. Oh dear god, please let the girls be hiding someplace. "We'll find them. They couldn't have gone far."

"Doubtful." Irena gripped Ella's nun-chucks in her shaky hand. "Ella wouldn't leave this behind unless she wasn't given the chance to grab them. How are we going to break the news to your brother and Martina? She'd freak out and this is not the time to lose one's cool." Irena chewed on her bottom lip. By her knitted brow, a plan was formulating in her head. But where to start?

"Let me deal with that." He rubbed the stubble on his jaw. "Why would they take Jasmin? She's barely four years old."

"The younger they are more money they fetch on the sex slave market. Plus, no doubt Fred will threaten to hurt Jasmin if Ella doesn't comply."

His already tight chest, clenched harder, squeezing the air out of his lungs. His dinner threatened to hurl up. "No way, Fred wouldn't—"

"He would." Irena nodded, her chin and hand trembled. How did she manage to keep her voice steady? "We need to find them before they are taken out of the country."

He raced after her to the hallway. He had to hand it to her for not allowing panic to take over her. If she lost her head, he wouldn't know what to do. Martina climbed the stairs, a bag of ice pressed to the back of her neck. His guts twisted a new. Maybe he should break the news to Ante first. He grabbed her elbow as they met on the middle step. "Where's Ante?"

"He's in the bathroom, retching. Why?"

"Do you know if the kids may be hiding in some of their secret places? They fancied sitting under the stairs. It was their clubhouse as they called it." Despite his struggle to hide fear, it must've shown on his face.

Martina's eyes widened and she snapped her gaze from him to the wide opened bedroom door. "Did you see Jasmin's stuffed toy? She never goes anywhere without it."

"Her bed is empty. No toys in there." By now Irena's voice trembled and so did her hands.

Martina's jaw dropped, fear flashed in her eyes, she'd freak out any moment. Instead, she ran down the stairs to the laptop on the coffee table in the den. "I'll locate her in a few minutes." Keys and charms jingled on her chain. She selected a small, black box. "Let's hope she still has her toy with her."

"Get Jasmin's location." Standing by the den's door, Ante pointed at the device in her hand. His jaw set hard. "They took my baby and they will pay."

Martina nodded, not taking her gaze from the computer screen. "Come on, load up you stupid page." She banged the mouse on the table. "Here." The clicking sounded and the map filled up the screen. She turned to Ante. "So you knew about GPS stuffed inside the toy. My brother suggested I should be checking up on you when you had Jasmin." Martina turned her head toward the three of them crowding her around the coffee table. "Speaking of my brother, where is Kris? Has anyone seen him?"

Dario crossed his arms over his chest and studied his brother's sharp face. Martina's admission was the truth behind Kris' sudden casement of shadowing Ante.

"Now we can pin down on her location. I'll go check on Kris." Ante scurried toward the door of the room at the end of the hallway. In a few seconds, he re-emerged. "Your brother's gone. His gun's not inside the display case either."

Ante's discovery twisted Dario's stomach tighter. If Kris took his gun, he must be hot on a trail of Fred's men. On the other hand, her brother would raise a bunch of his buddies to join him, and the hot-headed armed young guys meant more trouble than Dario wanted.

Martina's jaw clenched as she punched the combination of numbers and letters from the GPS into the Google maps. The position zoomed in on the screen. She turned the laptop toward Dario. "The stuffed toy is here, and if we're lucky our children are too. What is this place?"

Dario crouched in front of the screen and studied the map. By the name of the roads, he figured the location. "These are the abandoned military barracks on the army airport. How on Earth did they get there so fast? What time was it when you heard the thumps?"

"Around midnight." Ante's raw expression clenched Dario's chest. His gaze directed at the screen held snarky disdain. "We may be in luck here. Tom, Ana's...ex, was awarded one of the buildings there in lieu of monetary compensation for his war efforts and injury. He runs his kennels there—"

Loud knocking on the front door made them all jump. Dario stepped to the entrance and pulled them open, admitting the emergency workers inside. The police chief in his plain clothes stepped through and fixed him with a deadly serious glare. His sheer size filled up the narrow hallway making it appear smaller. "Dario?"

"Joe, appreciate you coming here at this early hour." Dario shook hands with the cop, but tension stiffened his arm.

The deputy scanned the scene. "What happened here?"

Dario glanced at Irena, her face pale and eyes wide. To hell with her instance not to involve the cops, the cop was here whether she liked it or not. "You told me to stay low and not do a thing with Fred. Now our kids have been kidnaped."

Irena's jaw dropped and she stared at Dario, then jerked her head toward Joe. "I told you no cops. He's most likely on Fred's payroll."

Joe put his hand up and took a step toward her. "No, I'm not. I can help you."

Her steely gaze stayed on Dario, coiled his insides. "Fine, let's go."

"You have a location on the kids?" Joe's eyebrows arched.

"The GPS inside the stuffed animal is telling us the girls might be at the old military airport." Dario hoped the girls were still there, not just abandoned toy emitting the signal.

The deputy nodded fast, his lips pressed into a thin line as if calculating the distance from their island to their destination. "Okay, we'll take the police power boat. It's faster."

The emergency people proceeded to check the vitals on Ante. Martina's father shuffled his feet in slippers across the floor. "Your mother is taking all of this pretty hard."

Martina stepped up to him and hugged him, but Dario caught the tremble in her voice. "I know, Dad. We'll get the girls back. I'll come see Mom in a few minutes. Stay with her and reassure her everything will be fine."

"He's good to go." The EMS tapped Ante's shoulder.

Ante got to his feet, grabbed Martina in a hug. Her chin trembled and her eyes brimmed with tears. "Go get our cricket back. Bring her home."

Irena heaved, sucking her lips between her teeth. "This is all my fault. If I never came here this wouldn't happen."

Exhaling loudly failed to loosen Dario's chest. He embraced Irena. "It's too late for ifs, too late for recourses. All we can do now is save our kids."

Ante released Martina from the bear hug. Irena slid next to her and touched her arm. "We'll get her back, you have my word."

Martina's stern expression mellowed and tears freely flowed down her face. "I know you're in the same situation. At least Jasmin has Ella. I know your daughter will protect her little cousin. Go now, bring them home."

"Stay strong and have faith." Irena embraced Martina then stepped away from her and gave her a single nod. God almighty, anyone else would fall apart, have a massive emotional meltdown, but not her. The worst fears have become the reality and now the years of training were kicking in and her toughness and determination held her intact.

During the brisk walk through the narrow and empty streets of the village, Dario speed-dialed Tom's number, but voicemail picked up on the fourth ring. He left him a message. If luck was with them tonight, the man would wait for them at his kennels, perps apprehended and girls safe and sound. That may be too much to hope for.

The police power boat bobbed on gentle swells in the snug harbor. The lines tied the starboard at the bow and stern to the wharf, stretching and creaking with a movement of the boat.

Dario swallowed against his dry throat. In less than an hour, they would discover the fate of the girls. They could be in hands of sexual deviants. What could they be living through right now?

Joe untied the lines and set the boat flush to the pier. With his foot planted on the starboard, he held the boat steady, then tweaked his head at the small party to start boarding.

Irena jumped in first. Dario followed her onto the small deck, Ante was right behind him. Joe turned the engine, the sea under the stern foamed. He retrieved the anchor and the boat inched away from the pier.

Irena settled on the seat at the stern, her jaw tight. The fine salt bullets assaulted the boat as soon as they cleared the bay and picked up speed. Ante hunkered low and found the shelter from the gusty wind on the starboard, flattening his back against the side. Dario wrapped his arms around Irena, sheltering her from the cold.

"Got a minute, Dario?" Joe called over his shoulder.

Irena gave Dario a nod and shifted toward the railing, pulling the hood of her jacket over her head.

Dario grasped for handholds, stepped to Joe who stared at the three beams of lights mounted on the rack above their heads, chasing the darkness from the boat.

"I saw you sparring with her and a younger girl at Kris' gym. They have some stealthy moves I couldn't pinpoint the type of martial arts, looks like some kind of hybrid fighting technique."

"Mother and daughter fight as a team." Dario glanced over his shoulder. Irena's face wasn't visible under her hood, her head resting on her bent arm. Perhaps she was gathering her wits and strength for what was coming. A warrior's tactic. He turned to Joe and continued, "I have a feeling you know more about Fred than you are willing to share. Why? Are you protecting someone?"

"Soon, you'll find out." Joe's face remained hard, his gaze set dead ahead.

"Irena thinks the police might be corrupted by this man."

Joe screwed his face. "Wouldn't be the first time the police chief's pockets got lined."

"She wants the ordeal to be handled discreetly and not to involve city cops unless necessary."

"I'm already ahead of you."

"Thank you, Joe. I knew I could count on you." By Joe's vague tone, Dario concluded, the cop was hiding something, but at least one knot loosened in Dario's guts.

"I alerted my bud, an ambulance attendant. Just in

case, they'll park on the road."

Dario couldn't decide whether Joe's words eased or upset him more. Could they need emergency medical help? Perhaps it wouldn't hurt.

"Good to know—" A long, shrill chirping of his cell phone had him reaching into his jacket pocket. The unknown number flashed on the screen. Should he take the call? It could be important. He tapped accept call button and pressed the mobile to his ear. "Hello?"

Loud breathing came through the line.

"Who is this?" Dario snapped. The last thing he needed right now was some prank call.

More loud breathing.

"I'm hanging up now, perv."

"No! Dario! Don't." The voice came broken up by heavy puffing.

"Who's this?"

"Andy."

"Andy?" Why did that name sound familiar?

"The receptionist from the Bastion hotel. Ella gave me your number. In case…you know…of an emergency." The loud swallow came from Andy's end.

Dario's mind blanked for a split second, he couldn't come up with right words. "Where are you?"

"At the abandoned military airport. My buddy and I just returned from fishing when this big speedboat comes into the harbor, set all the boats into the wild bob with the huge wake it raised. Then I saw a couple of guys toss Ella and another girl into a car trunk and drove off. We hopped on our scooters and followed them."

"Andy, those men are dangerous. You and your friend need to get away from there. We're on our way, will be there shortly."

"My bud's staying with scooters by the road."
Andy chuckled. "He chickened out. I can get the girls
out in no time if I can pick the lock."

"The lock?"

"Yeah, they are locked inside a dog's crate. I see
them through the broken window. They're asleep."

A dog's crate? Rage boiled inside Dario. Once he
got his hands on Fred, he'd stuff him in into a crate size
meant for a Chihuahua pup. "Andy, no. This is not a
joke. Listen to me—"

"I know these barracks. Hang out here with some
bad crowd." A huff sounded from Andy's end, then he
blurted, "In the past."

"Andy, get away from there before someone sees
you." Panic swelled in Dario's chest. He stuck his
finger into the free ear to hear Andy over the roar of the
engines and high winds.

"No one saw us. We were careful. Hey! Oh shit."

Muffled voices and shouts filled Dario's ear.
"Andy! What's going on?"

"Kid's curfew bell just rung," a man's voice
blasted through the line before it went dead.

"Shit!" Dario punched the console, then shook his
hand as pain shot through his arm. "They got another
kid, or possibly two. Can this boat go any faster?"

"We're already pushing at a top speed." Joe shoved
his arm toward the dark surface in front of them. "At
least the sea is calm tonight. And look!" He pointed
straight ahead.

Dario forced air into his lungs and peered into the
night. In the distance, islands loomed over the dark sea
like silent sentiments. A thin, hazy line of city lights

beaconed over the expanse. For the next twenty minutes, he kept glancing at his wristwatch. Only the drone of the engine cut through the heavy silence. The mass of land they headed toward grew bigger. Still, it seemed the boat moved at the snail's pace and he cursed each minute it took to bring them closer.

## Chapter 20

The police car sped down the country road, leaving behind the distant lights of the city. Shrouded in the moon's glow, the dense forest replaced cultivated fields. Irena snuggled in Dario's arms, and he tried hard not to think these could be their last moments together. Ante occupied the passenger's seat, clutched the handle above the window with each sway of the car, racing along the twisting road.

What waited for them at the old military airport? Would they make it in time to save his daughter and little niece? The girls faced horrible futures if they failed.

After several kilometers of heavy silence, a rusty signpost flashed in the headlight warned they were approaching what was once a military installation. The outlines of the abandoned barracks appeared in the distance. From his vantage point, Dario couldn't detect any activity.

The car slowed down and Joe pulled to the curb.

"Why are we stopping here?" Dario clenched and unclenched his fist, releasing the stiffness from the long grip on the door handle.

Joe turned to face him. "We're meeting someone. He's undercover cop and poses as one of Fred's thugs. Do as he says or his cover could get blown and we get killed."

Dario swallowed a lump in his throat. He let go of Irena's hand and the cold claimed his skin at the loss of contact. Her face was unreadable as she exchanged a hard glance with him, then stepped out of the car.

No sounds came from the clump of trees across the ditch, but winter still held its grip over nature. Joe turned on the small flashlight in his hand and pressed the button twice, the light blinked into the darkness. The same signal replied from behind the pines. A few seconds later a dark figure sidled into the clearing, his broad shoulders suggested a large man, a deep hood covering his face. He stopped several paces from them.

"Buddy." Joe gave the newcomer an acknowledging nod. "These people are in need of help."

"Buddy?" Dario directed his question at Joe. Could he put his hopes in someone who went by an alias and not very smart one?

"That's all you need to know about me." Buddy's deep yet quiet voice iced Dario's blood. The man was about to reveal something sinister.

"Your girls are fine...for now." Buddy shoved his large hands inside his hoodie pockets.

"You didn't even try to save them?" Ante's loathing look was directed at Buddy.

"No, I bide my time until Fred slips."

"You let them get away with kidnapping our kids." Ante tightened his fists, his breathing heavy. "How could you?"

"Just hear me out first." Buddy put his hands up in stop-right-there gesture. "For months we've been working alongside Europol on cases involving the disappearance of teens. All leads pointed to Mr. Penne, but all we had was mere speculations. We needed hard evidence or the case would get overthrown on circumstantial claims."

"I'm gonna kill you." Ante lunged at Buddy, threw a punch, but Dario grabbed his brother's other elbow and held him back.

Ante wrenched his arm free and jabbed at Buddy. He jumped back. Ante's fist punched the air again. His reddened face stood out even in the darkness.

"Dammit man! He's here to help us." Dario tightened his grip on Ante's arm, his nerves raw. "He risked his life to meet us here. Cool it now and do what you're told."

Irena stepped into the circle, yanking down the sleeves of her jacket. Dario glimpsed a brace on her right forearm. She grabbed Ante's wrist as he was about to lunge at Buddy again. "Stop it, Ante. Dario is right. We need to work together. It's hard to stay calm when our girls are taken, but if we want to get them back safe and sound, we cannot let emotions control us."

Ante dropped his arms, letting them dangle by his sides. "How can I? They got my baby."

"They took mine too." Irena's face mellowed. She hugged him, then stepped back. "It's hard, I know. But this is our chance to get hard evidence against Fred and stop him for good. So he can't do this to another child ever again."

Ante drew in a long breath. His shoulders rose and fell with his hard exhale. He nodded and turned to Buddy. "Sorry man. I lost it there."

"No need to apologize, I understand. Come, I'll take you to Tom where he's waiting with his men. Then I have to return before someone suspects I'm taking a too long piss."

Hope kindled in Dario's mind. "Tom's there? How do you know him?"

"We're war buddies. I got him a job after the war...he couldn't deal with the chain of command, as always. Guess he learned nothing in combat." Buddy nodded. "But enough of going down the memory line. Tom's kennels are there. Fred's men killed two of Tom's best dogs. He's furious."

Ante jerked his head toward the road. "What are we waiting for? Let's move. I want Fred's head before Tom gets to him."

"The lineup to Fred's head is this way." Buddy extended his arm toward the woods. The direction he'd emerged from.

Ante harrumphed but said nothing. By his pursed lips, he was still fuming. One by one, the men entered the wooded area, the dry grass and pine needles crunched under their feet.

Irena slid her gloved hand in Dario's. "Can we trust these men?"

He squeezed her hand. "I trust them more than I'd trust the police. By the way, why are you wearing an arm brace?"

"The vambrace is for protection, and for hiding a blade."

Blood froze at her casual tone. He couldn't find the right words. She was a brave woman, still, he couldn't comprehend she must carry such weapon. "Not to kill I hope."

"If I have to in self-defense, though I rather incapacitate. "

Buddy halted in front of them and raised his hand then signaled to crouch. Tall grass and shrubbery in the ditch prevented Dario from seeing what was happening on the gravel path above them.

Whoever was approaching with slow steps hummed off-key. Footfalls ceased in front of Dario. Close enough to make out camouflage pants tucked inside the black army boots through the blades of grass. In a slow and quiet motion, he slid the foliage apart enough to see the figure a few feet in front of them.

The man stopped humming and a flicked the lighter in his hand. A small flame drew Dario's gaze to the guard's face. Those long tufts of the man's hair anyone could confuse for a woman's. Before he could light the cigarette dangling from his lips, the night breeze smote the flame out.

"Shit," The man shook the Zippo in his hand and snapped the flame to life again. He took a deep drag and the tip of his cigarette turned bright orange. The illumination revealed his long face. Then he exhaled, and wisps of white smoke curled around his hand.

Ante gripped Dario's arm and whispered, "It's him."

"Who?" Dario mouthed.

"Justin." Ante hissed, but Dario shook his head. "Justin Trudich, the one who came asking for a job."

Dario's jaw dropped. That guard had come looking for employment the night Irena returned. Two days later their restaurant had burned and now the guy surfaced in Fred's employ. The dots started to connect. However, if their high school classmate had set fire to Mezzaluna, squeezing him for money would prove useless. Like most on Fred's payroll, the guy was flat broke.

The smell of cheap tobacco filled the brisk night

air. The guard blew out another long breath of white smoke, dug in his pant pocket and pulled out a familiar looking amulet.

With the cigarette in his mouth, he examined the rock, plucked the cig out and blew the smoke over the pebble, then kissed it. "Irena, I'll make you scream my name."

Dario exchanged a glance with Irena. Her upturned lips and protruding tongue confirmed he'd heard the dolt correctly. Guys had lusted after her in high school, the fact she wasn't a flirty girl and faithful to him, made the boys' fantasies hotter. But they all outgrew their teen days, matured and moved on. Proved how wrong he'd been.

Buddy jerked his head toward the guard, indicating he'd distract him while the group crawled to their destined spot.

Irena placed her hand on Buddy's shoulder, stopping him. "He's got something of mine."

Buddy nodded. "That amulet in his hand? I'll get it back." He motioned to Joe to continue on and Dario nudged Irena forward, following the lead in a single file. Buddy joined him after a few seconds, handing him the amulet. "The guards' rifle didn't have any bullets. What good is a fire weapon without ammo?"

"A scare tactic. Wonder if all of the guards are armed or if the guns are just for show," Dario said, placing the amulet in Irena's hand. He pointed at the long ground story building that still bore scars of the fighting from the bloody civil war over twenty years ago.

A small group waited hidden in the ticket a few feet away from the back entrance. A man approached them as soon as Dario led Irena closer. In his protective gear, Dario had a hard time recognizing Tom.

Tom's gaze shifted to Irena and a grin stretched his lips. "Irena Novak. Every guy from Tesla High's wet dream. Never thought I'd see you again. And you look mighty fine."

Dario seethed inside. Tom had admitted he too lusted after Irena, but respected the fact she was with Dario. Had their friend forgotten his vows?

"I never thought I'd see you either, Viper. Each time you and your sidekicks showed up at the school we knew someone was going to get their ass kicked and girls would be teased. Only the custodian wasn't afraid of you."

"It's been a while since anyone called me that." Tom's pout turned into a grin. "I'm on the good side now."

"Sorry to hear about your war injury." Irena gave him the once over as if to find out if he was disabled.

Tom patted his left leg. "Thanks to my lucky stars, the blast from the mine sent me flying backward. The explosion ripped the heel of my foot, but reconstructive surgery does wonders nowadays." He dismissed the reminiscing with a wave of his hand. "We have to make our move now. Fred's desperate to leave. Though I know he's not going anywhere." Tom pulled a long cylindrical object out of his vest pocket.

At Irena's and Dario's stunned look, he continued, "Came here two days ago, my dogs were quite timid. Did some snooping around and found a plane hidden in that hangar." He pointed at the depilated aluminum structure behind them. "Someone's using my property without my permission or knowledge. Today my guy calls me all panicky. He found two of my breeders shot dead. This won't go down easy. I had him move the animals to another location. When I found out it was Fred, I wanted to rip his guts out. If it wasn't for Buddy here who promised I'll get the first chance if I work with him, I'd have Fred's head by now. But the twat is holding hostages." Tom shook the object in his hand. "And I'm holding the starter from his plane engine."

"Please Vip...um sorry, Tom. We have to move now." Irena took his hand, desperation in her eyes and voice.

"First, you two need bulletproof vests." Tom waved his hand over his shoulder and one of his men rushed to him, two blue vests dangling in his hands.

Dario fastened the clasps of the vest, not believing he was wearing one of these close-fitting, protective garments. Would things heat up to such dangerous levels?

"Let's move," Buddy called over the group. "Dario, Irena, you are with me. Joe and Ante with Tom."

"It's about time," Tom grumbled, waving his rifle above his head. Three of his men piled into a single file in front of him.

Irena grabbed Tom's elbow, gaining his attention. "The guards' weapons may not be loaded. Please, I don't want anyone killed. These men are not trained soldiers, and most likely not aware of what they got themselves into. Order your guys to only shoot if they have to and not to slay."

Tom pointed at the two bound and unconscious guards. "Already figured as much."

Tom and three of his men split to take the other

doors. Ante nodded to Dario and jogged to catch up with Tom. Buddy cast her a weary look then entered the building first. Dario took Irena's hand and entered.

A dark and long corridor stretched before them. Light fixtures without bulbs hung from the crumbling ceiling. Debris of all kind scattered along the cement floor. Dario tried to avoid stepping on anything that would crunch or snap under his foot.

Buddy patted the gun tucked inside the shoulder holster and flattened his back against the dirty wall. "Fred and his main guards are in there. Kids are with them too. I'll go in and assess the situation."

Dario nodded but his throat lumped, his breathing erratic. He tried to catch a glimpse of anything as Buddy slipped through the double swivel doors, but saw nothing other than an upturned table.

Fred's voice boomed in the abandoned warehouse. "You stand to lose a heck of more than your pilot's license if you don't fly us out of here. I don't care that you're not a mechanic, fix it."

Muffled voices followed and Buddy burst out of the room, a tall man in tow. "Fred's expecting you. I must help the pilot get the plane ready." He leaned closer to Dario and whispered, "Joining Tom after I take care of the aviator."

Dario exchanged another uneasy look with Irena, but Buddy's winked ensured them he had the situation under control. Shoving her behind him, Dario led her inside the large room that at one point might've served as a canteen for the soldiers. Broken and upturned tables and chairs pushed under the windows indicated the objects had served as a barricade during the war.

Fred sat in the dark corner, Jasmin on his lap. She

was dressed in a lacy, red dress clearly made for an older girl, her lips painted in a red lipstick and her hair was pulled back into a messy bun. Earrings dangled from her ears, white beads encircled her neck. In her hands, she loosely held a fancy doll, but her shoulders jerked with spasms. Tears streaked her dirty cheeks and her eyes were red and puffy from crying.

"Who says I don't like girls?" Fred slid his hand down Jasmin's bare arm and kissed her hair. "See, I love them at this age. While they're still androgynous."

Dario's heart broke. If they did something horrid to his niece and daughter, Fred would beg for an easy death. "Jasmin, honey, it's okay. That man won't hurt you. Just come to me."

Fred lowered his head to Jasmin's ear. "Tell your uncle what will happen if you obey him."

Jasmin shook her head. Her whimper dug the knife deeper into Dario's heart.

"Come on, love, we talked about it, didn't we?" Fred brushed his knuckles down Jasmin's cheek, making her shiver. "I'll get you another toy when we get in our castle. What would you like? A pony? I know every girl would love a real pony. Now, tell your uncle what will happen if you're disobedient."

"The bad men will kill you." Her voice quivered as she spoke without making eye contact with Dario. "They are everywhere."

"Do they have bullets like the guards outside?" Dario glanced around the dark room, trying to catch a glimpse of hidden men who had their weapons trained on him and Irena. Instead, his heart stopped when he spotted Ella's lifeless body inside the dog's crate. Andy lay next to her, holding her hand.

269

"I see you found Ella and her friend. The boy protected her and took some beating. Still, the little cunt of yours broke two of my men's noses." Fred's smirked. Despite rage brewing inside Dario, he managed to stay calm.

"They stuck needles in her. Lots of needles." Jasmin blurted before Fred could stop her. "She fought them. They made her stop or they'd hurt me."

"Your daughter is still alive, for how long, I don't know." Fred set Jasmin on the dirty floor and got up. He strode to Irena. "It was fun watching you enjoy your happy life. I bet you started believing you could have it all. Now it's my pleasure to take it away from you."

Dario wanted to yell for Jasmin to run, but where would she go? Shots fired outside. She could get killed in crossfire or by an overzealous guard. No, she was safer here where Dario could keep an eye on her. He caught the glimpse of her feet as she pulled them behind the crate where Ella laid.

The fighting outside was subsiding, but sporadic shouts and confusion seemed to continue.

Fred snapped his fingers. Two men in black martial arts uniforms emerged from the side door. By their smooth faces and slim builds, Dario concluded the boys could still be in their teens. Their belts displayed ribbons they won at tournaments. They were about to find out street fighting was nothing like controlled competition sparring.

"Guys, here's your opponent. She prepared for this all her life. Don't be fooled by her appearance. She can kick your butt." Fred pointed to Dario. "You are to sit this one out."

"At least make the fight fair." Dario rolled up his

270

sleeves, ready to blow out some pent-up steam. And when Fred least expected, he'd turn on him.

"Don't say I didn't try to spare you." Fred took the seat at the end of the table.

"I could've taken these boys all by myself. Now I'll have to watch out for you. Try to stay out of their reach." She nodded to the guys and they took their fighting stances, feet apart, fists protecting their faces. "Jiyu Kumite!" At her command, the opponents bowed deeply.

One of them had a look of uncertainty on his face. He turned to his buddy. "A freestyle sparring?"

Dario crouched. Yep he assumed correctly, the two boys hadn't seen any fighting outside the dojo. Well, they were about to find out there was no referee to stop him from beating them to a pulp.

Irena stood still, her uncompromising glare at the man in front of her. What was she waiting for? He moved with slow motions, then threw a punch so fast the air snapped. She blocked his thrusting arm and grabbed his wrist, but he yanked his arm back. Dario's opponent roared and charged at him. The youngster's earlier uncertain expression replaced with cocky confidence. The boy took a timid lunge forward. Dario gripped his arm and pulled him forward. He wrapped his leg around the boy's and dropped him flat on his back. In a swift thrust of his legs, his opponent was back on his feet. In his low crouch stance, Dario waited for the guy to charge again.

Behind him, Irena battled the other. She parried each thrust by ducking down, swaying to the side or jumping out of the way. Her foe grunted in frustration, but so far had not cried out in pain.

Dario's rival kicked his foot high, connecting with his forehead. Pain ripped through his head, and a warm trickle reached his eyebrow. The karate kid should know the high kicks only looked good in action movies. Yet, he tried the same move again, giving Dario a good chance to throw his opponent off balance. By seizing his ankle, Dario twisted the assailant's leg. The boy's bones crunched under Dario's hands before he dropped him on his side. The youngster howled and clutched his limb close to his chest. He crawled backward on his behind and retreated from the match, tears streaking his face. If this was the top of Fred's crop, then Dario would love to see the rest.

"Coward," Fred roared, jumping to his feet. "Get back here and fight."

Dario snatched the chance and charged on Fred. To hell with his armed men waiting in shadows. There was no one there, or they would fill him with bullets.

He seized Fred by his bony shoulders and forced him to the floor. One hand curled into a fist, ready to pound on the skinny man's back. Damn it. He dropped the arm by his side. His parents had taught him never to beat a weakling, no matter how much they deserved it.

"No, Daddy, don't." Fred pleaded with the childlike voice. "Please Daddy, don't pull my pants down, I'm a good boy. Mommy says so."

Dario backed off. He just unlocked the secret of Fred's perversion and as much as he wanted to rip his guts out, he couldn't bring himself to do so. The lack of fighting sounds from Irena's direction had him pivoting to face the front of the room. She stood there. Her mouth agape, her eyes big and round.

Fred miraculously got over his childhood trauma

and rose to his feet. "You fell for that, didn't cha?" He shook his fist at the remaining boy. "Stop dicking around." He screamed at Irena's opponent. "Finish her."

The young man's eyes narrowed to thin slits. Before Irena could assume her fighting stance, he grabbed her arm and twisted. A piercing cry of pain ripped from her. Fred cackled and clapped his hands. "Now we're talking."

Dario rushed to help her, but she flicked the wrist of her free arm, releasing the blade. "I've got this. Help the kids."

Blood from the cut on his forehead dripped into his eye. He swiped at the crimson droplets and ran to the dog crate. The lock on the cage door stopped him from reaching inside. He slid his hand through the bars and touched Ella's forehead. Heat emanated from her skin. God, she was burning up with a fever. Andy placed his hand on his, showing he had comforted Ella.

In a fit of rage, Irena slashed the boy's wrist and he released his grip on her. Her arm bent at an impossible angle. Clutching his bleeding wound, he took a step back with each blow she administered, until he cowered in the corner. Irena hacked wherever she reached. The boy cradled his head in his arms, pleading for her to stop. Blood smeared his crisp uniform.

Tom and his men burst into the room, their weapons trained on Fred. Tom spoke. "Hard as it was, we didn't kill anyone but had to wound a few. Fred's men had loaded guns."

Fred's grin slowly turned into frenzied laughter. "You think this is the end? My lawyers will make a couple of phone calls and I'll be free."

Zrinka Jelic

"Not so fast." Irena grabbed the pistol from Buddy and pointed the gun at Fred.

Fred's smirk dropped from his face. He glared at Buddy. "I had a feeling you were a cop." Fred returned his mocking face to Irena. "Oh, please, whatcha gonna do with that? You're so fatuous. You'd end up shooting yourself. Besides, didn't cha know that I'm the Koschei the Immortal?" He sent another hate-filled glare at Dario. "That's right. I find out who you'd named me for, and to my delightful surprise, the name fits me."

"I doubt that." Buddy crossed his arms over his massive chest. "All of us who graduated under communist rule had weapons training in high school."

The sharp sound of metal pierced the heavy air as Irena cocked the gun. "You're not immortal. We're holding the egg, Koschei."

Fred paled and swallowed, then slowly raised his arms, but his glare stayed on Irena.

She lowered her arm. The sheer gloss of sweat on her face showed her pain. How much longer before she'd need medical attention? "You're not worth the jail time, or having you on my conscience."

The gun slipped from her hand and she stumbled, falling to her knees. Tom grabbed her before she collapsed to the dirty floor. "I'd kill you with my bare hands. First, you molest my kid, humiliate my woman, then slay two of my dogs."

"Your woman is a gold-digger, your kid is a weakling and running a puppy mill is illegal." Fred ran his fingers through his thin, messy hair, then straightened his suit jacket.

Tom glared at Fred. "You dumb idiot," he roared. "I run legit kennels here and my dogs are prized." He

274

took a threatening step toward Fred. "Insult my kid and my wife again and you'll be picking your teeth off the floor."

Fred snorted, taking a long step back, away from Tom's fist. "Well, it doesn't look like you're about to carry out your threat. If there's no one else who wants to kill me, I'll be off." Fred was about to step away from his pedestal, but Dario tripped him.

A skinny man in raggedy clothes pushed through the line of armed men. Days' growth of beard covered most of his face. He grabbed the gun from the floor and pointed the weapon at Fred. "Irena can't have you on her conscience, but I can."

"Put that gun down, Diego. We both know you won't shoot anyone." Fred pushed on the barrel, his tone, gentle as if addressing a little boy.

So this was Father Diego. The man's appearance didn't portray a priest, but a desperate man grasping the frail ends of his rope.

"From this distance, I can't miss." Diego's hand shook. "Yes, I gave the files from the school to the FBI. Your child prostitution ring is busted. You're, we're done…and so am I."

The flash and thunder of the gun, coupled by Jasmin's scream came so sudden. Horror filled Fred's expression as he watched blood soak into his white, neatly ironed shirt. He tried stopping the flow by pressing his hands over the wound. Crimson trickles rushed between his fingers. His legs buckled and his body dropped to the floor, the red stain spread over the broken tiles.

Diego took a step back then slowly raised the gun to his temple, tears soaking his face. Buddy's mouth moved, Dario couldn't hear, though the man thundered. In one stride, Buddy grabbed Diego's wrist and pulled his hand away just as the click of the trigger sounded. The gun shifted upward and the bullet wedged in the crumbling ceiling, sending the dry stucco into the air. Diego dropped the pistol on the floor and collapsed.

The next several moments passed in a blur. Dario wanted to carry Irena to Ella's side, but given her broken arm, he thought against moving her before her limb was immobilized. Divided between helping his daughter and Irena, he rushed from one end of the room to the next, stopping only to pat his jacket sleeve on his brow. The ambulance arrived and the attendant urged him to stay with Irena until they got Ella stabilized for transfer to the hospital. Then slapped gauze on his forehead and told him to hold the pressure. Jasmin rushed to Ante and cradled in his arms.

Ante glared at Fred's body on the ground. "So the priest got to him first. If it wasn't for our upbringing, I'd kick Fred's dead body until he's unrecognizable mush."

"Let it go, bro." Dario tapped Ante's back. "It's over."

He stepped outside. The sound of blaring sirens grew louder, the headlights flickering through the trees. Seated next to Joe, they followed the ambulance down the same winding road. The vehicle carried his heavily drugged daughter and his Irena with a badly broken arm and a dislocated shoulder. His world was still black.

## Chapter 21

Spasms jolted Ella's body and with each one Dario's heart clenched tighter. Uneven, fast beeping filled the tiny hospital room. At least the noise brought a nurse in on a whirlwind.

The woman turned off the sound on the machine and proceeded to check Ella's vitals. She tapped the drip bringing fluids to Ella through the tube connected to the needle inserted into her vein.

"The doctor is still waiting for her lab test so we'll know what's in her system." She studied the screen, then adjusted the wires connecting Ella to the monitor and pressed the red button. The beeping resumed, more steady now. Oxygen mask covering Ella's mouth and nose fogged up with her even breaths.

He took his daughter's hot hand and twined his fingers with her lifeless ones. His girl was suffering and there was nothing he could do for her. The tension in his neck and shoulders increased. A piercing headache in his temples caused him to shut his eyes tight. No amount of pestering the hospital staff would hurry those lab tests. He smoothed her hair and kissed her temple. What would he do if he never again heard her adorable giggle? Unimaginable.

His breath hitched and his nerves high-strung. "Baby girl, it's your dad. You're a fighter. Fight this and get back to us."

Ante knocked on the door. "Hey, how's she doing?"

"They took blood samples and are still waiting for the results." Dario lowered Ella's hand onto the bed but kept their fingers laced. He couldn't let the fear of losing this new life he'd found a little over a month ago overwhelm him. "Irena's in surgery. Her arm is mangled pretty badly. And I'm...."

Ante pursed his lips and nodded once, then joined him in his vigil over Ella. "Have you had that cut on your forehead looked at?"

Dario touched the wound. He winced at the contact of the bump under the dressing. His fingers came unbloodied. He was supposed to have had the laceration cleaned and taped, but he couldn't leave Ella's side. "It stopped bleeding."

The long pause between him and Ante stretched into an uncomfortable silence. Unable to listen to the beeping of the life monitoring machine, Dario asked, "How's Jasmin?"

Ante shifted in his chair, the metal legs scraping the tiled floor. "She's finally asleep. They gave her a mild sedative. Physically, she isn't hurt, but she'll have to be assessed by a child psychologist. I've never seen her so excited and chatty. The doctor says it's a defense mechanism."

Dario placed his hand on Ante's shoulder. "Kids are resilient." But that didn't excuse what Fred had done to her...what he tried to do. If Diego hadn't got him first, he'd strangle Fred with his bare hands.

More silence stretched between them. Ante exhaled loudly and leaned his head on the green wall. "Martina's on her way. Her brother returned to the island to take her to the city after he lost track of Fred's boat."

Dario rubbed his tired eyes. He was beyond exhaustion but had refused the sedative the doctor offered him. He needed his head clear. "It's a good thing or the bloodshed would have been worse."

"You got that right and Fred could've escaped. Kris is still a hotheaded teenager at heart." Ante yawned. "If he saw Jasmin in that dress and lipstick...God...I can't think of that." Ante shook his head as if to dispel the image. "What boggles my mind is why Fred put all his men outside while he sat in that dingy room with the kids."

Dario blinked slowly, his eyelids sticking together. "Who knows? The man was deranged."

Ante gave Ella's hand a soft squeeze. "You must pull through this. That poor guy, Andy, took a vicious beating while protecting you girls. Don't let his suffering be all for nothing." Ante returned his gaze to Dario. "How many youngsters would do that nowadays?"

Remorse stirred in Dario. Andy deserved to date his daughter. "His mother must be crushed."

"Yeah, I heard her wailing next door to Jasmin, so I went to see them. The boy's on the mend. He's asking about the girls." Ante tapped his foot nervously against the chair leg.

More guilt coiled Dario's insides. "I never expected Andy to find himself in the thick of it."

"Andy said Fred wouldn't allow his men near them. Fred would lose money if they weren't virgins. The priest got the worst of it. The kid heard him crying and begging. Joe found him naked, tied to some strange contraption, bloody and bruised on his...ahem...hind quarters."

Fuck! Fred was a monster. "Sick pervert. We all had good reasons to kill him, but that priest had most." Dario got to his feet and tried to shove the details in that room and Jasmin on Fred's lap...some porcelain toy from his memory.

What had Fred planned to do? Would Fred have kept her as his newest pet until her body blossomed, then discard her in his school where grown freaks would have their way with her? What kind of twisted sexual fetishes had those weirdos inflicted on children? Powerful people who should protect the young, instead they allowed the horrors to go on for their own sick perversions. The train of thought was entering a dangerous territory, churned his stomach. He needed a distraction. "Irena should be out of surgery by now. I'll go check with the nurse."

"Before I forget..." Ante dug into his pants pocket and pulled out Irena's half of their amulet. "Jasmin had this inside her dress. Fred let her hold it so she would stop crying."

"The amulet! Irena has my half Buddy took from that guard." Dario reached for the rock in Ante's hand. "Ella believes she can make it whole again."

Ante's expression of disbelief irked Dario, but he ignored his brother and approached the nurses' station. One girl in light blue scrubs typed fast on the keyboard, a pencil between her teeth.

"I'm sorry to bother you." He leaned over the counter.

"Yes?" she said, not breaking her glance from the computer monitor, keys clicking under her flying fingers.

"Are there any updates on Irena Novak?"

She plucked the pencil from her mouth. "Let me check." The nurse took the phone receiver and four beeps sounded as she dialed the extension. She doodled on the pad. After several um-hums and uh-has, and a couple of yes's and okay's punctured by chuckles, she finally hung up and turned to him. "They are just finishing up in OR and will transfer your fiancée to the recovery."

"When can I see her?"

"When she wakes from the general anesthesia and her doctor says she's fine to go to her room." The nurse nodded. Her hair pulled into a tight ponytail bobbed, then she returned to her typing. The phone on the nurse's desk rang and she swiveled her chair toward the sound.

He caught sight of Ella's doctor entering her room and hurried back.

The doctor pulled his glasses off and rubbed bloodshot eyes. It must've been a long night for him too. "Her tests are back. Traces of multiple drugs were found in her blood. On their own, none are lethal. Together, however, they can wreak havoc on the nervous system, especially of one so young. The Naloxone is the best treatment. I'll give her some other medication to stimulate urination and flush any remaining drugs out of her system faster. The next forty-eight hours are critical, but I expect her to recover."

Pressure eased from Dario's chest. Still, his Ella wasn't out of the woods. "Can she have any permanent damage?"

"It's possible, but a person who overdoses usually recovers fully with assistance." The doctor pushed his frameless glasses up his thin nose. The beeper clipped to his waist emitted a high-pitched sound. He pressed the button and tilted a narrow window up to read the message. "I've got to run. See a nurse for that cut on your forehead."

"Thank you, I will." Dario smiled for the first time since Irena accepted his proposal. Then she'd had her premonition and happiness vanished.

"Finally some good news." Ante patted Dario's back. "I'll try to get some shut-eye before Martina gets here. Hey, did I hear that nurse say Irena was your fiancée? Are congrats in order, bro?"

"They will be after we put this ugliness behind us. Go get some sleep." After his brother left Ella's room, Dario returned to his chair and brushed his daughter's hair. "You'll be fine."

Ella's lids twitched, but otherwise, she remained the same, pale and warm. Her chest rose and fell in equal intervals.

An older nurse came in to clean and dress his cut. At least the fresh bandage eased some of his discomforts. He glanced at the nurse from the desk who stepped into the room after the older one left. "Any news?"

"Yes, your fiancée's moved into her room. You can see her now."

He sprang to his feet, then locked his gaze on Ella. How was he to leave her and go see Irena? "Um...can my daughter get moved in with her mother?"

"No, they are treated for different things. Plus, the rooms are single occupancy. I can monitor her from my desk. If there are any changes, I'll page her doctor and call you over the hospital's PA."

He stared at Ella, uncertain, but the nurse in her pale blue scrubs pointed at the corridor. "The elevator is down that hall. Your fiancée is one floor up in room two-oh-two."

He stepped to Ella's bed and kissed her forehead. "I'm going to see Mom. Please wake up by the time I return."

The nurse gave him an encouraging smile. He headed for the elevators. He would run if he had the energy. His tired feet moved, one then the other on his wobbly legs and he almost believed those were not his steps, someone else was walking.

The sight of Irena froze him at the doorway, even in the dimmed light of her room. Metal spikes supported her left arm in a white cast from the base of her fingers to her shoulder. Her face bruised. Her beautiful pale blue eyes swollen shut.

He cleared the lump from his throat and stepped to her bed. "Hey, babe, how are you feeling?"

"About as good as I must look."

"You look fine."

"Liar." A shadow of a smile touched her lips. The effort made her moan and clench her jaw. "How are the kids?"

"On the mend." He couldn't burden her with Ella's condition yet. He straightened the covers over her chest. "Rest now."

"Stay with me. Until I fall asleep." She reached her right hand to him. "Tell me I didn't dream Fred's dead."

"He's gone, babe and can't hurt us." Dario pulled

the chair closer to the bed and took her hand. "I need my half of the amulet. You wouldn't believe it, but Fred gave Jasmin your piece."

"He had it all this time? Oh, God. I blamed Ella for losing it." Irena's voice held regret. "Why do you need it?"

"Ella thinks she could make it whole again." Dario's doubts surfaced. He believed in impossible, but unexplainable urge pushed him forward.

Irena sighed. "It's just a story I told her when she was little. It came to me in a dream. Kids at school were mean to her when she made a Father's Day card for you and I needed something to tell her how special she is. I thought she'd forgotten about it."

His heart clenched, his child had faced scrutiny from her peers for being fatherless, yet she loved him from afar while he had no idea she existed.

"What if that story is true? Ella told me of your dreams. I had the same nightmares." Had someone told him things he'd dismissed as absurd might be doable, he'd have a good laugh, but right now, he was ready to accept anything.

"God, that Gypsy woman from the fair would scare me every time. I was glad when the horror ceased. But what would that amulet do if it's whole again?" Irena rolled her head away from him and yawned. "Pain killers are kicking in. I need to sleep now."

"Yes, rest." He yawned too and lowered his head on the bed. The Gypsy woman had tried to communicate with them through their dreams. What had she tried to tell them? Something about mending, if he read her lips correctly. At the time, the message hadn't made any sense, now it seemed logical. "The amulet could have healing powers."

Irena muttered something incoherent. Her even breathing said she was asleep. With his family out of immediate danger, his mind and body relaxed. Listening to Irena's even breathing, he drifted to sleep.

****

Gentle fingers combed his hair and woke him. He rubbed his eyes and slowly sat up. Sleeping slouched over the bed had put a nasty kink in his back. At least Irena's swelling had gone down and she could open her eyes.

Sun shone through the slits of the vertical blinds on the square window. The new day promised beautiful weather. If Ella were conscious, perhaps the doctor would allow a short stroll in the gardens on the hospital grounds.

Ella! Could she have woken yet? The doctor had said forty-eight hours, but Dario hoped she might recover sooner.

He took Irena's hand, the one not in the cast, and kissed her palm. "How are you feeling this morning?"

The light of the new day revealed the true extent of her bruises. Her eyes were bloodshot and pain clearly reflected in them.

She moaned. "The meds they gave me during the surgery wore off some two hours ago. I paged the nurse twice and she hasn't come yet."

"Why didn't you wake me up sooner?" Dread spiraled through Dario. Irena's tolerance for pain was high. If she couldn't take it, no one could.

"You were so exhausted, I just didn't have a heart."

"I'll go find someone."

He stepped into the hallway. The nurses' station to

the left stood unattended. Which way should he go? A nurse came out of a room two doors away from Irena's. A young doctor followed her, walking backward, still talking to the patient inside.

"Doctor," Dario rushed toward the team. "My fiancée is in a lot of pain. She's in the room two-o-two."

The doctor flipped the papers on his clipboard and expelled a breath. "Oh yes, she's our next patient to see. We'll be there in a minute."

"Just bring something for pain." Dario hurried back to Irena's bedside, pulling his cell out and dialing Ante's number.

His brother answered on the third ring. "I'm sitting with Ella. She's still out of it. Jasmin is being discharged today, but won't leave without her big cousin. Martina's having a hard time convincing her Ella will come home when she gets better."

No! Dario's insides twisted. He had hoped she'd at least have stirred by now.

"Are there any signs of Ella waking up?"

"Her vitals are stronger and her fever has broken." His brother's chipper voice instilled Dario with hope. After a short pause Ante spoke again. "Her body needs a bit more rest, that's all."

Laughter sounded on the other side of the door. Dario gave Irena's shoulder an encouraging squeeze. "The doctor's here to check on Irena. I have to go."

The doctor and the nurse stepped through the door, greeting them with their cheerful voices. At least the morning crew seemed a bit more chipper than the overworked night one.

The doctor stopped at the foot of the bed. "I hear

the pain's too much for you."

"Yes," Irena panted, clutching her arm in the cast. "Can't you give me something? Preferably stronger."

The doctor glanced at the papers in his hands. "No, I can't do that, but let's see if this will take your mind off the pain."

He scribbled on the notepad, ripped out the top page and handed the sheet to her. She took it in her good hand. Her eyes widened then she stared at the doctor. "Really?"

"I wouldn't joke about this." The doctor smiled. "I doubt you suspected."

A grin lit up her face. "Oh my gosh. I did suspect, but..." Her melodious laughter replaced her earlier panting. She passed the paper to Dario. "I wanted to be sure before I told you."

Puzzled, he took the sheet with a shaky hand.

*You're pregnant*, the note read written in red ink. His jaw dropped and he gasped with excitement. Joy replaced all the dread and sadness he carried for so long. Careful of her arm and shoulder, he pulled her into a hug. They were about to become parents for the second time. Once the doctor and nurse leave, Dario would kiss her senseless.

"How's the pain now?" the doctor asked. "If this didn't work, I could get you a shot of Demerol."

Irena chuckled. "No need. Your miracle cure worked. I don't feel anything, but hunger. When can I eat?"

"Anytime, but keep the first meal light. The nurse will make you decent." The doctor left the room.

The nurse stepped to her bed and glanced at Dario. "Would you mind waiting outside?"

He kissed Irena's head "I'll check on Ella. Be back in five minutes."

He rushed out of the room, unable to restrain his giddiness. He would have to marry Irena before this baby came. No way would his second child be born out of wedlock.

The frosty paned double doors silently slid open and Buddy stepped through. "Hey man, how are your girls?"

"Better, but Ella hasn't woken up yet. I'm worried. They both need me and I'm stretched between the two of them on the different floors." His grin vanished at the thought his girl hadn't regained consciousness yet. Guilt for not telling Irena about Ella stung his core, increased his tension.

Buddy tapped his shoulder. "It'll work out, you'll see. I'm transporting Fred's men to prison."

Dario scowled. Had he known their rooms, he wouldn't have been able to control his anger and not done something stupid.

"What will happen to the Father Diego?"

"He was treated, in the ER, he left. There's no doubt in my mind he's a good man. He defrocked after he ratted on Fred. Fred got him before he could go into a protective custody." Buddy reached inside his jacket and pulled out a small envelope. "He left this for Irena."

Dario harrumphed, so he'd been right in his assumption about the cleric. "If it weren't for him, Fred's child prostitution ring would never be destroyed. Still, so many lives so callously wrecked. Fred's death isn't enough to right all his wrongdoings."

"Fred's corporation is ordered to pay damages, but they are in financial trouble. That school was their biggest money-maker. Fred's assets will be liquidated. Still, won't pull the company through. People are losing their jobs. It's ugly. Hard to believe their slogan is 'we value the person and always see others as people, not things'. Words on paper if you ask me. The company didn't adhere to their own catchphrase. Many can't believe nothing goes to his wife and child." Buddy's mouth twisted in an awkward frown. "Fred had Irena sign a prenup."

Dario examined Diego's neat handwriting on the envelope to hide the pain in his eyes. After their breakup, people assumed she'd naturally choose to marry money instead of living in poverty, but they were so wrong.

The nurse stepped out of Irena's room and called Dario. "She's asking for you."

Dario tapped Buddy's arm. "I've got to go. Thank you for all the help."

"Don't mention it. It's my job. Wish there are no more child prostitution rings to take down." Buddy waved over his shoulder on his way down the hallway.

The fact Irena wasn't getting a single red cent out of Fred's estate made Dario happy. They didn't need anything from her now dead husband. Hopefully, they could get a marriage license fast and put the last fourteen years behind them.

Irena's bed was raised to a semi-seated position, a couple of pillows propped under her head. Her smile warmed his insides, yet the fact Ella hadn't opened her eyes sent shivers down his spine. How was she to make the amulet whole again if she couldn't hold it in her hand?

"Bumped into Buddy in the hallway." He extended

his arm to Irena, envelope in his hand. "Father Diego, err...just Diego now left this for you."

"Opening this is a two-handed job. You'll have to do this for me." She stared at the letter clamped between his fingers. "And read it for me too."

He opened the envelope and pulled out a sheet with neat handwriting.

"My dearest friend," he began, taking a seat on the edge of Irena's bed. "You were still in surgery when I stopped by to say goodbye. It's with great sadness that I must leave you, but before I do, it is my turn to confess. Though I performed the wedding ceremony, I did not file the paperwork with the local municipality." Dario gasped and glanced at Irena's astonished face, her eyebrow arched and her mouth gaped. He returned his gaze to the short letter in his hand. "I hope you can forgive me. I was angry, jealous and, above all, confused. You are a free woman to marry and love whom you want. I'll find my solace in righting the wrong Fred did to this world. Farewell my friend, yours truly, Diego. P.S. Perhaps our paths will cross again."

Irena sniffed and shook her head. "I could never be angry at him, I only wish he told me this before. To rid the world of Fred's evil will take some time. At least you and I can marry as soon as this cast comes off. It'll take us a few weeks to organize the wedding."

A few weeks? Dario scooted closer to her and kissed her temple. "I waited this long, I guess I could curb my enthusiasm for a bit longer."

A knock on the door shattered their blissful moment. A young man pushed the wheelchair inside and set the brakes on next to the bed. A heavy stench of stale tobacco wafted from him. "I'll help you into the chair."

"I can do it, thanks." Irena flipped the covers and slid one leg at a time over the mattress.

The orderly's gaze fixed on her bare skin under her hospital gown. He cleared his throat and moved the wheelchair closer to her.

Dario smirked. *That's right, keep dreaming kiddo, she's mine.* He stepped to the wheelchair and grabbed the handles. "I'll take it from here."

The orderly nodded and left the room. Dario was about to push Irena out the door when he remembered the amulet. "I need that rock."

Irena pointed to the white cupboard by the bed. The small doors squeaked as he pulled them open. The panels wiggled and he was afraid they would fall off. His initial search of Irena's clothes did not produce the amulet.

"It's not here."

"It has to be." Disbelief colored her words. "Look again. I'd hate it if the amulet were lost again."

He dug through the cupboard. Grabbing onto the something hard inside, he pulled his arm out revealing the amulet safely stored in a plastic bag.

"Yes!" He pumped the air in excitement. Everything would work out just fine.

Irena's aunt, Divina, left Ella's room as he stepped out of the elevator.

Divina's face contorted in a mass of wrinkles when she saw her niece. She pulled out a lacy handkerchief from her black purse and dabbed her eyes. "Oh, you poor child." She enveloped Irena in an awkward hug. "Your mother sends her love."

Irena cast her a steely gaze. "Does she? Why

couldn't she bring her love down here?"

Divina patted Irena's un-cast hand. "There's one thing you must know about your mother, dear. She let others make decisions for her. When things went sour, she would say it wasn't her decision and no one could blame her."

Irena tilted her head toward Dario, her eyebrows knitted. "That's what she said to me the night I left for Canada. No one would blame you when your marriage fails, it wasn't your decision. I thought she assumed the marriage wouldn't last because in her mind's eye I was incapable."

Dario smoothed Irena's hair. "Let the past stay in the past. We have to live our lives for what tomorrow has to offer, not what yesterday has taken away."

"There," Davina said, patting Dario's elbow. "You should listen to him."

Irena squeezed Davina's hand and nodded. "Thank you, Aunt. There's still hope my mother and I will see eye to eye someday."

"As long as one of you is willing to extend a hand." Davina headed for the elevators, her sensible heels clicking on the hospital's floor.

Dario pushed Irena's chair in Ella's room and parked her next to the bed. Ante and his family sat around the bed. Jasmin on Martina's lap, sucked her thumb, her eyelids drooped, but she plucked her thumb out and reached her hands to him.

He hugged her and pecked her cheek. "Nice to see you smiling again, sweetheart."

Martina gave him a one-arm hug. A diamond ring on her finger he hadn't seen before caught the light from the ceiling fixture. Perhaps there could be another wedding in the family. "Thank you for saving her."

"It was a joint effort." Dario wrapped his arm around Martina's shoulder. "Your man proved brave too."

Martina jerked her head at Ante in a let's go gesture. Ante followed her to the door. "Need anything before we leave?"

"I have a feeling Irena could eat, but keep it light. We'll join you at the condo when Ella gets discharged." He turned to look at Irena. She stared at her daughter. The tears welling in her eyes broke his heart all over again.

In one step he was by her side. "I know it's hard to see Ella like this, but trust me, she'll be fine. The doctor says we need to give her time."

"The amulet!" Irena reached out her hand. "Give me the amulet and the other piece too."

He placed the two halves in her hand.

"Push this blasted chair closer," she demanded.

When she could reach Ella's hand not pricked with IV tubes, she lowered the rocks and closed Ella's limp fingers. Irena motioned to him to join his hand with theirs. He covered Irena's and Ella's hands with his. In a few short moments, heat radiated to his palm.

He stared at Ella's unchanging face. "Come on baby girl, make this whole again, make us whole. You can do it."

Her eyelids fluttered, then opened slowly. She stared at the ceiling, blinking, but her lids drooped again.

"No, Ella, wake up. We're here with you, baby." Irena's voice quivered.

Ella's eyelids opened again. This time she seemed

more focused. She turned her head in the direction of Irena's voice.

"Mom? Dad?" Ella barely whispered, but it was enough to loosen the dread from Dario's chest.

"It's us. You're safe, love." Dario removed his hand from their joined pile.

Irena followed suit. Ella opened her palm. The two amulet pieces, fused together as if they had never been broken.

"I'll be damned." Ante's astonished voice had Dario turning toward his brother standing by the door. "How did she do that?"

Dario cast him a wary glance through his narrowing gaze. "I thought you're getting us food."

Ante put his hands up. "Okay, heading for the cafeteria now."

Ella gave Irena a weak grin. "Mom, where's the little boy?"

Irena exchanged a puzzled glance with Dario. She turned to Ella. "A little boy with chocolate brown hair and piercing blue eyes, like Dad's?"

"Yes, him. Is he here? He led me toward the light. I didn't want to leave him in that dark place, but he said he's already in my world."

"I had the same dream during my surgery, only now I'm not sure it was a dream."

Dario rubbed Irena's stomach and beamed at Ella. "Could it be we're having a boy?"

Ella's wide-eyed glance traveled back and forth between him and Irena. "Mom's having a baby?"

"Yes, love. I am." Irena squeezed Ella's hand, a slight blush coloring her cheeks.

The way she looked at him made him feel alive.

"Maybe the boy we dreamt of is here after all."

The face of the Gypsy woman flashed before his eyes, a colorful bandanna covered the top of her head, thick curls of her dark hair hung loosely on her shoulders, and a wide smile lit up her young, vibrant face. The Gypsy amulet was whole again, its prophecy fulfilled, and The Fates smiled down on him.

Dario crouched between Ella's bed and Irena's wheelchair. Mindful of the cannula in Ella's hand and Irena's arm in the cast, he enveloped them in a protective hug as best as he could. His new, growing family was his reason for living. The years apart were nothing but a test of his love for Irena. She was always the one.

# A word about the author...

Zrinka Jelic lives in Ontario, Canada. A PAN member of the Romance Writers of America and its suspense chapter Kiss of Death, as well as Savvy Authors, she writes contemporary fiction which leans toward the paranormal, and adds a pinch of history. Her characters come from all walks of life, and although she prefers red, romance comes in many colors. Given Jelic's love for her native Croatia and the Adriatic Sea, her characters usually find themselves dealing with a fair amount of sunshine, but that's about the only break they get.

http://forromanceloversonly.blogspot.ca

Made in the USA
Middletown, DE
24 July 2018